Don Quixote

KATHY ACKER

Don Quixote

which was a dream

Grove Press, Inc., New York

First Grove Press Edition 1986
First Printing 1986
ISBN: 0-8021-3040-2
Library of Congress Catalog Card Number: 86-45260

First Evergreen Edition 1986
First Printing 1986
ISBN: 0-394-62085-2
Library of Congress Catalog Card Number: 86-45260

Library of Congress Cataloging-in-Publication Data

Acker, Kathy, 1948-
    Don Quixote.

    I. Title.
PS3551.C44D6   1986   813'.54   86-45260
ISBN 0-394-55018-8

Printed in the United States of America

Grove Press, Inc., 920 Broadway
New York, N.Y. 10010

5   4   3   2

Table of Contents

The First Part of Don Quixote: The Beginning of Night   7

The Second Part of Don Quixote: Other Texts   39

The Third Part of Don Quixote: The End of the Night   99

The First Part of Don Quixote
The Beginning of Night

DON QUIXOTE'S ABORTION

When she was finally crazy because she was about to have an abortion, she conceived of the most insane idea that any woman can think of. Which is to love. How can a woman love? By loving someone other than herself. She would love another person. By loving another person, she would right every manner of political, social, and individual wrong: she would put herself in those situations so perilous the glory of her name would resound. The abortion was about to take place:

From her neck to her knees she wore pale or puke green paper. This was her armor. She had chosen it specially, for she knew that this world's conditions are so rough for any single person, even a rich person, that person has to make do with what she can find: this's no world for idealism. Example: the green paper would tear as soon as the abortion began.

They told her they were going to take her from the operating chair to her own bed in a wheeling chair. The wheeling chair would be her transportation. She went out to look at it. It was dying. It had once been a hack, the same as all the hacks on grub street; now, as all the hacks, was a full-time drunk, mumbled all the time about sex but now no longer not even never did it but didn't have the wherewithal or equipment to do it, and hung around with the other bums. That is, women who're having abortions.

She decided that since she was setting out on the greatest adventure any person can take, that of the Holy Grail, she ought to have a name (identity). She had to name herself. When a doctor sticks a steel catheter into you while you're lying on your back and you do exactly what he and the nurses tell you to; finally, blessedly, you let go of your mind. Letting go of your mind is dying. She needed a new life. She had to be named.

As we've said, her wheeling bed's name was 'Hack-kneed' or 'Hackneyed', meaning 'once a hack' or 'always a hack' or 'a writer' or 'an attempt to have an identity that always fails.' Just as 'Hackneyed' is the glorification or change from non-existence into existence of 'Hack-kneed', so, she decided, 'catheter' is the glorification of 'Kathy'. By taking on such a name which, being long, is male, she would be able to become a female-male or a night-knight.

Catharsis is the way to deal with evil. She polished up her green paper.

In order to love, she had to find someone to love. 'Why,' she reasoned to herself, 'do I have to love someone in order to love? Hasn't loving a man brought me to this abortion or state of death?

'Why can't I just love?

'Because every verb to be realized needs its object. Otherwise, having nothing to see, it can't see itself or be. Since love is sympathy or communication, I need an object which is both subject and object: to love, I must love a soul. Can a soul exist without a body? Is physical separate from mental? Just as love's object is the appearance of love; so the physical realm is the appearance of the godly: the mind is the body. This,' she thought, 'is why I've got a body. This's why I'm having an abortion. So I can love.' This's how Don Quixote decided to save the world.

What did this knight-to-be look like? All of the women except for two were middle-aged and dumpy. One of the young women was an English rose. The other young woman, wearing a long virginal white dress, was about 19 years old and Irish. She had packed her best clothes and jewels and told her family she was going to a wedding. She was innocent: during her first internal, she had learned she was pregnant. When she reached London airport, the taxi-drivers, according to their duty, by giving her the run-around, made a lot of money. Confused, she either left her bag in a taxi or someone stole it. Her main problem, according to her, wasn't the abortion or the lost luggage, but how to ensure neither her family nor any of her friends ever found out she had had an abortion, for in Ireland an abortion is a major crime.

Why didn't Don Quixote resemble these women? Because to Don Quixote, having an abortion is a method of becoming a knight and saving the world. This is a vision. In English and most European societies, when a woman becomes a knight, being no longer anonymous she receives a name. She's able to have adventures and save the world.

'Which of you was here first?' the receptionist asked. Nobody answered. The women were shy. The receptionist turned to the night-to-be. 'Well, you're nearest to me. Give me your papers.'

'I can't give you any papers because I don't have an identity yet. I didn't go to Oxford or Cambridge and I'm not English. This's why your law says I have to stay in this inn overnight. As soon as you dub me a knight – by tomorrow morning – and I have a name, I'll be able to give you my papers.'

The receptionist, knowing that all women who're about to have abortions're crazy, assured the woman her abortion'ld be over by nighttime. 'I, myself,' the receptionist confided, 'used to be mad. I refused to be a woman the way I was supposed to be. I travelled all over the world, looking for trouble. I prostituted myself, ran a few drugs – nothing hard – , exposed my genitalia to strange men while picking their pockets, broke-and-entered, lied to the only men I loved, told the men I didn't love the truth that I could never love them, fucked one man after another while telling each man I was being faithful to him alone, fucked men over, for, by fucking me over, they had taught me how to fuck them over. Generally, I was a bitch.

'Then I learned the error of my ways. I retired . . . from myself. Here . . . this little job . . . I'm living off the income and property of others. Rather dead income and property. Like any good bourgeois,' ending her introduction. 'This place,' throwing open her hands, 'our sanctus sanitarium, is all of your place of safety. Here, we will save you. All of you who want to share your money with us.' The receptionist extended her arms. 'All night our nurses'll watch over you, and in the morning,' to Don Quixote, 'you'll be a night.' The receptionist asked the knight-to-be for her cash.

'I'm broke.'

'Why?'

'Why should I pay for an abortion? An abortion is nothing.'

'You must know that nothing's free.'

Since her whole heart was wanting to be a knight, she handed over the money and prayed to the Moon, 'Suck her, Oh Lady mine, this vassal heart in this my first encounter; let not Your favor and protection fail me in the peril in which for the first time I now find myself.'

Then she lay down on the hospital bed in the puke green paper they had given her. Having done this, she gathered up her armor, the puke green paper, again started pacing nervously up and down in the same calm manner as before.

She paced for three hours until they told her to piss again. This was the manner in which she pissed: 'For women, Oh Woman who is all women who is my beauty, give me strength and vigor. Turn the eyes of the strength and wonderfulness of all women upon this one female, this female who's trying, at least you can say that for her, this female who's locked up in the hospital and thus must pass through so formidable an adventure.'

One hour later they told her to climb up pale green-carpeted stairs. But she spoke so vigorously and was so undaunted in her bearing that she struck terror in those who were assailing her. For this reason they ceased attacking the knight-to-be: they told her to lie down on a narrow black-leather padded slab. A clean white sheet covered the slab. Her ass, especially, should lie in a crack.

'What's going to happen now?' Don Quixote asked.

The doctor, being none too pleased with the mad pranks on the part of his guest, (being determined to confer that accursed order of knighthood or nighthood upon her before something else happened), showed her a curved needle. It was the wrong needle. They took away the needle. Before she turned her face away to the left side because she was scared of needles, she glimpsed a straight needle. According to what she had read about the ceremonial of the order, there was nothing to this business of being dubbed a night except a pinprick, and that can be performed anywhere. To become a knight, one must be completely hole-ly.

As she had read – which proves the truth of all writing – the needle when it went into her arm hardly hurt her. As the cold liquid seeped into her arm which didn't want it, she said that her name was Tolosa and she was the daughter of a shoemaker. When she woke up, she thanked them for her pain and for what they had done for her. They thought her totally mad; they had never aborted a woman like this one. But now that she had achieved knighthood, and thought and acted as she wanted and decided, for one has to act in this way in order to save this world, she neither noticed nor cared that all the people around her thought she was insane.

SAINT SIMEON'S STORY

Simeon, Don Quixote's cowboy sidekick, told Don Quixote a story that night in the hospital, 'My father constantly publicly tormented me by telling me I was inadequate.

'Thus I began my first days of school. My parents sent me to a prestigious Irish gentry Catholic boarding school, so my father could get rid of me.

'There the upper-class boys wanted to own me. They regularly gang-banged me.

'Once a teacher whom I loved and respected asked me to his own house for tea. I went there for several weekends. He disappeared from the school. No one knew where he had gone – there were rumors. In his office the head of the school asked me what the teacher and I had done. I didn't know what he was talking about, but I knew there was something wrong, something about loving. I learned he had been dismissed for reasons which couldn't be spoken.

'A teacher at night told us to go downstairs. There he flogged us hard. The sound of flogging is now love to me.

'The teacher entered the classroom, sniffing. His nose was in the air. "One of you boys," the teacher said to the twenty of us quietly sitting in his classroom, "is from the working classes."

13

He sniffed again. "Now, I'm going to sniff him out." All of us shivered while he walked slowly around each one and scrutinized each one. He picked out the boy he sexually desired. The boy's blonde hair was floating around his head. "You, boy. Your smell is from the working classes. I know." Each of us knew what was going to happen. We could hear the sounds of caning.

'I want to be wanted. I want to be flogged. I'm bad.

'Thus I began my first days in school. I had two escapes from the school I hated: books; and even more, nature. Lost in books and in nature.

'They would find me asleep on a high tor and drag me back to their school. The sheep ate on the tor.'

THE FIRST ADVENTURE

Don Quixote set out to right all wrongs.

She saw an old man beating up a young boy. The young boy was tied to a tree. He was about fourteen years of age.

Don Quixote cried, 'Stop that! In this world which's wrong, it's wrong to beat up people younger than yourself. I'm fighting all of your Culture.'

The old man who was very proper, being found out, stopped beating up the young boy. 'I was beating up this boy,' covering up, 'because he's a bad boy. Being flogged'll make him into a man. This boy actually believed that I owe him money for the work he does in school. He demanded payment.'

'You're lying,' Don Quixote, knowing the ways of the world, replied, 'and your body is smelling. Free the boy!'

As soon as he freed the boy, the boy ran away.

'Come back here instantly!' the old sot yelled after the boy. 'We'll know how to care for you.'

'I won't go back to school. Never. I won't be turned into an old goat like you. I'll be happy.'

'Where're you going to, boy?' meaning 'Where can you go?'

The boy, being very unsure of himself, turned to Don

Quixote. 'Please tell me, ma'am, that I don't have to go with him.'

Don Quixote thought carefully. 'You have to go back, for your teacher, deep inside him, wants to help you and has just been mistaken how to help you. If he didn't care for you, he wouldn't want you back.'

The old man took the boy back to school and there flogged him even more severely. As he was flogging him, the teacher said, 'I have a good mind to flay you alive as you feared.' The boy tried to enjoy the beating because his life couldn't be any other way.

HOW DON QUIXOTE CURED THE INFECTION LEFT-OVER FROM HER ABORTION (SO SHE COULD KEEP HAVING ADVENTURES)

Seeing that she was all battered and bruised and couldn't rise out of her bed due to a severe infection and moreover, knowing that she was sick, Don Quixote couldn't rise out of her bed, which was the sidewalk outside her house.

'Who', St Simeon who had come to help his comrade asked Don Quixote, 'is responsible for this lousy condition?'

'No human's evil. The abortion.'

'Then who caused the abortion?' St Simeon was a highly intelligent young man, besides being holy.

'It's a hard thing,' Don Quixote instructed the saint, 'for a woman to become a knight and have adventures and save this world. It's necessary to pass through trials sometimes so perilous, you become mad and even die. Such trials are necessary.

'My heart's broken,' she continued, 'cause you demanded to be supported, cared for, and you gave nothing back. Either you clung like a child or you threatened to maim me. Now either you actually don't love me or else you're so insane, you don't realize how much you've hurt me.'

As these words were easing the old knight's and the knight's old heart, the saint re-questioned, 'But someone must be responsible for evil. Who's responsible for evil? For abortions?'

'I love you,' Don Quixote murmured. Aloud: 'I know who I am. The Twelve Peers of France and the Nine Worthies as well: the exploits of all of them together, or separately, can't compare to mine.'

Inside the house, her friends were talking about her:

– 'Is she going to die?'

– 'She's a very sick girl. She only knows how to do two things: When the sky's black, she lies across the sidewalk's length so the cars don't run her over. She indicates it's day by lying across the sidewalk's width. People, since they're forced to step over her, have to talk to her. I think she's lonely.'

– 'Why'd she have an abortion?'

– 'All she ever used to do was read books.'

'You're right,' the Leftist, who refused to drink in pubs, replied. 'She had no relations to other people. She didn't like them and she was aphasic.'

The Liberal: 'If she's evil, we must be evil too. No man's an island.'

'What about women?' asked the feminist, but no one listened to her. While the Leftist, who never listened to anyone but himself, answered, 'Books or any forms of culture're so dangerous, for they turn people mad, for instance Baudelaire or other pornographers, only our upper classes must be allowed to indulge in them.'

As he was stating this, Don Quixote was crawling into this room. 'I've had a dead abortion,' she said, trying to explain to her friends so they could love her, 'I mean: an abortion by a horse. I need you to take care of me.'

'It's because,' the Leftist, who always had to explain the world to everyone, replied to the knight, 'when you were a child, you read too many books, instead of suffering like normal children. The horse isn't responsible for your abortion. Literature is. You have to become normal and part of this community.'

In order to make her part of a community Don Quixote's friends dragged her toward her bed, which was a mattress on the floor, but just as they were dragging her across the floor,

16

they saw that she didn't have any wounds. They didn't need to care for or love her.

'My wound is inside me. It is the wound of lack of love. Since you can't see it, you say it isn't here. But I've been hurt in my feelings. My feelings're my brains. My feelings're now nerves which have been torn out. Beyond the hole between my legs, the flesh torn turned and gnashed, inside that red mash or mess, lies a woman. No one ever ventures here.'

Her friends, aghast at femininity, determined to burn it out.

Meanwhile, Don Quixote, having found the only true remedy for human pain, fell asleep.

A Dream Of Saving The World

I'm walking down a mountain. At a peak which was white, I traded something.

I and St Simeon're walking down a mountain. The foliage around us is luscious and light green. Trees have lots of little leaves. The path-down-which-we're-walking's dirt is tan and is winding slowly while it descends. The aerial freeway in a city. We're skiing. There're tiny blue yellow and orange flowers. We're running down a path. We're descending down a steep path. The path is reddish-brown. It's dangerous. We're at a curve of fantastic natural beauty: Thick thick bushes and leaves hang over waist-high dirt walls, are brushing our faces' skin. Beyond, the sky is blue. The foliage's so thick, there's only part of a sky. It's the beginning of night. St Simeon and I are at our little house at the foot of the cliff. The house's inside is beautiful. There're three bedrooms. A huge embroidered-blue-silk-covered bed's sitting in one of the bedrooms. Outside, the sky is lightless. A policeman is telling for a moment St Simeon who has a beer in his right hand to stop drinking. The cop grabs the beer out of Simeon's hand. Simeon runs after the creep. Since I'm knowing St Simeon has a bad temper, I'm running after the saint to try to stop him from doing anything stupid, the policeman's shooting me dead.

When Don Quixote awoke, screaming and raving on the floor, her friends told her she had to go to the hospital so that they could do something with her.

'Do you know why I'm screaming?' the mad knight told them. 'Because there's no possibility for human love in this world. I loved. You know how much I loved. He didn't love me. He just wanted me to love him; he didn't want to love in return.' Pauses. 'I had the abortion because I refused normalcy

17

which is the capitulation to social control. To letting our political leaders locate our identities in the social. In normal good love:

'It's sick to love someone beyond rationality, beyond a return (I love you you love me). Real love is sick. I could love death.'

Her friends, being kind, brought her food, for they knew the food where she was going stinks.

'I don't want this food. I want love. The love I can only dream about or read in books. I'll make the world into this love.' This was the way Don Quixote transformed sickness into a knightly tool.

PROVING THAT TRUE FRIENDSHIP CAN'T DIE

One day St Simeon went away. Don Quixote couldn't bear living without him. For St Simeon had taught her how to slay giants, that is to consider someone of more importance than herself. Even when she had been irritated then angry with him because he was younger than her – forty-two compared to her sixty-six years – she had learned to stay calm.

She didn't know why he had left her. She could only figure out that that evil magician, her enemy, had somehow enticed Simeon away from her. All she knew was that she had to have him back.

She sighted New York City. She was elated, for she was anxious to see her friend. She decided to wait until night which is when the city opens. Night orgasmed: it wasn't lightless: its neon and street lights gave out an artificial polluted light. Nothing was to be heard anywhere, but the barkings of junkies. Their whinings and mutterings deafened her ears and troubled her heart. Where was the heart? All the noises grew along with the silence. The knight took such a night to be an omen, but of what?, nevertheless, discounting the peril, she kept on.

About two blocks straight on, she came to a dark object. She saw that it was a tower. This old dilapidated boarded-up church inside of which rats cockroaches and occasionally junkies did their dealings was the principal church of the city. She thought Simeon, being a good Catholic, might be here. She was walking through the church's graveyard which was a blind alley filled with garbage. At its end, junkies were puncturing razors, for lack of needles, into their arms. 'It's probably the custom,' Don Quixote thought, 'in a land of revolution, to build major churches in broken-down scumbag sections, though it seems anti-religious. Every nation has its own customs: Even though I'm English, I must show some respect.'

Then she saw a number of well-dressed, obviously, society women. 'Don't be vulgar,' said a lady-like lady who was wearing a nice non-designer suit. A tall Givenchy-suited hideoso who had just found out the white-booted cowgirl was the reason her husband was divorcing her, even though the only thing she liked about hubby was his money, rapped cowgirl over the head. Cowgirl, turning around, kicked Givenchy upper-class slut. 'You can't hit me because I'm wearing glasses.' So cowgirl, taking glasses off, whacked skinny legs. Skinny legs whose legs weren't beautiful, down on ground cause also her legs weren't working, saw cowgirl's firm guinea-pig-like leg and sunk her teeth into its knees. 'I'll get you some iodine,' said the fat millionaire who was planning to turn or buy her young gigolo into a TV star. 'Get me a cure for hydrophobia.' Then skinny ugly legs sank down crying. How can such women live without men?

Desperate to find St Simeon, – this is the beginning of her desperation to find love in a world in which love isn't possible, – especially because she's so desperate, – Don Quixote's madness was beginning to reach a point beyond the imagination or human understanding. However the truth always wins. The truth was that Don Quixote had to be with St Simeon.

Not only was Don Quixote not with St Simeon. She was in a church.

Don Quixote had only one choice, for there's a remedy for everything except death. 'I *am* mad,' Don Quixote admitted to herself. 'Since I'm mad, I can believe anything. Anyone can be St Simeon, for anyone can be a saint. That's religion. If who I believes St Simeon doesn't believe he's St Simeon, I'll swear to it. If he swears he is, I'll whip him. But if he keeps on swearing he's not St Simeon, I'll tell him he's been enchanted.

'Where I spit,' Don Quixote said to herself, 'no grass will ever grow.'

In the United States, packs of roaming wild dogs now indicate a decaying urban area or an increasing separation between the universal military government and the national civilian populace. Don Quixote saw a pack of wild dogs coming toward her. One of the dogs lit a cigarette. A beautiful dog was walking by her. 'Mary darling, we've been waiting for you.' 'C'mon, Mary.' 'Leave me alone, Betsy.' 'What're you up to?' 'Shh.' 'How've you been feeling, Mary?' 'Shh. It's Gloria Grahame.' 'Anything for the gossip columns, darlings?' 'Shh.' 'Now, Mary. What's this about a doctor?' 'We all know about you and the doctor, Sylvia . . .' 'What do you know? . . . There's nothing between the doctor and I. He enjoys my company.' 'Oh.' 'Wait till I start talking about you, Mary. You're trying to break up my marriage, you pigeony X-wife, but you won't. S. . . is a gentleman. By the way, there's a name for you ladies, but it isn't used outside a kennel.'

'A malign enchanter,' Don Quixote thought that the leader of this pack was St Simeon, 'must again be pursuing me, this time outside my dreams, for he's transformed your hunky body into a dog's. I hope I don't look too bad.' Don Quixote looked for a mirror, but couldn't find one in the church. 'Nevertheless, dog, please love me because as for me I'm not so attached to appearances that I've stopped loving you. With us, friendship'll last forever.'

The dog tried to bite off the knight's hand.

While Don Quixote was trying to take her sick friend up in her arms, the dog saved her the trouble by kicking her. Since dogs aren't supposed to kick, Don Quixote knew this was really her friend. The dog, like all friends, started to run away.

'I'm always miserable,' Don Quixote whined. 'It's the way I am. If my best friend's a dog, what am I? How will anyone ever love me? I'm doomed to be in a world to which I don't belong.'

The dog, having smelled future dead meat in and of Don Quixote, had slunk back into the church.

'St Simeon. What lies concealed beneath your bark? Are you really good or evil? To tell the truth, I never noticed your ugliness, only your beauty, before this. Do you have any pimples now? Now, no one could really possibly love you except for me, because no one sees truly except for me, because I love.'

Because he was hungry, the dog followed Don Quixote, out of the church.

INSERT

I think Prince should be President of the United States because all our Presidents since World War II have been stupid anyway and are becoming stupider up to the point of lobotomy and anyway are the puppets of those nameless beings, – maybe they're human – demigods, who inhabit their own nations known heretofore as 'multi-nationals'. On the other hand: Prince, unlike all our other images or fakes or Presidents, stands for values. I mean: he believes. He wears a cross. President Reagan doesn't believe this crap he's handing out or down about happy families and happy black lynchings and happy ignorance. Worse: he might. Whereas The Prince believes in feelings, fucking, and fame. Fame is making it and common sense.

The Prince doesn't have any morals. Why? Because morals're part and parcel of a government which runs partly by means of the so-called 'have-nots'' or bourgeoisie's cover-up, (via 'Culture'), of the 'haves'' total control. Morality and 'Culture' are similar tools. The only culture that ever causes trouble is amoral. The Prince isn't moral: he doesn't give a shit about anybody but himself. The Prince wouldn't die for anyone, whereas Our President will always die for everybody while he's garnering in their cash.

Look at Prince's life. He's all-American because he's part black part white which is part good part evil. When he was thirteen, which is a magic number, he ran away from home just like Huckleberry Finn. He had nowhere to run to, cause there's nowhere to run to anymore. So he ran to a garage. He and his friend Cymone made music while they were screwing, sharing, and tying up girls. The Prince was the good boy because he didn't cuss and Cymone was the bad boy because he stole cars. Now Prince is twenty-six years old; he'll be thirty when he gets elected President of the United States. Thirty years old is the height of male cowboy American rock 'n roll energy.

Don't vote for a croaker again to run your life.

Does it matter that Prince doesn't know anything about governmental politics? I presume he doesn't. All political techniques, left and right, are the praxis and speech of the controllers. How can we get rid of these controllers, their praxis and speech or politics? Let the country go to Hell. By going to Hell, Prince, a good Catholic, might be able to save this country. Anyway, we'd have a lot more fun than now, now when we're slowly being turned into fake people who're alienated from themselves, or zombies. Our minds're floating in other bodies. The Prince is Dr Strange so he'll restore to us and restore us to those lowest of pleasures that are the only ones we Americans, being stupid, desire. Fucking, food, and dancing. This is the American Revolution.

It has been said that Prince presents nothing: he's dead, an image. But who do you think you are? Are you real? Such reality is false. You can only be who you're taught and shown to be. Those who have and are showing you, most of the controllers, are shits. Despite that, how can you hate you or the image? How can you be who you're not and how can you not be? Prince accepts his falsity. Prince uses his falsity. Prince, being conscious, can lead us. 'I'm not a lover. I'm not a man. I'm something you can understand. I'm not your leader. I'm not your friend.' We must be conscious in order to fight outside control. Make Prince who may be conscious the next President of the United States.

THE ADVENTURE OF MEN

Don Quixote decided that the only thing's to be happy. Since the sole reason she ever went out of her house was to fuck, she decided that to be happy's to fuck. She was riding her horse along, in order to find sex that wouldn't hurt too much.

At this point she saw three to four hundred men. 'My God,' she said, 'how full of air they are!' She turned to St Simeon who was now a dog. 'Fortune's guiding our affairs beyond our most hopeful expectations. Here're those giants I've been looking for.'

The dog said, 'Woof.'

'I'm going to get what I want from them.'

'Woof.'

'You have very little experience,' Don Quixote told the dog, 'in matters of this kind. Go along muttering, as all Catholics do, while I engage in these perilous untried unbargainable adventures.'

The dog muttered 'Woof' and hid from fear. Don Quixote went after the big men. The men began to run away. Don Quixote verbally dedicated herself to the cause of everlasting love or marriage, which is the most dangerous cause, cause it's no cause at all, then again and again went after the big men.

Some of the big men who didn't want to run away lashed out at this stalwart female. Again and again she rose up and went at them again. Nothing, not even a man, could stop her from going after them. She was inexhaustible indefatigable – a true knight. Nothing could stop her search for love, but death. Finally, a man hit her so hard she almost died. The dog came running over to her, but by the time it reached her, she could hardly speak, and it couldn't speak either.

The dog said, 'Woof.'

'Sentimentality,' Don Quixote, 'in time of war's more than useless: it's detrimental. Don't be sentimental, dog. Being severely physically and mentally hurt's no reason for me to stop my search for love. Being now so hurt I'm almost dead only means in a few minutes I won't be dead because change 'n life are synonymous. What's more: I know I've been hurt by a man who is so evil, women have to fall in love with him.'

'Woof.'

'Once upon a time, there were no evil men. In those days of yore, a man loved a woman who loved him. And vice-versa. Not like today.

'Why have matters changed between men and women? Because today love is a condition of narcissism, because we've been taught possession or materialism rather than possession-less love. Those people in days of yore didn't have proper language, that is, correct Great Culture. They were just confused and loved out of confusion. Today, our teachers call this confusion "poetry" (and try to define each poem so that the language's no longer ambiguous), but in those days "poetry" was reality.

'Today, only the knights who're mad enough to want to love someone who loves them maintain this order of poetry. I'm such a knight. Unless I'm mad, those big men over there who're totally dressed in black must be the servants of Simon, the evil man who makes women fall in love with him . . . '

The dog, hearing his name, said, 'Woof.'

'. . . For they have a woman with them.'

'They're worse than men,' the dog said.

'Why?'

'They're monks. Catholics kidnap young women not cause they're women but cause they look like boys.'

'Bitch,' Don Quixote replied. 'You don't know what you're talking about.'

Disdaining to listen to a beast's mutterings, Don Quixote walked up to the monk mass and cried, 'You lousy stinking shits! All you ever do is talk about good and evil. If you don't tell this woman you don't love her, I'm going to erase you.'

'Please beat us up. We belong to the Order of St Benedict.'

'I don't care anymore what you say. I know you don't love me. I know you don't love women. I know Catholicism is really a secret order of assassins.' With that intelligence, Don Quixote leaped on one monk who was so drunk, he passed out.

The dog bit the drunk monk's clothes.

Two travellers, who happened to be passing by asked the dog why he was doing this to a holy father.

'Woof.'

Since the travellers were humanists, they beat up the dog, left it for dead, and rescued the monk.

When Don Quixote saw her dead dog, she cried. 'Such are the laments of the pain from my love for you.'

ANOTHER INSERT

The Arab leaders are liars; lying is part of the Arab culture in the same way that truth-telling and honest speech're American. Unlike American and Western culture (generally), the Arabs (in their culture) have no (concept of) originality. That is, culture. They write new stories paint new pictures et cetera only by embellishing old stories pictures . . . They write by cutting chunks out of all-ready written texts and in other ways defacing traditions: changing important names into silly ones, making dirty jokes out of matters that should be of the utmost importance to us such as nuclear warfare. You might ask how the Arabs know about nuclear armaments. Our answer must be that humans, being greedy, fearful, and needing vicious power, have always known. The Arabs are no exception. For this reason, a typical Arab text or painting contains neither characters nor narrative, for an Arab, believing such fictions're evil, worships nothingness.

THE AFTERMATH OF THE WORLD

The dog gave a little quiver. It actually wasn't dead, just in great pain. It gave a little quiver again. Slowly, life was returning, in the same way that light makes its way into a sky that has lasted through the night. The dog like a baby began to crawl. Painfully, out of love, it inched over to Don Quixote and licked her feet.

'I'm the one who should lick you.'

'I'm sick of being so poor,' the dog howled. 'I don't like living in poverty. The poverty in which we're living isn't unbearable: it's creeping; crawling; restrictions; constant despair; gray; final disease. This poverty's more unbearable than unbearable screaming poverty because it can't shout it can't talk sensibly, it only mutters and moans, it hides itself in that terminal disease – gentility. Repression is ruling my world. Humans' most helpful and most pernicious characteristic is their ability to adapt to anything. First, Gestapo camps; now, here.'

'But you're not human. Not anymore.'

'I still need to eat. Take me out to dinner, baby.'

'Be patient. These things take time. In order to save the world, because this world's suffering, knights have to take on all this world's suffering.'

'Shit.'

'Suffering.'

'I'm sick of worshipping suffering. Those Catholic creeps who just beat the shit . . . '

'You mean "life."'

' . . . Out of me did so cause they believe in suffering. They're very powerful:' the dog was shivering from fear, 'cause due to their faith and belief in goodness and that what they're doing's always good, they don't question what they do.'

'Aren't you a Catholic?'

'I used to be until I was changed into a dog.'

'I'll protect you through this love from those monks,' Don Quixote cradled the dog in her arms, 'because I'm better than them. There's no man on this earth who's better than me. I'm strong. Valorous. Sincere. Slim and boyish despite how I look. When I have to be, I can be devious. As Hell. Charming. Cajoling. The most marvelous fuck in the world, as you well know.' The dog barked, 'Woof.' 'Totally devoted and totally callous just like Machiavelli. In short: a chameleon who has no goals except to change this world.' The dog, 'What's wrong with this world?' 'I admit that it's hard to live with me cause I

26

do keep going out on adventures. But when you get beaten up cause of me, you can always run to me. Have you ever, in any book, read about a human being such as me? Has there ever in history, that is, in novels, been a human being such as me? You have to totally love me.'

'I don't totally love you because I don't know how to read. I never went to public school. Looking at you, I think you're getting old. You're so fragile and physically debilitated, you can't even stand up without fainting.'

'I'm drunk.'

'What happens to a human when it dies – as a point of interest?'

'When a human dies, another human cuts the first one in two. Next, the second human glues these two body parts together – Plato told us this – and pours medicine down the first human's throat.'

'If human death isn't final, what's the cause of human suffering and pain?'

'Traditionally, the human world has been divided into men and women. Women're the cause of human suffering. For women are so intelligent, they don't want anything to do with love. Men have tried to get rid of their suffering by altering this: first, by changing women; second, when this didn't work because women are stubborn creatures, by simply lying, by saying that women live only for men's love. An alteration of language, rather than of material, usually changes material conditions . . .

'Women are bitches, dog. They're the cause of the troubles between men and women. Why? Because they don't give anything, they deny. Female sexuality has always been denial or virginity.

'This's why there's no love in this world, dog. The milk in the breasts of mothers all over this world is dry; the earth is barren; monsters, instead of children, run through our nuclear wastes. In Our Bible or The Storehouse Of Language, we tried to tell women who they are: The-Loving-Mother-Who-Has-No-Sex-So-Her-Sex-Isn't-A-Crab or The-Woman-Who-Loves-That-Is-Needs Love So Much She Will Let Anything Be Done To Her. But women aren't either of these. A woman is she who stuck the stake through the red Heart of Jesus Christ. By refusing suffering, women have made armies of men into corpses. Their shut-up breasts, instead of giving men suck, brush over the once-populated Egyptian sands and the now even more decimated Russian snowy wastes where our dead bodies are lying on top of each other, unseen whites, our corpses' mouths're intertwining with each other's. This is the only love we now can know because women don't want anything to do with love.

'"What the Hell do you know!" screams Medusa. Her snakes writhe around nails varnished by the Blood of Jesus Christ. "I'm your desire's object, dog, because I can't be the subject. Because I can't be a subject: What you name 'love', I name 'nothingness.' I won't not be: I'll perceive and I'll speak.

'"What if," the bitch, (excuse me, dog), continues, "by 'love' you meant I was allowed to want you? Then we'd both be objects and subjects. Then sexual love would have to be the meeting-place of individual life and death.

'"Do any of you allow this transcendence?

'"As long as you men cling to your identity of power-monger or of Jesus Christ, as long as you cling to a dualistic reality which is a reality molded by power, women will not exist with you. Comradeship is love. Women exist with the deer, the foxes of redness, the horses, and the devious cats.

'"When you love us, you hate us because we have to deny you. Why? Objects can't love back. Your Man Of Love is a man of hatred. Human hatred, being functionless, turns back on itself: your love has to drive you to suicide.

'"You who own this world are dead corpses: Our friends the pigs're eating your ears. The foxes're nibbling at your cocks 'n you're coming. Poor men needing mothers. Poor idiots. You're worshipping suffering, in every possible fetish, and we like our freedom. All being is timelessly wild and pathless, its own knight, free."

'As I have explained,' Don Quixote told the dog, 'there's no human suffering that humans haven't created.'

HISTORY AND WOMEN

Finally Don Quixote understood her problem: she was both a woman therefore she couldn't feel love and a knight in search of Love. She had had to become a knight, for she could solve this problem only by becoming partly male.

It was necessary for her to delve deeper into this matter. Did she really have to be a male to love? What was a woman? Was a woman different from a man? What was this 'Love' which, only having dreamt about, she was now turning around her total life to find?

'Therefore, who am I?' she asked St Simeon.

'Who cares.'

'Of course I'm not interested in personal identity. I mean: what is it to be female?'

'To be a bitch,' the dog answered.

'If history, the enemy of time, is the mother of truth, the history of women must define female identity. The main tome on this subject or history was written by Cid Hamete Benengeli, a man. Unfortunately, the author of this work so major it is the only one is an Arab, and that nation is known for its lying propensities; but even though they be our enemies, it may readily be understood that they would more likely have added to rather than have detracted from the history.

'"Be assured," this book starts out, "that the history of women is that of degradation and suffering." (True,' she said to herself, rubbing her wounded cunt.) '"Nevertheless, history shows us that no woman nor any other person has to endure anything: a woman has the power to choose to be a king and a tyrant.

'"Let us examine this history of women in its details:

'"The first woman recorded by human history was Amadia of Gaul. Gaul, you know dog, was an ancient city. Amadia fell into the clutches of her mortal natural enemy, Arcalaus. Arcalaus made her prisoner. Then he stuck two knives into her thigh flesh. Then he bound her to a pillar in his court-yard, for

29

he was a rich man so he could do whatever he wanted. It's a well-known fact that he lashed her body two hundred times with his horse's reins solely for her own pleasure. A certain female chronicler, anonymous or dead as women in those days had to be, recorded how this woman, hair as white and red as the Bloody Body of Christ, left in a room alone, a trapdoor opens beneath her feet, she drops into a deep underground pit of shit. The shit smells. She finds herself again bound hands and feet. Arcalaus liked this form of torture. Servants made her drink down a bowl of sand and ice-cold water.

'"'Please love me.'

'"'Why should I love you?'

'"'Hit me.'

'"He hit her hard across her face. She looked up at him with her eyes open wider than usual. 'Hit me again.' He hit her even harder.

'"'Oh.'

'"He slapped her face's right side twice. She wondered if there was a danger of her ear being damaged. 'I'm hitting you because I love you.'

'"Already she was in a trance in which every one of her moments was coming. She couldn't live without this pleasure: the possibility that he might love her because he was giving to her without taking. Since he wasn't vulnerable, she had no way of knowing whether he loved her.

'"She was dangling from a long hook. She had never wanted before. 'Slap.' 'Slap.' She would do anything to make him love her."'

'Then how have women come up in the world?'

'By magic.'

'That makes a lot of sense. Magic's really done a lot for this world.'

'Don't be a bitch,' Don Quixote told the dog. 'You only say that because the only thing you can perceive is history. History's a fiction, and, as such, propaganda. Just as death destroys pain and time memory, so magic does away with history.'

The dog scratched its head. 'As far as I know, the real pain is death.'

'Without personal history or memory,' Don Quixote

explained, 'you wouldn't know. Then everything would be possible. In the immortal words of Hassan i Sabbah, who was Cid Hamete Benengeli's friend, "Nothing is true, everything is permissible."

'It's not history, which is actuality, but history's opposite, death, which shows us that women are nothing and everything.' Having found the answer to her problem, Don Quixote shut up for a moment.

A SCENE OF THE MADNESS AND/OR THE DREAM OF DON QUIXOTE

Having decided that heterosexual love's possible, Don Quixote looked up a brothel's address in the telephone book, then walked toward it. One of the madame's favorite prostitutes, seeing a woman or potential money staring at the house, ran toward her. Being female, she could see that Don Quixote was sick with love.

So she put Don Quixote in an attic and took off all of her armor. Laid her upon four smooth planks. Don Quixote had been hurt for so long, so deeply, she took pleasure in all of this. The prostitute tied a white blindfold around the knight's eyes so the night'ld feel easy and learn to trust her. She covered Don Quixote's bruised body with sheets made out of saddle leather.

The madame, entering this wretched attic, was short skinny hunch-backed and one-eyed. She and her girlfriend pulled down one of the leather sheets, rubbed oil into the knight's flesh to heal the deep bruises, and covered her from her head to toe with plaster. At times, they kicked the bitch.

As the madame looked at the deep black blue and purple bruises on the knight's body, which she couldn't see cause plaster was covering them, her girlfriend explained, 'She's sick from heterosexual love.'

Don Quixote, being plastered, couldn't speak. Her dog spoke for her. 'These aren't the marks of heterosexual love, but of Catholics. Catholics, since they're celibate, throw stones.'

31

The girlfriend: 'I prefer whips to rocks, myself.' She again kicked the dog. 'I often dream I'm falling down from lofty rocks, my stomach goes, but I never touch the ground, and my fear changes to freedom. When I wake up, I see I'm covered with bruises.' She again kicked the dog.

The dog: 'Such are the bruises of love.'

The madame: 'Who's this bruised-up victim?' She kicked the dog.

The dog: 'A knight.'

The madame: 'But it's white, not black.'

The dog speaking for itself: 'It's the person I love.' The girlfriend kicked it again.

At this point Don Quixote due to her constant habit of imagining any possibility to be true conceived of as wrong a reality as can be imagined. She imagined that the madame was beautiful and had fallen madly in love with her. For the madame had promised that night, and every night, she would sneak to the knight and lie in bed with her, so that their hearts would cease to ache throughout the long night. Thus Don Quixote spake thus (via her dog): 'Beautiful lady, thank you for your treatment of me, which has been pretty lousy, which I will remember for the rest of my days. Will you marry me since I love you? I don't need to tell you who I am, so you can put the name down on the marriage certificate, because you don't give a shit. Our love, or rather my mind's idea of love, is written down in everyone's memory for all eternity; my heart through all the varying vicissitudes of life, however much we'll be parted, will adore you. I would to Bloody Christ that this love between us didn't hold me an insane captive. What are such love's laws? It scares me to love you more than to love my life. How can I live and how can I live responsibly fully when I love this way? Your eyes are the mistress of my freedom.'

Don Quixote's mentality was so mad, she, maddened, took such mental perceptions to be facts. She had visions:

Her first vision was of human love. A person whom she loved loved her.

Her second vision was of a handsome man. This man told her that he loved more strongly or possessively or madly than she loved. If this is true, then men're more capable of love and vision and life than women. If this is true, women can survive. For, as I've said, as soon as a woman loves, she's in danger. Why? Because the man for whom she'd do anything because he beats her up makes her almost die: Because she's the one who loves, not him, from not knowing whether or not he loves her, she becomes sick, yet she can't give him up. She loves him so much, she becomes pregnant, but she can't have a child alone. Her dilemma of love or she is her abortion. If a woman insists she can and does love and her living isn't loveless or dead, she dies. So either a woman is dead or she dies. This's what the handsome man told Don Quixote.

Is it the same for a man? Men're inscrutable things.

Can Don Quixote solve this new problem? Can Don Quixote figure out how to love and live? Can Don Quixote fight this handsome man?

This is the way Don Quixote fought: 'Man. I don't accept your argument. If you're realistic, I'm mad. My madness is love. It isn't possible for your Culture to judge or explain my love.

'For how can anyone judge if another person's sane or mad?'

A judge, who showed up, said that being rational he couldn't decide.

All reality and madness are trying to destroy each other. Bam! Bam! Wop! Swop. Madness, because it's a thin old debilitated aborted knight, is too weak. It had no chance of doing anything. It can't think. It fails. As it falls to the ground, the invincible reality of malehood puts his sword to its pulsating throat.

'Either become normal, that is anonymous, or die,' the handsome man told Don Quixote.

'I can't be normal because I can't stop loving.' *How can I stop loving you? I must stop loving you. You are my life. Please help me. I don't need help.* 'I won't go against the truth of my life which is my sexuality.'

In the face of her insanity, the man, being as kind as Jesus Christ, gave the woman another choice. 'Become a normal person and stop having visions for at least a year. That way you'll be allowed to live.'

33

I've stopped loving you.

All of this happened to Don Quixote in her madness which was a dream.

MARRIAGE

Now that Don Quixote couldn't love for a year, which is as good as forever, she no longer knew what to live for. It's not that she had to have a man: it's that without faith and belief, a human's shit and worse than dead. Worse than being shit and dead, Don Quixote knew she was no longer a knight but shit and dead, that is, normal. Better to be a businessman.

She decided she'd rather be dead than worse than dead.

The dog told her it could solve this problem. Since it wasn't human and didn't believe, it could believe without dying.

'What're you going to believe?' Don Quixote queried.

'I believe I'm going to die instead of you so you can love without dying.'

'How're you going to die?'

'By whipping myself.'

'I've no objection against that. I just don't understand how a dog can believe.'

'That's why you're going to have to pay me a lot of money for me to die. How much's your life worth?'

Don Quixote, being a knight, was an idealist. 'Filthy lucre has nothing to do with faith! I won't pay you a bloody cent to die. Human love occurs only when a human suffers for no reason at all. You can't give me my life if I give you anything because then you're taking, not giving.'

'Thank God I'm not human and rational. Give me money or give me life.'

Wanting to live, that is feel, Don Quixote agreed to pay up.

'How much?'

'A hundred.'

'Five hundred.'

'Two-fifty.'

'Four-fifty. My life isn't dog shit, but dog.'

'Four hundred. You're not a real dog. As soon as you beat yourself up so much you suffer, vision'll take over this world.'

They found a powerful and flexible whip made out of a donkey's halter. That very night the dog, beginning to beat itself to death like a good Catholic, whispered, 'Please beat me,' to itself.

After two of these fierce whiplashes, the dog asked Don Quixote for eight hundred dollars. Suffering greatly, Don Quixote agreed. The dog began to hurt itself as much as possible, and more again, and since each lash or scratch or wound had no reason, for money doesn't exist for an idealist, each blow tore out her heart.

At the sound of its agonized wails and the thud of the cruel lash, she came running up to the dog and snatched the twisted halter that served as a whip out of its paw. 'I love you too much for you to hurt yourself. If I have to, I'll be normal and dead.' It was in this way that Don Quixote's quest failed.

Inasmuch as nothing human is eternal but death, and death is the one thing about which human beings can't know anything, humans know nothing. They have to fail. To do and be the one thing they don't know. Don Quixote realized that her faith was gone.

DEATH

'Thank God, I'm so happy.'

'Don't you believe that humans suffer?' the dog asked.

'I don't know anything about what they're always telling me. The media. I know what's around me. All this love crap and do-good crap's an illusion. I feel great and this world's wonderful and no humans suffer.'

All the people around Don Quixote decided she was mad. She was the maddest child they had ever seen. They had to get rid of her.

They tried to explain to her that human love and good deeds are good things. Humans should live for love and goodness.

'We love you.' That statement confirmed Don Quixote's belief that all their statements were hot air. 'In the past, romance was my joy and utter pain. Now I know it's all nothing. I have to be very precise now: I have to explain to you the exact truth. Here's my will:'

Anyone who knows enough to draw up a will must be sane. Her family was willing to re-own her. They began to cry because they felt so much.

Only Don Quixote was a feelingless monster.

'Here's proof that I'm sane:

'TO THE DOG: I give my dog everything. Please, dog, forgive me for my selfishness; please, all the ways I have not understood you, for I haven't been intelligent enough and known what love is. I will the rest of your life to be very happy and, more, I know it will be, for you're strong and patient and willing to understand, moreso than me, even if you are crazy.'

The dog interrupted, 'I don't want you to go.'

Don Quixote: 'We must do what we must.'

The dog: 'You're dying because I didn't love you.'

Don Quixote: 'No.' Don Quixote turned back to her last will and teaching,

'TO MY ABORTED SON: If you marry anyone, male or female, who isn't totally rich, you'll be poor. Otherwise you'll be poor.

'TO MYSELF: I was wrong to be right, to write, to be a knight, to try to do anything: because having a fantasy's just living inside your own head. Being a fanatic separates you from other people. If you're like everyone else, you believe opinions or what you're told. What else is there? Oh nothingness, I have to have visions, I can't have visions, I have to love: I have to be wrong to write.'

When she had finished writing down all these smart teachings, being old and worn-out, she reaffirmed her belief that human love doesn't exist and died. 'For me alone you were born, and I for you. We two are one though we trouble and hurt each other. You're my master and I'm the servant; I'm your master and you're my servant. I'm sick to death because I tried to escape you, love. I yield to you with all my heart or

36

mind. This mingling of our genitals the only cure for sickness. It's not necessary to write or be right cause writing's or being right's making more illusion: it's necessary to destroy and be wrong.'

The Second Part of Don Quixote
Other Texts

BEING DEAD, DON QUIXOTE
COULD NO LONGER SPEAK.
BEING BORN INTO AND PART
OF A MALE WORLD, SHE HAD
NO SPEECH OF HER OWN. ALL
SHE COULD DO WAS READ
MALE TEXTS WHICH WEREN'T
HERS.

TEXT 1: RUSSIAN CONSTRUCTIVISM

1. Abstraction

Petersburg, my city.

Petersburg steeples triangles bums on the streets decrepit churches broken-down churches churches gone churches used as homes for bums for children forced away from the abandoned buildings they run.

Son.

1.

City of people who weren't born here who decided to live here who're homeless, trying to make their own lives: poor refugees artists rich people. People who don't care and care too much. Homeless. You, baby crib, only you've been financially shuffled off by the USSR government.

You, city, along one of whose streets a hundred bums're sitting standing and lying. Three-quarters of these bums're black or Puerto Rican. The concrete stinks of piss much more than the surrounding streets smell. A few of the creeps smoke cigarettes. One half of the buildings lining the street're a red brick wall. Mostly the bums don't move or they move as little as they have to.

How is this City of Cities divided?

This new holy city is a reality not only without religion but also without anything to want or seek for: without anything. The city whose first characteristic is it gives nothing, breakdown, and so its inhabitants individuals, no its communities, have to make everything for themselves.

As taught in school, Petersburg has five parts: its main part is the Nevsky Prospect.

St Petersburg is actually the Nevsky Prospect.

The Nevsky Prospect's an island joined by bridges once on

its northern tip, twice on its southern, and once at its eastern edge to the rest of Petersburg. Though Petersburg is the capital of the USSR, most Russians who don't live in Petersburg hate and fear the Petersburgians: they think they're murderers, dope addicts, and perverted by fame.

Is there such a thing here as true love: that violence that's absolutely right?

Lamplights hang over the edges of the park running through the vertical center of the Nevsky Prospect, from its beginning at St Isaac's, about fifty blocks north, to its black section in the depth of the seventeenth line. The geographical divisions are actually racial: ghettoes, each one on the whole about nine to sixteen blocks large, don't mingle. This past year the ghettoes're beginning to physically cross cause the rich're now trying and will take over this whole city by buying all of its real estate.

The islands especially Vasilyevsky Island are the drug oases. The hooker centers're the Millionaya, again Vasilyevsky Island (pimps always get their puppets hooked), the large black bridge across the Neva, and the Winter Canal. The languages are less than 50% Russian, then, (heard less often in this order), Spanish, French, and German. Petersburg isn't Russian: it's a country on its own. Since it has no legal or financial national status; it's an impossibility, an impossible home; it's tenuous, paranoid. Its definitions and language're quantum theory, Zen, and the nihilism found before the Russian Revolution.

Squares quadrilaterals concatenations of imaginations who lack other necessary sensualities. The flesh which touches flesh has to resemble Martian green gook. City of simultaneous inner and outer space where each day a new human disease appears, whose inhabitants, like rats, through sickness remain alive and work. Who can tell me I'm too sick to be alive? My sickness is life. You, my city, romanticism of no possible belief:

In Peter one morning, the female weight-lifter fell out of her loft-bed. It was a beautiful day, late in September. Larks were singing and drops of sunlight were filtering through the navy blue Levelors (through the clouds through the pollution through the surrounding buildings' walls) which she hadn't opened since she bought them cause she didn't want to see junkies shooting up.

A newspaper below her fallen body:

CITY OF PASSION

a non-achiever
non-leader, non-
and non-romantic,'
former classmate
lentine.
he was 18, George
stined to end up a
then a horrifying

George was totally wrapp
up in the fantasy world
comic books.
'He was also cons
with TV – especiall
ture shows,' said
By high scho
had withdrawn

Meanwhile, in the alleyways,
Dear Peter,

I can't stand living without you. I hate this day-after-day constant waiting-for-you: you're not here: all my hours spent in longing for what's not here. I won't stand for living like this. Then I realize I'm falling in love with you. There's no one to turn to: again and again I realize I have only myself.

Sixteen hours until I see you again. 1 2 3 4 5 6 7 8 9 10 11 12 13 14 15 16. I can count 16, but you'll probably not want to see me. If I see you, I'll want you. If I don't see you, I'll die. I'm going nuts. I don't care about this writing. I just want time. I can get rid of this night by closing up my eyes with work, brain calculations, dumbie-making TV: you have leapt into my arms, madness: I'll wait for you forever if you'll only come to me, for there's no time until I see you. Love makes time and life. I must be blind: you're poor. Your life is shambles. The more you want something, the more you deny it to yourself. You: my nightmare; I don't care. You've conquered me. You, kookoo totally untogether, make me as irritable and change-able as you are, so I've made myself into your Rock of Gibraltar in order to capture you but I don't want you, I don't want you to break up your marriage, I don't want you to do anything that'll hurt you: I have to lose. But if you don't see me tomorrow, I don't have to lose because you don't love me. So: real love is strange and any simplicity between us has to be a lie.

I don't know what I'm doing. You're the only life I've known in a very long time. How can I let go of life again? You're my day and night. Forget it, little baby, he's told you clearly he doesn't want to have sex with you and he only wants you so he can revenge himself on his wife cause she once left him for a richer man. You are my madness. Come in me, my madness, and since you've already taken me, I beg you with everything that is me to take me. I'm sold, but not yet enjoyed. The day I'm going to see you I'm happy and the day I'm not going to see you I'm miserable.

(My nurse enters and binds me up.)

Nurse: Shut up, brat.

Myself, to Myself: I don't talk cause I can't talk about you. I guess I am obsessed possessed. Spain needed a revolution, a far more profound revolution in fact than that being attempted by the Republic. I'm bound by cords cause you aren't fucking me. (Aloud, ((Allowed))) Cords're binding me cause you aren't fucking me. You're going away from me.

Juliet: You're going away from me. It's still dark and black and hideous: you don't have to leave me yet.

You: It is daytime; there are candles. The beginnings of clouds can be seen. Since this world for her light no longer needs the stars, like the jealous bitch she is, she's shut them off. Day like total revolution's waiting to infiltrate. I have to get away from you to keep my life going.

Juliet: The light's that's coming within you for me's as violent as mine for you. As you say we've nothing to do with nature: the fire between us competes with the sun. I'll keep your unnatural solitary fire going! I'll follow you in disguise. You don't need to ever leave me. Don't go.

You: OK. I'll stay with you and I'll die. I give way to your love: These beginning light lines in the sky are the streaks of blood on your colorless unspeakable thighs. The unseeable approaching daylight isn't a day but just moon to your energy and grace. Since without you I die and with you I die, I chose

44

to die with you, my life, and besides, I've no choice. It's dark and black and hideous still.

Juliet, resigning herself: Go. Get out. This world stinks. We can't pretend this world doesn't exist. The Fascists have taken over. All that's natural and beautiful're dividing us. Since natural is now unnatural and unnatural is natural, those who love can't know. How should I know what to do? It is the day: get away from me!

Dear Peter,

Please understand me. Please believe what's in my mind at this very moment. I do everything you want. Now you want to be away from me cause you're fucking your wife. You're the only one I love and this moment's infinite. I'd do anything to phone you right now. Cause I can't phone you, I hate you. Cause I hate you, I'm never going to phone you ever again, cause I hate you. I'll say your name so the whole world'll know, cause what you fear most, your only morality, is what you think other people (whether or not they know you)'re thinking of you. King Sunny Adé. King Sunny Adé, I hate your guts. You were my sun and your house was my home and you threw me out like a kid without a home, (you) saying, 'All you want is security so you don't love me at all,' and then you didn't even understand that I love you. That's why this moment's infinite.

Why do I like you cause I know you're so self-righteous you'd holocaust the universe faster than Margaret Thatcher; you don't understand what art is cause you're so scared of your wildness with which, you artist, you're frothing, you're trying to eradicate every weakness mainly those in other people cause that's what you see so you demand certain behaviors and accept nothing else; when people act differently, cause you've buried your wildnesses more anger volcanoes out of you than I've ever felt from another human being? I like you cause your eyes look at me a certain way and cause your nose twitches; your mental capacities're at least as sharp and rapid as mine; when you're not being (ridiculously) ruled, you're as decadent as I am. Why do you give a damn about social rules? Why not become an artist? I'm going to fuck lots of men now if they'll fuck me cause I need that physical reassurance and I'm sure while I'm doing this, there'll still be thoughts of our fucking:

Between you and me was a madness which's rare. Not just sexuality. Who're you kidding? That this anger and fear (appearing cause I touched your madness too closely or cause you care about society) are more powerful than your sexuality? Only a man who adores fucking comes near me. What's love? Love's the unity of friendship and desire. I messed up with you. I didn't care enough about friendship. I fought too hard against your desire to be socialized which, if I love you, should be as important to me as my ways. Can you be patient – I'm willing to fight myself to be with you?

You don't think our friendship's important. Maybe you're so young, you believe there're an infinite number of mad relations.

I agree with you: I was too frightened you didn't love me and not terrified enough of imposing on your love. Please remember, you also feared I didn't love you and you begged me for reassurance.

I hope your wife'll make you happy forever. I'm saying this cause I want to be friends. I want my desire for friendship to waken your love for me –

Walking the streets.

Tatlin designed a city. Tatlin took unhandlable passion and molded it.

It all comes out of passion. Our city of passion.

Biely wanted to fuck his closest comrade, Alexander Blok,'s wife until the duel between them in 1906 (which never happened), then Biely left Russia for a year. When Biely described this passion, he constructed language as if it was a building. If architecture wasn't cool cold, people couldn't live in it. I have to figure out why I'm hurting so much. Recognition: I'm really hurting. One of this hurt's preconditions is I'm in love with you.

A city in which we can live.

What're the materials of this city?

Is sensuality less valuable than rational thought? Is there a split between mind and body, or rather between these two types of mentality? Why's a Cubist painting, if it is, better art than a Vivienne Westwood dress? Is our city abstract?

When you talk to me on the phone I'm hurt and maddened by your lack of sexual and emotional communication. Art criticism, unlike art,'s abstract.

I'll mold my love for you: I can't say over the telephone what I want to say to you: 'Please touch your cock because I can't touch your cock now and I have to touch your cock.' What's mainly not allowed? Time's the main non-allower. I can't touch your cock right now because one event can't be another event. (Time is substance.) Three thousand miles now between the events of you and me, or three hours. Absence to a child is death. This is death. Time's killing me. Time's proving you don't love me. I have to mold my passion for you out of time:

2. The Poems Of A City

On Time

desinas ineptire
et quod vides perisse perditum
    ducas.

The subjunctive mood takes precedence over the straightforward active. The past controls the present. The past.

fulsere quondam candidi tibi
    soles,
cum it hurts me to remember I
    did act up today, a way of
    saying 'I'm not perfect,' forgive
    my phone call, ventitabas quo
    puella ducebat (on a leash:
    leather Rome)
amata nobis quantum amabitur
    nulla.

The first future tense. What do words really say: does this future propose future time?

ibi illa multa kisses on kisses
    between us
your hands your flesh unending
    time into time
the past wasn't past – how do I
    transform the past: that awful
    prison cause it ends?

fulsere vere candidi tibi soles.

By repeating the past, I'm molding and transforming it, an impossible act.

New section:

nunc iam illa non vult: tu quoque, impotens can't fuck any boyfriends these days, bad mood no wonder I'm acting badly, noli NO

nec quae fugit sectare, nec miser vive

My present is negative. This present becomes imaginary: The future of amabitur and the subjunctive at the beginning of the poem?:

good advice sed obstinata mente perfer, obdura.

vale, puella. (My awful telephone call. This's my apology, Peter. Do you accept?) *iam* (ha ha) Catallus obdurat,

nec te requiret nec rogabit invitam:

> I'm a good girl

I have, behave perfectly.

at tu dolebis. The imaginary makes reality, as in love, cum rogaberis nulla

scelesta. Scelesta nocte. My night. quae tibi manet vita without me?

quis nunc adibit? without me cui videberis bella?

quem nunc amabis? with me you fuck whoever you want.

Let the imagination reign supreme. quem you now fucking? cuius esse diceris huh!

quem basiabis a stupid question? cui labella labula mordebis? (allied to death?)

at tu, Catullus, destinatus obdura

to facts, for only the imagination
lives.

The imagination is will.

Will Versus Chance

no more sighing blackness nihilism
and senile old fogies' blathers
as snot falls out of their nostrils
all more worthless than the two bums I saw talking today.
suns rise and set I never see them –
for you my love and me a few brief hours of sun
then no consciousness blackness perpetually.
take it kiss me do it grab me
grab my arms grab my ankles grab my cunt hairs
the only nights of light the only eyes we have.
conscious.
so much so much so many phenomena we can no longer think
understand, realizing we're not responsible,
so no bourgeois or moralist can touch us
or know anything real about us.

Time Is Identity

No one he states my boyfriend'ld rather fuck
than a duck, than me. Even if Psyche herself begged him. He said to me. But what a man tells
any woman who loves him is lost in these winds and squalling
    waters. My lover is changing water.

Loneliness

Lines one through four. Emotional thesis: on always being
    away from you. I'm not scared of dying. I fear dying
    (absolute absence)'ll take away your love for me.
Lines five and six. The supplementary thesis: death or absence
    destroys love.
Lines seven through ten. The antithesis: love can and does
    fight this absence.

Lines eleven and twelve. The synthesis: My love for you is making me your mirror your object, fuses, whether I'm with or away from you. So this love's overcoming and becoming, through identity, one with death.

Lines thirteen through eighteen. The next thesis is based on the above synthesis: when I'm dead and absolutely apart from you, I'll still love you. No matter how long you stay alive, we'll eventually be together forever.

Lines nineteen and twenty. The supplementary thesis: our love is absence.

Lines twenty-one through twenty-four (the first section which isn't just one whole sentence. The three short sentences of this section syntactically reflect their verbal content). The antithesis: This life or these constant changes may destroy our love. Like death, love is infinite.

Lines twenty-five and twenty-six. The synthesis: while we're alive right now we have to love each other as much as possible cause love has nothing to do with time. (I can never say anything this direct to you cause I love you too much.)

The overall sentence syntactical structure is and concerns the relations between several kinds of time. What is the verb structure? Verbs're Latin's grammatical backbone.

The first kind of time, lines one through four, is linear time. The first main verb is *is*, an *is* which isn't Platonic. This common *is* leads to the first person subjunctives, *fear* and *hinder*, as well as the *is*' subject noun, *fear*. This kind of time or the world makes human fear.

Common time's other or enemy is death. *Is* is bounded by death. So the other of *is* is *be without* in the present tense.

Since the past is like the present in this time model, lines five and six, death or absence also destroys memory. Here's another reason I'm afraid.

Since the only certainty I can have in common human time is that which has to be most feared – the end of time – , all I can feel is more and more pain.

The second temporal model begins with human will, when I will to enter the realm of death. Line seven. This is exactly what I can't do, the antithesis, the necessarily imaginary.

Because we're apart, our sex because it has to continue, is false, imaginary. Line nine. Love makes me dare. I'm coming, masturbating, in the darkness. Line ten. Blind. Because I love you I want to die. My main verb is *orgasm* in the mythological past tense; in the realm of blackness the mythological's more powerful than the temporal present. (What is the time model of my will?)

If I've died to you am dead, who am I? Because I love you I've destroyed myself: I'm you. Lines eleven and twelve. Love destroys common time and reverses subject and object; the verb acts on itself; I'm your mirror; identity's gone because there's no separation between life and death. Line twelve. The final model of time is that the mirror reflects the mirror: time is our love.

But my whole body's aching and I'm crying uncontrollably every night because you're not here:

Now all tenses and moods, *may come had given*, like and equal to all other phenomena appear out of nothing or death, line eighteen, which is also the ideal, lines fifteen and sixteen. But my whole body's aching and I'm crying uncontrollably every night because you're not here:

Now all tenses and moods, may come had given, like and equal to all other phenomena appear out of nothing or death, line eighteen, which is also the ideal, lines fifteen and sixteen. But my whole body's aching and I'm crying uncontrollably every night because you're not here, lines nineteen and twenty. The subjunctive tenses grammatically reflect this new model of common time: change is time.

I'm fighting the phenomenal that has to happen. I'm scared. Line twenty-one. So all the verbs are now subjunctives; all verbs are change. Again: loving you is making me feel pain. The final verb, *is changed*, grammatically reflects its opposite in content: the mirror. Time: love or fusion exists side by side with change:

I want you. That's all I can think. This is our absolute present. Line twenty-six.

Time is Pain

last night I couldn't sleep at all, then I woke up in a sweat though I wasn't crying tears fall from my eyes. I'm

in pain I phone I want to suicide you
over and over again my brain revolves you
focus obsession I see nothing else. You're my world
blindness' opening my heart. This 'love'
between us (your name) to me is *blood*.
Everywhere you slept you touched you came
in this house is your blood.
I would do anything to fall asleep. At night. But as
each dream passes
each absolute reality shows itself temporary
I obsess you. At times I hurt
like hell. At times I'm dead. Every other night
there's been a morning when I can
stand up from this bed.
Now there's only night: each night
unnatural is the ornament of your blood.

Time Is Made By Humans

I hope there's some relief writing
this you: otherwise, none. I've never felt such pain.
Day after day pain after pain how do
I count these days? It's pain to count.
Pain to have a mind.
Worst: at the moment when sleep's ease should come,
(no coming. no you.) and thoughts are loosened,
but I don't want these thoughts.
I phone: I don't like life.
So stopping the mind up, no
life no utterance, jail within jail within
jail, what can days dates
time matter? Only this ease
of verbally sobbing out ugliness.

3. Scenes Of Hope And Despair

The girl's happy because she knows the man she loves's in love
with her.

   The girls sitting around: Peter didn't call me. You've got a date tomorrow with him, don't you? Should we eat? Did they fuck yet? Great fun, seducing girls. These men have the most fun. The most we can have is getting revenge. That is fun. Did they fuck yet? I don't know. Peter still hasn't called. I bet he forgets his accent. Uh-oh. Hurry back. Oh oh, she's drinking champagne. That means she's in love. I say, men just want you to suffer. They're so fucked up. They not only break up with you suddenly, they want this big dramatic thing. After you've broken up whenever a man starts talking about who's guilty, I tell him I couldn't care less I'd rather drink champagne. I think Peter's a little lame I mean he's always making dates and kind of forgetting the time but at the same time I could tell he really cared for me so his not calling me now doesn't mean he's off me. Edward's breaking up with me has made me think a man can't want me. All she does is cry. Englishmen fall in love too often so it doesn't mean anything to them. We always tell Englishmen, we only go with American men. This film is dumb.

Why do you want? I want love. You're not going to get love. OK. You're going to get hurt again. I know. The main thing is to always giggle. All the last week when I really hurt, I felt like I had a disease. Being hurt is having a disease.

The girls cross their legs and laugh. 'What should we do now?' 'I need food,' she, fainting, said. Her arms draped over the pillow. 'We're caught in our own trap,' she said laughing.

Right now the first girl is thinking about the man she wants to fuck. 'We can,' she says to her friend, 'by fantasizing, increase our possibilities and joy in living, more important, understand how things work. Why's this? Examine these two events: 1. Last night I fucked with you. 2. I'm fantasizing fucking with you. But these events are now only my mentalities. Therefore there's no distinguishing between the two of them. But what if we hadn't fucked? Take another example: We don't love each other. Is it possible that by fantasizing we love each other, we can love each other? Possibly? Fantasy is or makes possibilities. Are possibilities reality?'

The other girl lay in her red bed and crossed her legs. 'There're always possibilities,' she said. 'I always prefer drama.'

'I fantasize I desire and know what desire is. This's how

fantasizing allows me to understand. Every possibility doesn't become actual fact. So knowing is separate from acting in the common world.'

'I'm caught in my own trap cause every event for me can only be my mentality.' The girls looked at each other.

'I know you know a good many of my New York friends and I've always wanted to talk with you about your work.' 'Come inside.' 'Are you reading Husserl?' 'After college I was a political theorist. Then I worked for Austin.' 'Ooo. What's he like?'

What did we talk about?

'What's the relation between practice and theory in your filmmaking? I mean: does writing criticism stop you from making films?' 'They're just two different kinds of activities.' 'But they're also two different ways of thinking.' 'When I make a film, probably partially because I always work with other people and also due to the film's economic situation, I know even before I start to make the film exactly what I'm going to do in the film.' 'Ugh: If I knew what I was going to write before I wrote a book, I'd be bored.' 'It's a different business. When you make a film, you have to consider who's going to see the film the popular culture.' 'Why do you care so much when you work how other people'll judge your work? I first consider my own pleasure.   Do you think there's something fishy in the semiotic theories, especially in Deleuze's and Guattari's?' 'There's a gap now. You have to realize that semiotics hit England before it hit America. We got Lacan and Althusser, rather than the later semioticians . . . Derrida . . . Foucault . . .' 'Foucault isn't really a semiotician. He was always on the outside. Who, then, 're you reading now?' 'I have a theory that we're at the end of a generation. Semiotics's no longer applicable. At the moment there's nothing.' 'I remember in New York when semiotics came only it was Sylvère who brought it over, what it really did was give me a language with which I could speak about my work. Before that I had no way of discussing what I did, of course I did it, and my friends who were doing similar work we had no way of talking to each other. A critical way of talking about my work allowed me to go one step further in my work. Now it seems, as in the pre-semiotics days, practice's prior to theory.' 'The age of theory is over . . .' '. . . absolutes . . .' '. . . so there's only what I do at any moment.' 'Pleasure. Even Baudrillard in his new book . . .' 'He's a semiotician and dead.' 'Not anymore. . . . says our language is meaningless, for meaning – any signs – are the makings of the ruling class.' 'But he's still using meaningful signs to say this.' 'Oh, the black plague. Is it good?' 'I've read all about plagues.' Kiss. We don't stop kissing each other now. Your physical touch is incredibly gentle. But I can't physically feel anything cause I've been through a six-week relationship at the end of which the man kicked me out as fast as possible cause he decided he didn't know what he wanted. I must be shy of getting hurt. I think you're intelligent and lovely. Your face is keeping changing its shape. Maybe I'm hallucinating? It's not possible I can feel again after a winter and spring of no sexual love then for the second time in five years I moved in with somebody. That failed violently, forcibly.

4. The Mystery

'How, exactly, does my body feel pleasure?:

'I'm remembering fucking Eddie: I'm remembering situations of power. This's the way he likes to be fucked best: I'm on top of him. My arms reach straight to the pillow on either side of his black head. My legs slide from a sitting position straight down inside his legs so that my inner thighs nearest my cunt're rubbing his cock and so that I rising up and down am fucking his cock with my cunt. As I do this I think to myself that he likes this position more than I do. I don't come as easily in this position as when my legs're sitting on top of him because I have to be accurately acutely aware of his reaction to make sure his cock stays in my cunt and, I can't let myself fully go. I reach over Peter so my mouth is on his nipple. Or my wet tongue is flicking his nipple tip. This makes me excited more subtly than when I'm being touched: I don't come as much as violently, but I'm sort of coming all the time. I'm sort of coming all the time. Other times I stick my right hand's third finger into Eddie's asshole. It easily enters. He bucks and looks at me with surprise and openness unusual for him. Openness makes me open. My finger is reaching up and toward his cock. That opening. As his thighs're reaching up for me, Sometimes I coldly turn him over, spread the asscheeks, stick my tongue into his asshole. I don't mind doing this though I usually mind doing this on men. When I do this he groans very loudly so I know he's receiving tons of pleasure. Peter's asshole's too tight for my finger to wiggle up and I don't want to force anyone to do sexually what they don't seem to want to do. When I once mentioned, innocently?, that I had a whip back in New York and he said "I'll have to try it", I was surprised and thought maybe it's a go between us.

'Peter's sexually scared for instance he never comes with me cause he's trying not to be in love with me cause he loves his wife or cause maybe he doesn't want to come. Whenever Eddie comes, I instantaneously come he usually turns me over I've been fucking him. He's on top of me. Now I remember. My legs clasp his waist and touch each other because he likes this. I can't come in this position. Legs open up so feet rest on outer sides of ass. Rubbing bone above clit against cock-bone. Come. So as he about to come he almost stop moving. First my arms have to curl around his neck as tight as possible clasp each other. Soon as he about to come; now now, almost no movement. I'm not going to come even though I've come. Soon as he starts to come and there's almost no movement, I automatically come.

'How, exactly, does my body feel pleasure?' The girl's telling the other girl about her former lovers.

'No no. I can't talk about anything directly.'

'There's a definite difference in my physical being or body between when I'm being fucked and I'm not being fucked. How can I say anything when I'm totally uncentralized or not being fucked?'

'There's no sex anymore. I'm not going to have any sex. I'm not going to open up. This is me: the image. A man's suit. Look at me. I'm a woman who looks like a delicate boy and I'll never change. You can't touch me. I'm impervious. This's the way I'm happy. I'm totally elegant.'

'You're out of your mind.'

'Better than being laid, then sticking razor blades through my wrists.'

'Living isn't so black.'

'Living is a present. I'll never say otherwise. I wish I was together enough to say or do something.'

'Touch me. An open quivering clit. The little red animal wiggles.'

'Art, since its very beginning in prehistoric caves, has been, in our present ways of speaking, conservative.'

'Art's more interesting than sex . . .'

'More rewarding. We ARE getting old,' the fourteen-year-old says. 'At least art doesn't end up with razor blades stuck in the wrists.'

'. . . only according to the art critics and they only lie about dead artists.'

'I've lied down for enough artists cause I prefer men who hurt to men who want to own me.'

'No one sexually owns another person. That's the province of art. Provenance. Roman art made dumb Roman politicians into gods. Christian art justified or rationalized the controller belief system. So what's my sexuality apart from all that's been shown me?' The other girls throw up their hands in disgust.

'Then who's responsible for the human violence in this world? Those who make. The artists.'

'Who's this person I'm fucking?'

'If I'm just reflecting, I don't know. When I'm making love with you, my loving is seeing your face. The only thing I'm seeing my only identity is you.'

5. Deep Female Sexuality: Marriage Or Time

'When Eddie was kicking me out of his house, I put a razor blade into my right wrist in order to stop Eddie from saying "You don't know how to love. No man will ever love you." The people who saved me from death're my friends.

'Two men are fighting each other with cudgels. They're standing knee-deep in water. There's an overwhelming monster whose waist and hips are so soft, he looks like a woman. His right arm doesn't look like an arm. The man is puking against my building's corner wall. He doesn't flinch as I watch him. A man as he's facing out from this wall masturbates. He has a typical grin across his ugly face. I have to tell you how I get sexual pleasure. The women, rather than turning away from him, look at his exposed cock and laugh. Toward the point of death.

'Therefore I love you. Knowing that in the face of about to touch absolute darkness, there is the one rescuing that happens between two people and in the face of full knowledge. Of not only pain and incomprehendable evil and death: The real knowledge is that I want this I want to die. Horror! Knowing this – what're our jealousies our endless sexual maneuverings our social deviousnesses compared to this: we know what love is?

'What's the function of darkness? Of being ignorant?

'You said, "Light light. Those who survive must learn mathematics." For me there's just love, I'm scared of love. I run away from any immediacy.

'One of my legs is extending outwards. You're owning me. A sky of hot nude pearl until . . . crickets in these sheltered places . . . the wind ransacks the great planes. You are taking over control so I can relax. I'm alone on an island. I'm all by myself. Here, I'm waiting for what is to follow my collapsed dreams. I'll be more precise: I'm waiting for you cause I can't know anything and everything's whirling. His hand put itself on top of the clitoris and pressed. It didn't move. Her own hand was resting on her clitoris. His hand pressed down, through her hand, on the clitoris.

'I'm alone again . . . on this island. I've my books around me. I don't know why I feel lonely. This is my life, if you put it that way. You know what I mean. My life has been hard. I'm not easy and I've been, probably irreparably, scarred. People say that someone who lives like me, in this much nothing, is sick. I'm at ease.

'You're owning me. You've touched me and I'm scared because I've decided to love you so now I'm trying to break this ownership: I phone you you're a malicious beast: I know in the past years and now you fuck lots of women and tell them you love them madly. You can't love everybody madly, (I do). You're doing the same thing with me. I can't mean anything to you. I'm not special. You're shitting on my face. I hate you. I don't want to need you because I already, probably most, probably one-twentieth of me, is needing you. So after I yell at you for being as sexually romantic as I am, the next day I tell you "I love you" when you don't want emotion. I want to die and not have responsibility.

'"I'm only interested in abstract thought." But what do you and I do, not so much with our bodies, but with our needs? I remember waking up. First, I see your head. I see your eyes're open and you're looking at me. I have to smile because your obvious love for me makes me smile. My thumb and second finger my left hand hold between them your nipple, my bones. Your right hand's fingers're on my left nipple and my right hand's fingers're on your left nipple. My right hand's fingers're pulling back the extra skin of your cock tip and your lips're contorted from the scream that's coming out of your mouth, as your head turns right as I lift my body so that your cock finally hard is entering my cunt and you have to scream I remember waking.'

The women are shaving their heads.

TEXT 2: *THE LEOPARD*: MEMORY

It was a long hot summer. She lay moaning on the fields where the straw grew. The sun's blaze was so hot it had turned the grass into straw. One of her hands crept down to the pale printed old material as a slight breeze fluttered under it. Her hand was resting on her knee. She wasn't aware of what she was doing. A slight restlessness made her turn her knees, bent, just to the right. The sun was blazing her face. She felt that. Placing her hand on her cunt hairs, she cupped the slope; then, raising her hand, the third finger tip running lightly up the flesh turned to the inside. The flesh was as red as the burgundy of the country.

Behind her the hills were yellow. Not the color of gold but a yellow that is greenless: dry shrubs tiny little animals who have nowhere to hide long dusty roads minute hills roll up and up so that before each hill there seems to be one long upward rise then roll; the real hill equals the roll, the rise of the earth's breast. Its nipple is dry yellow-as-dust holding-shrubbery-tossed-together-with-stones; but nothing's visible except the rise, for light almost blinds the eye. A carriage would be lost to human sight: a tiny black speck. Speck among specks. Another stone. A slingshot caught among rocks. It goes on and on. There're no decisions. Rising part way up one of the hills, in the middle, there's a carriage. Three brown wagons follow the closed carriage. They move around a curve, then aren't seen again by the non-existent human eye. The human eye sees again always new.

It was the year 1860. The Garibaldis had just landed in Palermo. Then the Prince and his huge family fled from the Garibaldis through these hills. All around them the yellow wasn't gold but white: parched, waterless. They weren't hopeless, but just uncomfortable always maintaining over discomfort, even when it becomes pain, that rigidity of control, that is, appearance apparent. The family's women aren't delicate and don't faint; the men who've spent their lives laying back in lawn chairs and feed gaping-mouthed cockers are. The priest, a short fat man who sides with Garibaldi but has to do as his master dictates, shrinks into one corner of the carriage.

The youngest son, actually a nephew but since he's treated as a son is, is gorgeous. Black hair black eyes and white skin fighting each other parallel the sun's whitening of the earth. His clothes in contrast to his family's aren't rumpled, but slovenly in a manner that denotes the highest bohemian elegance. He just fought with the Garibaldists. Wounded.

When they returned to Palermo, the town had already, though not yet openly, welcomed the Garibaldini. A sleazy toady who has plenty of brains but keeps them hidden within his unctuousness is the new mayor. The Prince's old flunky, a thin man in a tan coat torn every which way possible, is keeping his mouth shut. The women look up to the men as if they want to be raped. When The Prince walks in to vote, out of respect the mayor halts the election. Tiny crystal cordials hold brilliant red, clear, and brown liqueurs. The Prince votes for Garibaldi and when his fat priest hesitates, The Prince says, 'You're not allowed to vote because every priest's a foreigner.' Nothing in the town had changed: The Prince still ruled Palermo.

That night there was a festival in honor of Garibaldi's unanimous victory. The Prince saw the mayor's daughter as she stood on the balcony and listened to her father who was orating with pride. The Prince desired her. Her eyes were fixated on her father.

Human desire creates a story.

During a long hot afternoon while The Prince was hunting with his flunky, Ciccio, he asked Ciccio Ciccio's opinion of their new mayor: 'How did you vote in the election?' 'I thought voting was supposed to be secret.' 'It doesn't matter now.' After more egging, 'I voted against Garibaldi.' 'I told you to vote for Garibaldi. He's the better of two possible evils.' 'How can I remain faithful to you and at the same time vote for Garibaldi? I voted against Garibaldi, yet the new mayor announced the vote was unanimously pro-Garibaldi. So it's as if I never voted; I don't exist.'

'Do you know the mayor's wife?' 'She's an animal. She can't read nor hardly write. She can't speak. The sleazy Mayor keeps her under lock and key. But I've seen her because one afternoon I spied through a hole in the church wall while she was praying. She's beautiful.' Some while later as they're standing between a leafless tree's arms: 'What about their daughter?' This is the question The Prince wanted to ask all along, but he was unable to ask directly. 'She's as good and clean as her mother's an animal. She's paradise.' He kisses his fingers, 'She loves animals and everyone loves her.'

'Don't talk that way, for now she's part of my family and above you. I'm giving her to my nephew in marriage.' 'You can't do that! This connection'll ruin your family: her grand-father's a low peasant they call "Mr Shit".' 'Her father's now politically powerful and wealthy. Don't be a fool.' The Prince's desire for the daughter's making him marry his elegant nephew to her.

The Prince to himself: Alone. Alone my heart. This, for

you. I've decided I love you. This is a decision. I like being alone and I love you. Black dress all rumpled up into the sofa. I want to say this: this is *I love you*. I hope that we'll carefully fashion, though there's no human who can do anything, our loving because it's slow and sure and we're smart. Are we smart? I'm doing this for you because I love you.

:My heart.

:I woke up this morning and I needed you. I screamed. 'She's going to leave me.' I know I don't know if you're going to leave me. I screamed, 'She's going to leave me.' The scream is my realization I need you. There's nothing I can do about it. Nevertheless I'm calm, though I might end up in disaster; either there's disaster or there's happiness.

Red and navy and umber and deep purple.

Soldiers descended on the town. Red white and blue clothed soldiers lay dead on the street. Tancredi, the nephew, had just fought at Palermo against the Garibaldinists. The Prince exulted in the return of the monarchy. The priest informed him that a sexless and spineless female relative of his adored and wanted to marry Tancredi. The Prince replied he was about to marry his nephew to the mayor's daughter cause he wanted money for his family. The mayor's daughter's absolute sensuality owned him now. The Prince commenced to act:

The daughter and Tancredi physically and mentally obsessed each other. Their lips were on each others':

The Prince: I don't want you if I'm going to have to feel this pain. I don't want you, or rather I don't want these feelings of wanting you more than anything else in the world. If having these feelings which you blithely call *love* means most of the days I live through are spent in wanting that which can't be relieved: this is no fucking way to live and I won't stand for it.

:I have to erase you out of my life so I can keep on living. No matter how passionate no matter how perfect no matter how deep love, it fades and there's nothing. I won't stand for it.

:I've never felt anything such as this in my life. No. Those are your words. I'm too tired to speak now, my darling.

:I refuse to give up a love which I believe's good. I believe it's good because it's not linear, just an obsession; but calm, rich, and many-angled. Her father visited me. The mayor's physically little and apparently a fool. Since his social idiocy masked social power allied to intelligence, I welcomed the fool.

The Prince: Since from far away, since from far away in my mind, I watch them kiss, I know I can't have her. When she kisses him, her eyes're looking at me. She has told me that she knows she owes everything to me including her marriage. I answered she owed me nothing. I loved her. She put her right hand on my cheek and with it, she kissed me. It's very easy for a woman to tell a man she loves him.

:When she tells me 'I love you', she means 'You'll never have me.'

:My cock's full for no reason at all.

:The first room in my castle: I can't talk: it hurts too much. Sexual desire dumbs. Sexual desire stops

:The second room: I've got to talk, I've got to tell you sexual desire's making the world impossible. You've a future husband to whom you're faithful. You only want me because you want a boyfriend in another country who doesn't quite want you so you're safe imagining you're running to and adoring him. Does your marriage demand this fantasy? At the same time, since you want a love strong enough to force you to break up your marriage, you're pushing for more and more emotional violence despite your wanting this person who doesn't quite love you. Such a world isn't possible.

:The third room: You don't exist: When you're with Tancredi, he owns you. He tells you which people you're going to see. He tells you how you'll be occupied during each of your waking hours. He controls the money. He allows you to fuck other men. He gives you your work.

Abandonment:
The world is memory. I don't remember anymore because I refuse to remember anymore because all my memories hurt.

The Leopard equals these memories. I'll remember: I won't repress I won't be a zombie, despite the pain, I will have life. This's why *The Leopard*'s romantic.

Band. The Mayor's Daughter: I was wearing a red velvet

flounced though cut to the thigh skirt black velvet cut equally close though without shoulders or neck above, tiny black suede bowed shoes, ebony-and-silver around the neck. I brought the man who was living with me who was intelligent. He was going to abandon me the next morning. I've finally learned manners. I greet my hostess innocently, slightly haughtily, and distantly. Such distance is a grace which allows other people to act as they wish or need without fearing my judgement. Though my background and my manners have been considered poor, now I have enough money and I'm so beautiful, many men want me. I don't know if they want more than this image of affluence and sensuality. Men now announce, from a distance which they've chosen, they adore me and haven't ever met any girl like me. But anyway people're treating me as if they look up to, rather than down on, me; so I find it easier to be at a ball, at this ball, and I can start to pay attention to what I'm seeing.

The Prince finds all this death-in-life in bad taste, especially since he's aware he's going to die soon. Sexual desires no longer interest him: he's hurt and been hurt too many times. These older women have been his mistresses. Once sexual desire has passed, its object always disgusts. These young women're no longer beautiful . . . except for Tancredi's fiancée.

The Prince: Since I want her and I know my sexual desire's declining and I've little time left to live, my desire is violent. Italians eat too much starch. Because I'm finding my own mental processes increasingly fascinating, I'm tending to have less to do with that or whom bores me. Less and less I know the rules of normal (social) reality; less and less I care about such ignorance. I'm anonymous: I'm at this party just like I'm watching a movie. No event touches me

On Death:
The Prince: As if I'm in a ball, I'm looking. For a long time I've been looking from room to room, gorgeously decorated room after sumptuous silk room, dreamed room after sumptuous silk room, looking for I don't know what . . . Or why? . . . Rational knowledge: Nothing matters. No one here knows me. I can do anything I want in a social situation. My sexual

desire, sometimes overfull and sometimes minimal, is distant from me.

The Prince's rationality: Only intelligence can grab me. I want an intelligent friend. Since I've no such person, I've no language.

:In this world of nothing-and-no one-matters, what is there? A palace which I've created or rationality. Every day the palace is larger and stronger. It's the place through which I'm walking. It's the place in which I'm less and less tired.

The Prince's irrationality: (:I'm ((again)) in the old house which is taller than wide and wood. I'm climbing up narrow gray ((carpeted)) stairs. At the same time I'm descending. The middle rooms, which I've seen before, 're libraries or like libraries. Books cram their shelves. Each room is more magical.

(:For the first time I've reached the bottom room. The room's larger than the others and different. Its walls aren't dark or wood, but light green. In some of its ends clean white tablecloths cover banquet tables. Although a number of people mill about, the room is more than half empty. Unlike the other rooms, there's lots of light.

(: ((A party? An art party?)) A white wood door, almost in the center of one of the room's longer walls, swings open. For the first time I can walk through. I look through the partially open doorway. I feel no emotions: there're no emotions. In the next room I see girls in some sort of Catholic ceremony, walking ((in formations?)); each one is carrying a white china plate on top of which's a slice of chocolate layer cake. One ((several?)) of my friends walks through the partially open doorway. There my friend takes one of the small white china cups filled with dark coffee which is being served out of a large silver-colored coffee-maker. When my friend's ((friends')) in the light green room, I ask how the coffee tastes. It's real coffee. I want some. I say aloud that I'm not going to drink any because I don't want to go into the other room. I decide not to die yet.)

The Prince's rationality: Since nothing matters, every event is every other event. This's called 'manners'. Decadence is aristocracy is rationality is gold is death-in-life. This's why aristocrats're rich. Being a rational man, I'm an aristocrat. I'll kill the Vietnamese and the Nicaraguans and I'll fall in love with whomever I please. Rationality has made me a totally free man and my country a democracy.

The Prince's lust: Why do the bourgeoisie shit? Bourgeoisie, you're not apart from the world. That's not your myth. You are the world. You don't create my palace: you're greedy for sensuality. You want want beyond all measure, Don Calogero, and you're poisoning this world by your greed. We control money or devaluation, and you control greed or things. 'This suit must'a cost a lotta moola,' my future daughter-in-law's father, Don Calogero, says to me. Insect, crawling along my suit lapel. Bourgeois shit.

The Prince's feelings: Maybe you're unhappy. You hold me in your heart with your large hands. This perception of humanity breaks through isolation and judgement.

:Yes, I love you. I'm beginning to trust you and give you my heart, that is, my trust. The only thing there is the only possibility against rationality which is shit and death is trust; you say that you want it.

:When I stop believing trust, I decide to die.

The end of the ball.

The Prince: On My Death:
:OK. I'm growing old. What does that mean? I know I've less and less energy. But I'm focusing more clearly so I don't have less energy. When I'm not focusing I can feel the energy's weaker:

:I'm no one. I'm no longer a personality.

:It's as if there's (me's) this black statue whose being is obsessed in and is its work. When the work goes, the being goes. The world obtrudes: there's only universe.

:I want writing is the world.

:Is courting writing, courting death?

:Approaching death changes your physical appearance. Just as when a fashion designer takes hold of your body, you no longer recognize your physical self. You act as you would never act, such as you shit in your pants in front of people. You have to flee from this self.

:Fleeing makes me want to die.

66

:Even though I'm more and more tired, I know there's more and more no need of sleep, cause soon I'm going to sleep forever. I have to be as conscious as possible every of these few moments left. I want to taste: I remember I've savored most of my experiences; I will enjoy.

:What do I enjoy? I'm apart from the world its social identities. I enjoy the mentality that leads to the world. The palace. (The world isn't separate from death.) All kinds of events're equally real. Memories're now the events most available for me to taste. As I care less and less about the world its social identities, I forget memories. I luxuriate in appearances. Every appearance or change's perfect. The closer I get to dying, the more time is perfect.

:I'm in the hospital. Cold tiled floors beneath the feet. Pale green walls pale green ceiling pale gray floor tiles. The hall outside this room: nausea-yellow walls nausea-yellow ceiling pale gray floor tiles. This is as far as the eye can see. This room is called 'a luxury room'. Even though (I remember) I've got money history etc., all my perceptions're narrowed down to this. My narrow bed in a box. I'm a narrow bed in a box.

:My perceptions're going.

:There's no one in this world of whirling. I've no one to turn to. I have to face the formal nausea alone. The formal nausea's absorbingly interesting: swirls of red slight lines of yellow some white within the swirls. I have to garner, and am, all my energy (me) to deal with this. Those who're in the world should deal with the world. Every human with where they're in. Giovanni, Stella, Frabrizietto: my blood, you should take care of blood. But you don't think anymore; you go after objects: it's the end of the aristocratic world, still mine, and the beginning of the bourgeois.

:I no longer exist.

:It's not only that my senses've been deprived shut in on themselves; now they're sending me in the priest whom I hate. Reality is taken away from me. I hate His cockless thighs. I hate the snot, cause He has no sperm, drooling out of His genitaless beard. They're making me do what I most don't want to do just when I'm my physical weakest. Priests're harbingers of death. I want booze, drugs, orgasms, sexual dramas, connivings, slaughters, the greeds of politicians, pre-adolescents giggling in the snow. At least I want a glass of champagne. A glass of champagne rather than Him! Of what use is all this – drama, tribulations? What is my life? Just phenomena? Even all that I've thought, I've spent my whole life contemplating, I've meditated. What're these theories and abstractions worth? Are they just the preoccupations of humans who don't have anything better to do?

:Humans who don't have anything better to do are rich. Are the world's controllers. Did I admit early enough I was controlling the world?

:Was I? I, an upperclass member. What I wanted most was love. What I want most now, even as I'm dying, is love, though the sexual component has disappeared. I would have this love which is neither control nor being controlled.

The Prince: What People Say About Me After I've Died:
:'He fucked every female in sight. He had to have females, especially famous females. I'll tell you what he was like . . . '

:'. . . a ladies' man . . . '

:'he was so sex-struck, you wouldn't have to be nice to him for it.'

:'I hear he's the best in town.'

:'He's dead.'

:'I hear he's the best in town: It isn't exactly what he does; he doesn't do anything special; it's that he shows he likes to fuck so much, he makes you feel good and that you're the only woman who exists, the only woman who can please him, and what he needs most in the world. You wouldn't feel insecure.'

:'As a race, Jews're remarkably insecure and need to be needed.'

:'He'd persuade, by his voice's timbre by his eyes by his desperation by his desperate emotion by his sweetness, that he needed and loved you while he was refusing to fuck you so he could lean on and depend on you to get you to help him in his sexual affairs. He used these women who were the ones he really loved.'

:'His friends regarded him as a piece of embalmed flesh.'

:'He didn't like being sucked because he felt guilty.'

:'Part of him wanted to be a female.'
:'Cause that part was too babyish to be a male.'
:'Cause that part was too scared to be a male.'
:'Potency in a man is limited because a sadistic element linked with it requires it to be repressed.'
:'His friends ran away from him before he died.'
:'He didn't know what love is.'
:'I'll tell you whom he loved. The one person he loved.'

TEXT 3: TEXTS OF WARS
FOR THOSE WHO LIVE IN SILENCE

:I need you.

:Because you had to be out of my life, I closed myself off to all other men. I didn't want.

:Now, I'm very scared. Every other living being is a nuisance to me. My being alone is my only absolute pleasure.

:I won't accept the norms I've been given.

(Explaining to others): We've decided to rebel:

:If I can't get Heathcliff into my arms because we're too poor, I'll go off adventuring:

:Wars are raging everywhere. Males dumber than non-human animals're running the economic and political world. I want. What do I want? Is it wrong to want life?

:The liberty for love, the liberty for instinctual roamings, the liberty for friendship, the liberty for hatred, the liberty for fantasy: all of these have faded.

:Civilization and culture are the rules of males' greeds:

:The sun was no more than a degree or so above the horizon, where it stays when it is the end of the world. From the still-heated surfaces of the water – not thoroughly cooled by the former blackness – a slight low mist begins to rise; hovering; a mist so thin it is invisible to human eyes, yet strong enough to make the pale sun indistinct and brighter, hot. The edge of this disc touching the longer more elliptical slate of the ocean turns it darker, into a frown: our ocean is now deeper, and hints, in this brooding, of the real presence of evil.

:The second underground nuclear test took place on a small island somewhere in the South Pacific. Prehistoric monsters were born returned. Blue geysers rose up. The monsters were coming back now because culture and/or humans had been erased.

:At this time a typical American family was sporting in one of the lovely blue lakes near the island in question. Dad heard the first sounds of the quake. He looked around: all objects unusually, abnormally were rolling. One of his Japanese kids started to scream for help. The lake boiled up. What, they inwardly questioned, is happening to us? As an answer, daddy shot his rifle into the blue sky. His little boy was riding a plastic horse float up and down the boiling waters which were now a monster. Dad grabbed him away from the evil sexual water and they all ran. Would they be able escape increasingly abnormal nature?

:In the distance the Japanese people were watching this abnormality. White mists rose.

:One of the Japanese was a space scientist. Evil men overturned his private home. His closest friend chased the criminals into their car. But unconsciously, they had left tiny grains of an unknown substance that looked like sand on the space scientist's floor.

:'Why have criminals invaded this home? Will they also invade our bodies and soil and sky as the Hiroshima bomb had torn us apart?'

:Exhaustive analysis revealed that the sand-like grains had to be from a thirty-miles-below-the-sea-bed stratum or from Easter Island.

:'Has evil always been part of human nature? And is nature evil?'

:That is: Now that we and our world're at the edge of destruction, we have to figure out what evil is.

:If everything including us were evil, evil wouldn't be a problem. Since evil's a human problem, nature, naturally, isn't evil. So the young Japanese scientist, Mr A., can make a robot. Then the criminals returned to his home, killed him and his friend in order to own the robot. Were the criminals after the robot?

:CSeaSee-topia is an island. All the Ctopians wear white. Overlooking a weirdo lake, an Easter-Island-like statue gazes down on five dancing girls. This is paradise.

:Why is Ctopia Paradise? Because humans use nuclear weapons, whereas the Ctopian populace want to keep their waters breathable. They've now realized they have to fight to destroy humanity in order to erase nuclear weaponry. Since they desire to kill all humans, the Ctopians are evil.

:Already, with all this nuclear waste that's in our air, the poisons that have had to filter down even to the very core of Earth have turned Ctopia red, then blue; then, poisoned, Ctopia in turn, naturally had to pollute the world above her. There's no getting rid of poison except via destruction. So the Ctopian government sent Megalon the Monster up here to eradicate us. Since Megalon's primary cause is human violence and human violence's finally powerless, Megalon, being a mirror, was an insect.

:Actually the young Japanese scientist isn't dead but is now (along with his kid) bound up in ropes in the back of the human criminals' truck. These human criminals and all human criminals aren't Ronald Reagan and the post-capitalist money powers who have put Reagan into power because human evil finally is indefinable and unknowable to humans. Zoom the truck moves on. The truck is moving toward mysterious Easter-Island-like island. Megalon the Insect is standing there. Waiting. Is there no escape from all these different forms of terror, of evil?

Mr A. runs away. But escaping doesn't solve problems.

Because of what you've done, The Insect conflagration disintegration destruction erasure lobotomy control dispersion is destroying everything. Total destruction is rational because it comes from rational causes. Why are humans beings still rational, that is, making nuclear bombs polluting inventing DNA etc.? Because they don't see the absolute degradation and poverty around their flesh because if they did, they would be in such horror they would have to throw away their minds and want to become, at any price, only part-humans. Only Godzilla who not only isn't human but also wasn't made by humans therefore is unidentifiable and incomprehendable to humans can give the human world back to the humans.

:Planes shoot at The Insect. Huge, The Insect stomps on the planes. Blues and reds, from explosions, own the sun. The two monsters, being nonhuman, are mindless. The two monsters, the future rulers of our world, have the following conversation:

'Anti-rationality.'

'In the modern period, exchange value has come to dominate society; all qualities have been and are reduced to quantitative equivalences. This process inheres in the concept of reason. For reason, on the one hand, signifies the idea of a free, human, social life. On the other hand, reason is the court of judgement of calculation, the instrument of domination, and the means for the greatest exploitation of nature. As in De Sade's novels, the mode of reason adjusts the world for the ends of self-preservation and recognizes no function other than the preparation of the object from mere sensory material in order to make it that material of subjugation. Instrumental or ossified reason takes two forms: technological reason developed for purposes of dominating nature and social reason directed at the means of domination aimed at exercising social and political power.'

'This tendency, predetermined by the drive for self-preservation, now pervades all the spheres of human life: this exploitation or reduction of reality to self-preservation and the manipulable other has become the universal principle of a society which seeks to reduce all phenomena to this enlightenment, ideal of rationalism, or subjugation of the other.'

:The monsters created from human beliefs and acts will no longer follow human orders.

:Throughout the Second World War, the United States was planning, then actually preparing (for) its role in the future post-war world. If there is to be such a world. Emerging militarily and economically unrivalled from the Second World War, America was uniquely and fully able to impose its hatred of nonmaterialism – its main ideal – on the remainder of the world. This belief in total materialism is or intimately connects to economic hegemony, for the economic base of this new order is large export markets and unrestricted access to key materials.

:Americans, having learnt from the British, inflicted this order by eliminating trade restrictions via the creation of the OAS, establishing organizations such as the World Bank and in 1944 the International Monetary Fund to stabilize currencies, opening international banking institutions to aid investment, and developing backward areas. International finance (that is, American finance) is a war strategy, a successful one, which the Japanese copied.

:The interests of these banks and companies are truly global, for the United States controls, or believes it controls, (does 'believes it controls' mean the same thing as 'controls'?), the globe. Thus the multi-national corporations form an integrated economic system which must be protected: this 'Cold War'. In order to maintain 'The Cold War' or economic control, we Americans believe (have been taught) the following ideology: 'The domination or control of the political institutions of any American state by the international Communist movement, extending to this Hemisphere the political system of an extra-continental power, would constitute a threat to the sovereignty and political independence of the American states, endangering the peace of America . . .' (the Caracas Declaration, a 1954 amendment to the Monroe Doctrine).

:An amendment to this amendment: 'I have the most conclusive evidence that arms and munitions in large quantities . . . have been shipped to the revolutionists . . .'

:American General Smedley D. Butler: 'In 1914, in the interest of American oil companies, in Tampico the transfers of Mexican prisoners were common. None of the shits were allowed to talk. Around five P.M. each Wednesday we selected the transfer prisoners. We led each of the men, one by one, to the infirmary, to the doctor. There was no need to give any man a garment to shield him from the cold. In the infirmary, our doctor told the prisoner, each one privately so the prisoners couldn't by comparing notes understand what was happening to them, that the prisoner was being sent to another camp so was now being given an injection to protect him from the radically poorer conditions of this new camp. The shot was only a sedative.

:'These sedated men were then driven by lorry to the Tampico airport where they were put into one of the navy's Fokker airplanes. At a certain point over the Gulf Stream, we dumped the prisoners out of the plane. They were still alive. You can understand these weren't normal drownings. The attitudes of the drowned people showed that they fought against the sea: the finders could see the despair on their faces. Fish had usually by now mutilated the bodies. A number of the dead men had severed hands. Most of the dead men were nude. Sometimes they wore briefs. One body had been packed in a nylon bag.

:'The dead prisoners were people whom the Argentian government had known or suspected were subversive or "left-wing" because they were spreading ideas . . . contrary to Western and Christian civilization.'

:Somoza García persuaded Sandino to withdraw his arms. A few days later, picking Sandino up as he left a dinner at the National Palace, Somoza García machine-gunned him to death. In 1956 Rigoberto López killed Somoza García. Then Rigoberto López wrote the following poem:

> The seed of your sperm Sandino blood
> ashes our ragpickers' buildings our blood
> Blood multiplied
> blood is rain.
> The victims' blood covers
> all eyes is the future
> destroys all people
> murder. The crime of Cain.
> Then peace'll rain
> olives and trees peacocks' squeels
> lift and fall all
> dashed. Able to feel.

:Able to feel.

:Three men are talking. These are the men who cause war. One of these men is wearing what I see as a Renaissance-type

74

hat or else he has genetically-flawed hair. Since his right eye is larger than his left, this man is smirking as his shoulders curve inwards. Except for the hat unless it's hair, the man's naked.

:A short person who has deformed that is loopy fingers faces him. All of these men who cause war are deformed, therefore, recognizable.

:Another of these men, light-haired, since he's looking into a handmirror,'s a female. She wears an armless white T-shirt.

:Almost directly in front of her but slightly to her right. This man is ugly. This man has ugly monkey lips. Black greasy hair is dripping down his neck. A white toga, which signifies the highest form of human culture knowledge and being-in-the-world in our Western history, is hanging off of his hairy ape-flesh. Since reality/my seeing can't be clear, he's either eating a half-peeled banana and/or holding a cross. One of our rulers is a monkey and/or a high religious figure.

:These hideous monsters being in the sky being above all other people are controlling the world Our Father Who Art All men're created.

:The ape monster looks down at these territorial holdings (us or the world): acres after acres of clear fields streams running a few trees: Nature. I can't tell the difference between tree and tree-shadow or tree-image. Nature is either a reflection, or else nothing. I'm a reflection or else I'm nothing.

:The humans're both dogs and skulls. Both humans and dogs need to eat and feel heat. The skulls don't need either. Human-dogs eat and feel heat in a kitchen. This kitchen is a den of iniquity. Whereas a den is the province of men, women control kitsch but there are no women among the human-dogs or maybe the humandog whose face is anonymously or nauseously also approaching-skull (simultaneously either-or life and death) is male and or female and it no longer matters. Since a broom's sweeping hisandorher bald pate, heandorshe is a which. The dog who stands up like a man stares at the broom and behind him a male skull laughs, but at what is he laughing? Another humandog pisses on the floor because they're bums pissing in concrete doorways. This isn't scenes of war this is war.

:The paw on her tit shows the big dear's making love to the woman. That is: he wants to fuck the woman. Since his horns are beautiful, since he's horny as hell; horniness or lack of love is Hell. Being a beast, he's bigger than all the humans: now animal is superior to human. The woman who's holding a baby, all babies should be dead whenever they open their mouths, is looking at him with longing because he's deigning to desire her. Since the old crone who's almost disintegrated into a skeleton, who's in front of the woman, is holding her baby which is a skeleton (it must have opened its mouth) up to the monster, he must be a guru or a leader. The moon pukes. One of the old bitches who's behind the monster has half-way become a skeleton.

:What world is this? Behind the monster, the Virgin Mary and her cohorts exist. The Virgin Mary and her cohorts are palely fading away and don't have facial expressions because they don't have faces. All the other beings who all worship The Beast wear togas because they're classical. Dead children're lying between the classical humans. This human world is human religion and culture.

:Then, what is nature in this world? One of the humans who's fat and female bears a stick, her banner, over her left shoulder. Dead babies hang from her stick or banner. Likewise, the earth is dead: The soil is barren. The hills behind are barren. The sky is barren. The sky is always nighttime.

:The only foliage in this world occurs around The Beast's horns.

:This world is sick. Why? No reason.

:Since there's a monster in it, this world's sick; since this world's sick, there's a monster in it. Human understanding can only be circular; humans can't understand much.

:What I see I am: since I can see only roughly, almost unforms, I only partly am.

:The perception of wartime.

:A dog sticks its head over a barricade. You can't tell what the barricade is. The only event you see and you can see is the dog's head.

:'Woof'. The only language you hear and can hear is 'Woof'.

:I thought I was at home. I thought I was lying in my bedroom by the moors. Because I'm weak, my brain becomes confused, and I unwillingly unconsciously screamed. Don't say anything. I've got to have someone. So stay with me. I don't need someone: I'm alone. I hate solitude. I need —— so I can be in paradise. I dread to go to sleep now: my dreams shock me: I don't sleep anymore. Oh, if I were only but in my old bed in my old house! And the wind sounding through the gables sounding in the firs by the lattice. Do let me feel – the moors, the solitude come straight down to my heart – let me be alive! I am no better than a wailing child.

TEXT 4: WEDEKIND'S WORDS

1. The Selling Of Lulu

On the street, outside the professor's house.

Lulu sits down on the plinth of a column, sorting her flowers. She doesn't at all look romantic or virginal or anything at all. This is what she looks like: she isn't even a kid (being a kid is romantic): she's 18, perhaps 20 years old. She wears a little French-ish hat, where she got this one we'll never know, which has been exposed for more years than she has to London soot wind and rain and has seldom if ever been brushed or loved. Neither has her hair. Her hair's color's natural; she's not a punk; it's mousy. She wears some kind of black coat which manages to touch her knees. The coat's too tight around her chest. Her boots, likewise, are something-or-other. She is as clean as she can be.

But she's had a hard life.

Compared to real ladies, she is dirty. Do we see any ladies? Are there any ladies to be seen? Like all women, she needs unnaturalness.

Lulu to Schön, a dignified professor: Cheer up, captain, and buy a flower off a poor girl. (Her hand is reaching for his wallet.)

Schön, politely: I'm sorry. (He sees her hand on his wallet, as if he's almost not acting grabs this hand, and brings her to her feet.) Something is going to have to be done with you poor people.

Lulu: I ain't done nothing wrong. I'm only trying to sell you a flower. I have a right to sell you a flower if I stay off the curb, don't I?

Schön: Why're you scared of me? Do you think I'm trying to hurt you?

Lulu: I don't know *what* you are.

Schön: *Who* I am.

Lulu: Who I am.

Schön: You do not know who you are because you do not know how to speak properly. A woman who utters depressing and disgusting sounds has no right to be – anywhere – no right to live. Certainly no right to sell flowers. Remember that you are a living being with a soul and thus with the divine gift of articulate speech. Your soul's language is the language of Milton and Shakespeare and the English Empire. Wouldn't you like to be able to speak properly?

(Lulu doesn't say anything.)

Schön: Come along now. I have to do something to help out the poverty-stricken in this country.

Inside the professor's house.

Schön, to The Maid: Take her clothes.

The Maid: Yes, sir.

Schön: By George, the streets will be strewn with the bodies of men shooting themselves for your sake before I've done with you.

Lulu: You've got no right to touch me.

Schön: I have no desire to touch you. I'm going to find out whether I can change you. I'm going to find out whether I can make a poor . . . member . . . of society into a member of society. It's a social experiment.

Lulu: You can't change me cause there's nothing to change. I've never been.

Schön: Well, now you are. Or hopefully, you're going to be. Think of this: You shall marry a socialist politician who controls the arts. His father, who's a conservative member of Parliament, disinheirits him for marrying you. But when he finally realizes your exquisite beauty, your fine manners, your dinner parties, his Lordship . . .

78

Lulu: Shit.

Schön: What?

Lulu: Shit. I gotta shit.

Schön: Oh. If you are naughty, and idle, you will sleep in the kitchen among black widow spiders and be hit by my chauffeur with his huge car rod. If you do not do what I tell you to, you will be guilty.

– Outside and inside Schön's house.

A day-laborer, actually whatever's worse than a worker, manages to knock his hand against Schön's door. His name is Schigold. Since he has nothing else to do, he keeps on knocking. After a long while, Schön opens his door.

Schön: Excuse me.

Schigold: I want my daughter. That's what I want. See?

Schön: I thought she doesn't have a father.

Schigold: Everyone has a father. If a child didn't have a father, it wouldn't know how to want.

Schön: Then of course you want your daughter. Take her. Back.

Schigold: Take her back? Just like that?

Schön: Why should I pay for her? Why should I pay for her wants?

Schigold: Somebody's got to pay. *What* do you think she is?

Schön: *Who. Who* do you think she is? She speaks the same . . . language . . . as you.

Schigold: Now now, look here, Governor. I don't know what you're saying. The girl belongs to me. You got her. Don't you believe in free enterprise?

Schön: Only for the free. Since she belongs to you, she isn't free. Take her away.

Schigold: No, Governor. Don't be so hasty. Haste makes waste and you've wasted my daughter, so I want something in return.

Schön: This system isn't capitalism.

Schigold: No, it's decapitation. Listen, Governor. I don't want my daughter to waste her life. I want her to have the chance to be something.

Schön: Someone.

Schigold: To own something. A girl needs to have a man. You and me is men of the world, aren't we?

Schön: No, we are not just because we are both men. *Of* and *own* are two different worlds.

Schigold: All I ask is me rights as a man. You're a man, aren't you, Governor? A man is a man. Or are you a thief? Would you take away a man's bread-and-butter and give back nothing? Are you a slaver?

Schön: Only if you're a slave.

Schigold: I'm not a slave: I know what money is. What's a fifty to you? What's Lulu to me?

Schön: Lulu? Is that her name?

Schigold: Of course not. What's in a name?

Schön: Are you a white slaver?

Schigold: Not in a general way I'm not, but to oblige a gentleman like you I'd do a good deal, I do assure you.

Schön: Fifty pounds is not a good deal. Fifty pounds of flesh.

Schigold: Then forty.

Schön: Here's a tenner and good riddance. (Schigold grabs the money and weasels away.) Moral questions are exceedingly difficult.

2. The Creator And The Creation

The Creator

Schön is pacing around his study. His study looks like a room in a Renaissance painting where a room is both a microcosm of the whole world and reflects endless numbers of microcosms, for there is no other reality than anthropomorphism. Thus: no escape for man from himself. The ideological revolution that began in Renaissance Italy was men's new belief that they, not God, were the centers of the world. That they can do anything. That they can do whatever they want. So Schön, who is now rich, believes that he owns the world. He is surveying his room: the world:

Schön: Thrones, Dominions, Princedoms, Vertues, Powers I now possess, as Lord, a spacious World, to Heaven little inferior.

I was a working-class boy.

I didn't have any security. Of course I didn't have any schooling.

With my own two hands, I made a kingdom. All this:

Not only with my hands, with my very body, like Hercules, I wrestled Fate, the nine-headed snake, the Hydra of the poor. Like Hercules the hero, I won.

How does a working-class boy become a hero in this world? By his own two hands: by fraud and bribery. Every time I successfully seduce a man with money, I steal that man's will: he is then lifeless, a robot; he can be controlled. In this manner I extended my economic control, for economic control is only the control of other humans. I know.

There are those who dislike me. There are those who dislike me. There are rats. There are rats everywhere. They creep. They sneak. They have brains. They carry diseases. I cannot get rid of my rats. Rat!

I have been forced to take drastic measures against those who want to hurt me. This is not my fault. But I always have to be careful: they might attack me at any moment, the humans whom I don't fully control. Every second of the world I have to be at the trenches.

My world is rotting.

The rat rot is deep, deep: there are so many enemies and people at war that sooner or later the world is going to end.

When the world ends, there'll be no more air. That's why it's important to pollute the air now. Before it's too late.

After the end of the world, also, all the technological advances which have been made in this century, which could at this very moment allow a leisure society for all but a few technicians, and a few women with wombs, – so that there will, I mean there could, be no more social class – after the end of this world when humans are no more, the machines for human paradise will run on their own. Just as McDonald's now runs.

After the end of the world, there will be no more time because the world has ended. Since there won't be any more time barriers, all the airplanes'll be super-Concordes. Anyone, even a woman, can travel anywhere in human reality instantaneously. Therefore after the end of this world, feminism will be viable.

81

It's the women who're doing this! It's her. The bitch. The one for whom I did everything. The one I brought out of nothing to make into a decent human. My very creation is turning against me. She's a traitor.

In the same manner as when England deigned, out of the goodness of his heart, to turn the black devils in Africa into decent social products and did so then their human products turned on them devilishly and are still turning on them devilishly, so for those in power good deeds are always mistakes.

Bitch: I'll give you what's coming to you. Why should I turn you into anything but nothing so you can turn against me?

Lulu, yelling from offstage: Daddy!

Schön: This child is now an abortion.

The Creation

Lulu enters.

Lulu: Do you love me?

Schön: Parents always love their children.

Lulu: That's why I'm asking you: Do *you* love *me*?

The Maid, who's always in the background: You have to respect your father, Lulu.

Lulu: You *don't* love me.

The Maid: Lulu. Do what your father tells you to do. Go to your room.

Lulu: You don't love me! I'm nothing. You've made me nothing. (Schön hits her. Lulu, from the floor,) Daddy, you have given me everything. I don't have anything else but you because I don't know anything but you.

If I lose you, I am not.

What could I've known before you? It's not possible for a child to know anything prior to her father.

How could I know anything besides you? Is there anything else here? This is your smell. These are your objects: your touch. Everything that I see and touch is yours. My smell is your smell. My touch is to touch you. My eyes cannot see beyond you. Who are you, daddy?

It must be true because if not, nothing is true: I am yours.

Daddy, I am yours. Can't you love me?

The Maid: Your father wants you to go to your room.

82

Lulu, directly to Schön: Don't you realize what this lack of love is? I'm not denying that you picked me up from nothing and made me. But if you do not love what and who you have made, for all is living, what you have made is polluted and an abortion. Just as your world is now polluted and an abortion. I am polluted and an abortion.

I was better off before I existed.

Don't you see what you're doing because you refuse to love me? Look. See.

Schön, finally speaking: I see a disobedient child. I see a child who has no respect for her elders, for the culture into which she was born, thus, for society, I see someone who will become amoral, if not worse. I see. I can't even say 'a person', of whom I am deeply, Lulu, deeply ashamed.

Lulu. From now on, you will be confined to your room. I have nothing more to say to you because you will not be worth speaking to until you learn to be a person and to act in manners acceptable to this society.

(Lulu looks around her and no longer bothers to speak to anyone because IT ISN'T WORTH COMMUNICATING ANYMORE.)

Their End.
While both Schön and Lulu are absorbed in their own realities, Schön in paranoia and Lulu in autism, Schigold, who is now so old worn-out and poor he looks exactly like death, sneaks into the room: He might as well be Death or dead for all Schön or Lulu care about him.

Schigold: My home! My home my kingdom!

Farewell happy fields where Joy forever dwells:

Hail horrors, hail infernal world, and thou profoundest Hell

Receive thy new possessor: One who brings A mind not to be chang'd by Place or Time:

Me.

The mind is its own place, and in it self

Can make a Heav'n of Hell, a Hell of Heav'n.

Where's some booze?

(Looking about him. Finding it.) Here at last we shall be free.

(Drinking.) Here we may reign secure.
Better to reign in Hell, than serve in Heav'n.
I own everything here! I do.
You only need to ask and you shall have:

3. False And True Love

Waiting For Godot
Schön's study is now too dark to see clearly into.
Voices:
The Maid: What're you waiting for?
Lulu: I'm waiting for my brother.

May The Rich And The Poor Join Hands
Schigold is now alone in this study of the world. But he's
pickled. He looks even poorer and more down-and-out than
death. He looks as if he's living in urban USA.
Schigold: I'm a worthless piece of something-or-other.
Humanity. I'm not even that good. I'm not even good enough
for the bombers of humankind.

I hope they kill me off fast because this slow death is killing
my guts. Where's more liquor? (He looks around the study for
more booze, but, like everything else, it's hopeless.

(Being intelligent, he changes his mind:) I'm not going to
have anything more to do with them.

You know what they said to me when I was good enough –
well-dressed enough – in a suit, – for them to take a little
notice of. A little.
Maybe I could enter that society. They said, 'Here, dog. Play
along with us and we'll let you into society so you'll begin to
have a few friends.' What dog wouldn't lick a little? What man
here is so naive that he is too purist to survive? But I'll tell you
something: the tongue that licks their hands, even slightly, is
torn out. They are the masters of intelligent torture.

(Looks around him. Confused:) Who are they? Who's out
there? Where are you, people who hide in total sufficiency and
your lack of need, you people whom I hate?

(Lulu enters this study. She is now rich. Jewels are making
love to her nipples and hairs. Her gown is Chanel, not Claude

Montana nor Jean-Paul Gaulthier. Money, not being Marxist, is worshipping humanity, as it should.)

Schigold, looking up to her: Please help me.

Lulu: What are you doing here?

Schigold: I'm your father. I used to take care of you.

Lulu: I'm terribly sorry. (She has learned how to speak.) I'm waiting for someone.

Schigold: I know who you're waiting for. You're waiting for a man. Aren't you?

Lulu: Do you want me to get you a drink? (Thinking that if she gets him drunk enough, he'll be non-existent.)

Schigold: Get me another bottle of Jack Daniels. (As she looks for a bottle of anything,) You can't fool me, you know. I'm your father. I know about you: I know you've got a man around here.

Lulu: You're drunk.

Schigold: I am drunk, but I will tell you something no other man ever tells you: No man respects you. Not one of the men you have anything to do with has any respect for you. I'm the only man, Lulu, who cares for you and more important has respect for you.

(He starts crying.)

Lulu: Look. Daddy . . .

Schigold: I care for you: I can make you happy.

(Almost unconsciously he is searching for her breast.)

I'm the only man you should trust.

Lulu, pulling away: Why don't you do it with my mother?

Schigold: Your mother doesn't do these sort of things. She's dead.

Lulu: You'll have to keep your hands off of me if you want me to let you have anything to do with me in the future.

Schigold, crying, and sucking her nipple: You can't trust men, Lulu. I'm the one who's taken care of you and paid for you all these years. (The doorbell rings.)

Lulu: Shit. (She adjusts her breasts and jewels.) Hide in the bathtub. Stop weeping like a woman. (Schigold manages to crawl only to a curtain which he wraps around him ostrich-style.)

The Theatre

When Lulu opens the door, Alwa, Schön's son, enters.

Alwa is a successful theatre director. He is bald and has a slight stomach from drinking too much beer and never eating. Even though he's a slight sadist, as are most theatrical directors, he ignores this and all his other personal attributes by allowing only work in his life.

Alwa: I've been thinking about the new play.

Lulu: Why do you have to think about work all the time? Don't you have any feelings?

Alwa: What I really want is the actors to have freedom. I want the actors to find their freedom. But they won't do this. That's the problem.

Lulu: I have to talk to you. Personally. I've been waiting for you all day. You're the only person I can talk to because you're my brother.

Alwa: I have to make my actors take their freedom. You're my actress, Lulu. How can I do this? I know what I want to do, but I can't do it.

Lulu: I have a problem. (With increasing realization that she can't talk to him because he isn't her brother. That she has no one.) I'm very lonely.

Alwa: I know what to do. Listen to me, Lulu. Just shut up for a second. Sit down. Is there anywhere we can sit down? We have to talk.

Lulu: Here. Would you like anything to drink? What can I do for you? (They sit down on a couch; rather, Lulu on the edge of the couch, and Alwa on a nearby hard chair.)

Alwa: I know how I'm going to do it. I shall push my actors until they're forced to take their own freedom: they're forced to revolt against me. At that moment the play will begin.

Lulu, sadly: That's a brilliant conception.

Alwa: It's conceptually correct. This is Sartre's notion of freedom.

Lulu, shaking: Will you hold my hand?

Alwa, not holding her hand: Lulu, you're the one who's inspired me. I've learnt most of this from working with you, for your relations with men teach me what happens when a woman's pushed too far.

Lulu, sadly: I don't understand what you want with me.

Alwa: I can't afford to disrupt my emotional balance when I'm in the middle of a play. I have to give all my attention to the play. Look, Lulu: it isn't easy between us now because, since you're my father's wife, I would be destroying this familial stability if I felt anything for you.

Lulu: I want a brother.

Alwa: Wait until the play's over. (He french-kisses her goodbye. Lulu clings to him and kisses him. She wants to ask if he loves at all, but can't because such language isn't allowed. For reasons unknown to her he kisses harder and she embraces with all the need of her inability to talk or loneliness: her need for a brother.)

4. *LULU* In Hell: Casting The Devils Out Of Hell

for Elegguà, lonely spirit, friend to violent warring Ogun, causer of all automobile accidents, you my black lonely spirit, loneliness, Holy Guardian Angel who joins Yemayà from whose bursting stomach comes out the world. To cast out what is dead inside (which is outside) my mind.

for the peace of the heart.

Hell: The End Of Affection

The scene continues from the end of Act III: Schön, entering his study, sees his wife kissing his son, but doesn't say anything. They don't see him.

Lulu, drawing back from Alwa: I want to know if you're going to fuck me.

Alwa: I told you: I can't afford to disrupt my life. You're married to my father.

Lulu: Are you even sexually attracted to me?

Alwa, lying: What man wouldn't be? You're the femme fatale.

Lulu: Just put your arms around me. Hold me. (Not even caring what the reality is or what the effects will be as long as she gets hugged. Over his shoulder, as he's hugging her against his will, she sees Schön.) Daddy!

Casting Out Devil One By The Lack Of Causality

Lulu: Daddy. Why're you staring like that? What's wrong?

Schön: I neither cry nor speak a word, nor will I, until a new sun looks down upon a cleaned-out world.

Lulu: I'd feel better if you'd show your anger, if you'd take your anger out on me. If you'd punish me. If you'd touch me. How many times have you told me that I am only cause of you: by the grace of your tongue I have a name; by your money's power I am clothed. Justly punish me. Strip me! There's nothing in this existence I want. (The two men are watching her as if she's their stripper.)

Schön: You're a stranger to everything decent; your flesh is corruption. I don't know why this very earth (his foot strikes either concrete or plastic) tolerates your presence on it.

Always, Lulu, you have been a piece of shit. You were always unlike every other person. You did everything wrong. You are genetically wrong. Your very being is proof that you should die.

Lulu, bending to floor: Kill me. Take away my life. This is the only way I can get affection. (The play director, disgusted by this scene, has turned away from Lulu.)

(Schigold, who's been in a drunken stupor somewhere or other, is attracted enough by this scene to wake up enough to move toward them.)

Schön: What do you want? (Schön takes out a gun and points it at Schigold. Schigold doesn't see it because he's staring at Lulu.)

Schigold: Hey. You're cute. I want to fuck you.

Schön, to Lulu: You see: you're a whore. You're a toilet men use, an empty hallway any men wander in and out of. You are nothing.

Schigold: I'd like to fuck the shit out of you. I'd like to stick my thingy-dingy up your witchy-washy. I'll rub and dub you until you scream for help.

Alwa: Why don't we all sit down and try to straighten this out. A glass of wine mi. . .

(Schön pistol-whips his son. Alwa falls to the floor.)

Casting Out Devil Two By Innocence

Schön, looking down at his son: The night's coming up. (He grasps his gun even harder.)

Schigold: I'm not so confused anymore. I think I know what's going on.

Schön, looking at Schigold: The air in here stinks. (Showing him the gun.)

Schigold: Don't hurt me. Don't hurt me. I never did anything to you. I never hurt you. Let me out of here.

Schön: There's nowhere to go.

Lulu to her fathers: If memories are realities, this world is a prison.

Schigold to Lulu: Lulu. At least I can look at you. Do you know, when you were a child, you were always smiling? Your mother called you 'Sunshine'.

Lulu: I had a mother? I thought she was mad.

Schigold, on his knees again, clawing to grasp on to Lulu's legs: Lulu, don't leave me. Never let me go, child. All that we have is blood!

Schön, kicking him: Get your filth off.

Schigold: No. Never. Innocence is all that we can proclaim! (He is biting Lulu's knee so hard, it bleeds.

    (Schön shoots him.)

Schön: Shit. This world is a piece of shit.

Casting Out Devil Three, The Father, The Last Of The Holy Trinity, By Murder: The Battle Against Love

Lulu: No.

Schön: What're you saying?

Lulu: You don't love me. You don't love anyone.

Schön: If I loved no one, I'd love you because you don't exist.

Lulu, to herself: Since I've been submitting my soul to my appetite for being loved, I have put myself in prison. (To Schön,) You said that parents always love their children. Fathers always love their daughters . . .

Schön, interrupting her reason: You're not my daughter: You're a dead man's daughter.

Lulu: . . . This is so: The child is born into a situation of love. Being born into a situation of love, the child must love. A child cannot not be love. Don't you see?

Schön: You are not my child. I do not love you: I hate you, hole.

Lulu: I can not say 'No' to love to my appetite for love, and yet I must. To survive I must not love. Don't you understand?

Schön: I understand everything. (He puts the gun to his head.)

I was once a man, but now I'm as dead then rotten as a forest after a conflagration's lived in it for days. The entire world that I see is dead and rotten.

All your emotions. All your emotions – these needs – whatever you speak about – are nothing, trivial, in this total pain that is. You still do not see how deeply you are nothing to me. (He is still holding the gun to his head.)

Lulu: I see. I won't deny that I love you even if it costs me my life.

Schön: Can you love ash? Can you love fish rotting on the burnt-up sands? If you can not understand, if you are so stupid that you are unable to 'feel' – as you phrase it – what I see and am, at least spare me your tender emotions. Your love.

What you call 'love', if I paid any attention to it, would rip me (and this world) apart. Get out.

Lulu: No. I know now what's right. (She puts her hand on the gun.) You'll shoot me before you shoot yourself.

Schön: You still do not understand. All of you are shit. You're not worth anything. There is nothing.

Lulu: You're wrong. You must be wrong, but I can't understand anymore. It can't be mistaken to need someone else to love and yet only human solitariness allows human survival.

If you won't kill me, at least someone kill off this heart and mind! (They wrestle for the gun. Schön wins.)

Schön: I will not have you show me love. You are nothing, nothing. I will not have you break into my world, break me up, destroy me. (He points the gun at Lulu.)

Lulu, coming to her senses: You're mad. This is a world of madness. All of my memories of you and of my life are valueless. (She takes the gun out of Schön's hand and shoots him.) I have no more memories.

5. An Escape

Before the Beginning:
There are no spoken words here. Lulu is in jail. She is about

to be killed for her murder of Schön. At that moment she begins to speak her own words:

Lulu: When the soul and the heart, for the soul and the heart are the eyes, are so desolate that every incident is pain, when the nerves have been scraped into shreds for so long that only fantastical torture is real, when there is bottom: DIVINE HOPE IN THIS WORLD still pursues her way and is saying, 'There is something better: your ideal.'

These are the days of my romance:

The Home Of Childhood

Lulu: I was on a ship. I left the ship; I walked through a village; I came to its other end.

This happened in Spain where drama is reality. I kept on walking.

When I raised my head, I saw a massive house, a house so grand it seemed to be a force detrimental to the existence of human beings . . .

I have nowhere else to go but home.

The Beginning of Inside: Before The Beginning Of The World

Lulu: The inside of the house – downstairs – was a huge room.

Inside this extended kitchen there were three women.

Lulu, to the women: I'm looking . . .

Witch-Bitch: Are you looking for someone special, dear?

Lulu: The first old woman was hideous. She was a hundred years old if she was a day. Her skin, hanging in long folds, couldn't have been skin which any man or woman would want to touch.

And her breasts, visible through shreds of some material, vomited down as my grandmother's breasts used to wave here and there on the waters of her bathtub.

Old age appals me.

Lulu: I'm looking for a friend.

Thin Witch: Yes yes yes. Your little friend's been here.

Lulu: The second old hag wiggled her finger-frankfurter at me while her head kept on bobbing as if someone had almost succeeded in cutting it off or as if she was listening to rock'n roll. This biddy was as fluffy as a puffed-up parrot: She had fluffed-up or watered-up skin so white it seemed about to burst and flood the world.

The two old women chattered to each other about my friend with such rapidity I could neither tell what they were saying nor did I know about whom they were talking. I thought I heard the names of cards.

I drew up whatever courage I had from my solitude and asked them for food. I was hungry.

The oldest hag asked me if I was looking for someone special. Her sister chimed in: Wait until the morning, the morning, she said, when the world will be able to begin . . .
Lulu, to the two sisters: I'm looking . . .
Lulu: A young girl, the only other person in this world, brought a bowl of steaming broth and a piece of bread to a wood table. She watched me like a starving cat, a beast of wet sexuality. If I moved, she would eat me. Already her eyes ate me so deeply, these eyes were empty, They contained nothing. She gave me my food and squatted on the ground.

She said, 'The archbishop once slept here', spat on the floor, and rubbed her left thumb in the spit until the spit disappeared.

I replied I wasn't looking for an archbishop.
Young Girl: You've been looking for a long time, haven't you? You're tired, aren't you?

The archbishop once slept here.
Lulu: She spat on the floor and rubbed her left thumb in the spit until the spit disappeared. The puffy old dame told me I'd have to give them money if I wanted to sleep there. Since I was tired, I gave them money. They wanted all my money so I could wake up in the morning.

The young girl handed me an oversized plastic motel key. She told me I could sleep in the archbishop's room, a holy room.

Through The Rooms:
Lulu: I was following the young girl up some stairs.

At the top of the stairs was a long dark hallway. Rooms branched off of the hallway. As we passed by each room, I had to look inside, I had to see, but I didn't know why I had to look.

The first room was the room of childhood:

When I was a child. My parents owned a summer house by the Atlantic Ocean. I would spend my days playing on the beach. A number of us – girls – formed a gang. Our purpose was to tease boys our age either by kissing them (mentally killing them) or by burying them in sand (physically killing them). The boys were weaker than us.

On this beach, a woman, who is sitting on a fat woman's lap, is looking down at an earringed man. The earringed man smiles and hands the first woman a fish. The first woman thanks him for the fish.

I am sleeping on the top of an ocean full of monsters, of double-fish. On top of a headless man, a man who is only his sexuality, who's lying on one double-fish, a woman sits. She sits on him; she is a pirate. I am lying on top of the ocean of monsters, but I'm safe because I'm on a ship. When I was a child, I wanted to be a pirate.

Young Girl: This isn't the archbishop's room.

Lulu: The second room was the womb of art:

An artist, who's a man, is sitting on the floor and holding an easel or a mirror. He can only stare at what he sees. All he sees are women.

To his left, a woman wearing silvery armor is standing in absolutely calm water. Behind her a male corpse's legs are sticking out from the calm water. In front of her a young woman whose tits are lovely and who's wearing a slight pink slip is holding the black oar upward: Either butch or fem, the women the artist sees are warriors.

Behind the pirates, the men do the more menial work: rowing and flute-playing.

The women the artist sees on his right are all enslaved or imprisoned: A woman who's a mother is sitting locked up in a tiny bird-cage. Big-beaked bird is guarding her. This cage rocks on a row-boat on the same sea as the pirate sea. I see. Another woman, in front of the row-boat, is crawling dog-fashion out of the sea on to a sliver of sand or security. Because all men are above women, a lowly hotel valet bearing a king's crown on a silver platter is riding the bitch.

Are women pirates or slaves? According to whom?

On no side, from no perspective, do women and men mutually see each other or mutually act with each other. Art, also, is fetishism.

I left behind all that I had known, I have left behind all that I know, so I go into the room of my death:

The top half of this room is a mirror of its bottom half. The bottom half is pale yellow, pale and dark green, and violet-blue; the top half is pale yellow and violet-blue deepening into dark blue.

In the middle of the floor, my mother lies in a coffin, in the non-possibility that is death. The skin of her face is bright green; her hair is yellow; her mouth and eyes are open in a scream.

Around her coffin are lots of flowers.

To the left of this coffin either a doctor or a butcher or a doctor who is really a butcher is standing over his patient who's a woman, just like my mother. My mother is adjusting her stocking – she always wore a white garter belt and sheer silk stockings. I remember. Since in this world men and women have nothing to do with each other, my mother isn't looking at her own doctor.

My mother used to take dexadrine so she could diet and then valium and librium to come down from the dex.

To the right of this coffin a naked woman is sitting on a dark blue-purple fish-face. Just as the doctor and his female patient didn't pay any attention to each other, men-fish and women who're fucking each other don't have anything to do with each other.

My dead, my suicided mother's mouth is shaped in a scream!

The reverse of this floor or life is the ceiling or land of death. In death, right is left and up is down.

In death three black tuxedoed men, the preacher men, sing and swing; they have lots of aspects, many faces; they don't have to say what they mean, cause they don't mean: they sing. Having more than one face and one set of eyes, the minstrels see each thing from all sorts of perspectives: in death there is no more human judgement, no more human moralism. Sing! Don't just look, Lulu: sing!

Now a walrus-like-head whose eyes are red is giving head, I

mean, what is the mean, is sitting on the non-existent head of two fishy tales. Near him and/or her, a white pussy is an angel. My pussy has a hard orange cock, when it gets hard, and he blows his horn. Oh, Lord, mama! He's blowing his music right out!

Two purple something-or-other's are, snakelike, wrapping themselves around the self, for each one is a self unto its oneness or selfishness. The self might be a bird; the self might be the unnamable spirit; the self might be me: the self might be language. Sing!

My mother's mouth is open in a scream. I will sing!

The Young Girl: This isn't the archbishop's room.

Lulu: Then we came to the fourth room. The room was empty. The gypsy girl left me alone.

I couldn't see anything.

Inside The Room

Lulu: I knew that, in order to make it to the morning, to light to sunshine, I would have to go to sleep.

I couldn't go to sleep. I was face-to-face with myself. I was face-to-face with my hideousnesses. I had to see my characteristics. I was deeply bored. I wanted to run away, into having no mentality, but there was nowhere to run.

I was stuck with myself: some hideous, because known, blackness.

I hate solitude!

I sat down on the bed. There was nowhere to run: suicide wasn't possible because my mother had committed suicide. I had to sit on the bed.

I had no choice: I had to see. My eyes became accustomed to the darkness.

I saw a window. I saw that I was sitting on a huge bed. Attached to this bed, above my head, was a canopy. I saw a wardrobe so huge it had been made for a giant. It could be that humans are giants.

Something was the matter.

How did I know something was the matter? I didn't see anything that should have frightened me. What is this act of seeing? Is it just physical seeing?

I grew more and more frightened. I hated myself the more I became frightened:

Rapists were going to get me.

I had no friends.

Stop it. Calm yourself down because there absolutely is nobody who is going to take care of you. Just look:

I walked over to the window. The window was barred from the inside. I looked under the bed. Nothing. I walked over to the huge wardrobe. It had two large swinging doors. When I pried one door open by my fingernails, a dead body fell on top of me as if it wanted me.

I was looking into his face, his eyes. They were dead. I screamed.

I wondered if they were going to kill me. I was face-to-face with my fears; with death; my fears now were real. I had to act.

I wanted to disappear, I wanted to escape. I have never wanted any pain, any world which includes pain to be real. But if I am to survive it doesn't matter what I want, it matters if I can do what I have to. I opened my eyes and looked at the corpse.

Neither his body nor his clothes showed signs of violence and he was too big, a sailor, to have been slain without a struggle. I looked even more closely at the dead sailor who was next to me:

Since there were no clues to what had happened on his body or clothing, like a lover I looked into his eyes. Dead men say nothing. He had nothing to say to me.

What good is love which dies?

Truly, there is nothing.

In despair and fear I sat back down on the bed. I was so wrapped up in helplessness and fear, in nihilism: I didn't see anything.

With a last attempt of the will, I looked up. The bishop's canopy, lowering, was almost touching the top of my head. As I rolled off the bed, on to the dead sailor, the murderous canopy crushed into its ground and cracked.

Again I was looking fully into the sailor's face.

I quickly took his clothes off him, rolled them into a rope, and lowered myself through the now unbarred window.

As soon as I reached ground, I ran to the sea.

6. To See The Sea

Continued from Act V. Lulu is standing in front of the ocean.

Lulu: Now I must find others who are, like me, pirates journeying from place to place, who knowing only change and the true responsibilities that come from such knowing sing to and with each other.

Now I am going to travel.

The Third Part of Don Quixote
The End of the Night

DON QUIXOTE ACTS:

DON QUIXOTE IN AMERICA, THE LAND OF FREEDOM

A Brief Introduction: The Coming of Night.

Don Quixote: 'He whom I love is my eyes and heart and I'm sick when I'm not with him, but he doesn't love me. He's my eyes; he's my I's; I see by my I's; he's my sun. My son lets me see and be. Thus he's my and the Ⓐ. I've said it in every book, mainly porn or poor books, I've ever written Ⓐd nauseam even in nauseam, for love hurts badly. I'll say it again: without I's, the I is nothing. Or without feeling the body's dead. Now, without my heart, the malicious winds're blowing about my reactionless body. They do what they want with me. The evil enchanters.

'They've separated us. The evil enchanters of this world such as the editors of *TLS* or Ronald Reagan . . .'

'But you don't even know this man,' a dog-catcher whom Don Quixote had met on her American travels interposed.

'Ronald Reagan?'

'The one you're always talking about . . .'

'Ronald Reagan . . .'

'The love of your life.'

'Oh. That's not Ronald Reagan; that's a dog.'

'A dog,' the dog-catcher said excitedly.

'They're all dogs in this city,' Don Quixote was in New York City.

'Where are they?' The dog-catcher looked around and saw garbage.

'. . . but mine's a real dog.'

The dog-catcher nodded understandingly. Her pink tongue appeared between her lips. 'Then he's worth catching?'

'St Simeon.' Don Quixote could barely utter that name without tears appearing on the skin below her eyes. 'St Simeon the dog may or may not be real because the St Simeon in my heart is certainly my idea. In fact, I guess it doesn't matter whether or not St Simeon loves me.'

'If you don't care whether he loves you, why do you care whether you see him again?'

'Because of the evil enchanters!' Don Quixote expostulated. 'They separated us because they knew that the only thing that'll destroy me is to be apart from the dog. The dog (or saint) and I're two peas in a pod. Evil enchanters such as Ronald Reagan and certain feminists, like Andrea Dworkin, who control the nexuses of government and culture,'re persecuting and will continue to persecute us until they have buried and downed, drowned us in our own human forgetfulness.'

'I don't get it.'

'As soon as we all stop being enchanted,' Don Quixote explained, 'human love'll again be possible.'

'But why do Ronald Reagan and certain feminists give a shit about you?'

'Because they know that I'm about to defeat their evil enchantment in order to regain love,' replied the night.

Superficialities
In order to defeat the evil enchanters of America, Don Quixote first had to find out how the American government works:

For the Kennedy and Johnson administrations Spurgeon M. Keeny, Jr's job had been to clear State Department and Pentagon policy cables to points overseas. It thus could control such policies. When Nixon and its pal Kissinger came into the White House, Kissinger barked that Keeny, Jr could stay, but it no longer had any policy control cause Kissinger had all the control. At the same time Kissinger was woofing to everyone that it wanted openness in terms of policy control for the first time in the White House. Only its hypocrisy troubled Keeny, Jr. When Gerard C. Smith, the newly appointed head of the Arms Control and Disarmament Agency, offered Keeny, Jr the post of assistant director for science and technology, Keeny, Jr ran to it. Lee A. DuBridge, having been recently appointed science adviser by Kissinger, was never able to meet Kissinger. When Kissinger finally met it in a basement, Kissinger immediately took a phone call from a friend and stayed on the phone. Larry Eagleburger in the hospital barked to Roger Morris, 'Don't bark about anything on your phone. You're being tapped.' Both Eagleburger and Morris were members of the NSC staff. Kissinger was acting not out of greed, but out of fear. The USA government is run out of fear.

Kissinger barked about Nixon: 'The President is not about to be persuaded by opposing points of view. It feels threatened by them, obviously doesn't want to hear them. When ambassadors would go in (to pay courtesy calls) it became almost a joke. You know, American ambassadors going abroad would see the President and always raise two or three things, parochial concerns in those countries. I never sat in but would hear about them later. Nixon would start getting very cool and friendly and smile and appear to be agreeing and obviously had no intention of doing it but wasn't about to argue it through or confront it. Let the ambassadors woof it and go away and then write them off as fools for having misused their time with the President to try to get something out of it.' Halperin, at the Pentagon, barked about Nixon: 'Nixon basically is a dog who doesn't like to be pushed into a corner.' Is this an example of fear? It continued barking: 'If you got in to see it while it was President, and you asked for something and you pushed it – eventually it would bark, "OK, you can have it." And then when you walked out the door, it would pick up the phone and call Haldeman and bark, "I've just promised the Secretary of Transportation – or whoever – something. One, it is not to get it, and two, I never want to see that dog again. Send it down the shark chute."' The New York City art world for obvious economic reasons modelled itself politically on the White House realm.

'Where shall I go?' Don Quixote, wandering, woofed questioningly to nobody. 'Is anywhere in this world of despair, this post-war endo-colonization, somewhere?'

In the early 1960s Thomas A. Pappas had persuaded the

Greek government to grant it the right to build a 125-million-dollar oil, steel, and chemical complex in partnership with Standard Oil of New Jersey, but when George Papandreou, the head of the Center Union Party, came into power in 1963 and '64, he forced Pappas to renegotiate some of these contracts at a loss. Three years later the restored junta restored Pappas' prosperity and Pappas, according to Elias P. Demetracopoulos, a prominent Athens journalist, laundered 'hundreds of thousands of dollars from the Greek KYP . . . for the Nixon campaign.' The American CIA, which had been born in 1947, had spent hundreds of millions of dollars in directly financing, training, and supplying the Greek intelligence service, the KYP.

An old friend and operative of Nixon's, Murray Chotiner, barked to Demetracopoulos to '. . . lay off Pappas. It's not smart politics. You know Tom Pappas's a friend of the President.' In 1976, Henry J. Tasca, a career Foreign Service officer who had been Nixon's Ambassador to Greece, woofed on oath to the House Intelligence Committee that Pappas had been a conduit. Tasca died in an automobile accident in 1978. After the junta's seizure of power, the Pentagon began to sell defense materials as 'surplus goods' to the junta. They couldn't sell them as defense materials cause the American dogs disapproved of the junta. Hypocrisy's greed's tool. With every year, the total worth of these military goods climbed by ten million dollars. The USA government is run by greed.

Anxious to extend their profits Nixon and Kissinger wanted to ship these goods openly, but unfortunately, at this moment, the American public disapproved of the junta's policy of torturing political prisoners. So Nixon and Kissinger quietly leaked to *THE NEW YORK TIMES* that the renewed flow of arms to Greece was linked to an ongoing national security crisis in the Middle East. The USA government is run via the media by dogs' greed.

Don Quixote's First Battle Against America: The Letter
'I will be a mercenary,' Don Quixote barked. 'For what other kind of soldier is there who isn't an owner, even of ideas? I don't own anything. I don't even own St Simeon, the dog.

'An example of my not owning St Simeon is that now St Simeon is living with someone else. I have no idea where he's living because I have no ideas.

'Therefore America's fucked. How do I know the profound almost incomprehendable fact that America's fucked? Because the owner of my New York City apartment's an artist. Due to its high leftist ideals, its artwork's successful. As part of these leftist ideals, it promised its tenants, in return for their building their raw, and I mean raw, spaces up to C/of/O standards, to keep their rents stable and to return their building investments if and when they decided to leave. Unfortunately the tenants' leases neglected to mention rent stability and at the same time allowed the tenants to pay all building taxes, heat costs, and further building fixture fees. Does the law agree that any lease is legal? Does Shylock get his pound of flesh these days?

'No! For there's no legality in New York City. There's only imagination in this home of artists. My landlord is the Imagination of the Left in America.

'One plus one equals zero. There's no way I can directly fight America because there's no way I can fight the landlord. There's no legality here because lawyers win everything.

'I'll have,' Don Quixote decided in her heart of hearts, or cunt, 'to destroy America by more indirect methods. So, one, I will have to ignore my daily life or everything that I know. Two, I will have to make battle with and in a situation about which I know nothing.

'The civilization I know least about – there're lots of civilizations I know nothing about – is Africa because Africa is so far away and because there are so many myths about niggers here. Are all myths lies? Now,' Don Quixote began to ask herself, 'what's happening in Africa?

'Where there is can I interfere?'

Unfortunately for the night there didn't seem to be any trouble in Africa. Biafra had just declared its independence and the USA was supporting Biafra. Why was the USA acting so romantically? Cause the Biafran Ibos were Christians, mainly Catholics – Jews always prefer Catholics to Wasps on account of the tribal systems. – whereas the Right-Wing (there) was Moslem or Black. Political motivations aren't always economic which makes politics complicated. It was hard for Don Quixote to know what to do. 'While America is not the world's policeman, let us at least act as the world's conscience in this matter of life and death for millions . . .': Nixon about Biafra during its 1968 presidential campaign.

Don Quixote, having the knightly virtue of patience, hung around.

Two years later she had her chance. About one and one-half million Biafrans were starving to death. In some of their villages no one older than seven years old remained. Although Kissinger according to Kissinger, cause it had human emotions, wanted to help the Biafrans, the State Department was stopping it. So, in order to get the Nobel Peace Prize, Kissinger barked an order to Morris to woof negotiations secretly with the Foreign Minister of Biafra in the *SATURDAY REVIEW*'s editor's apartment. It didn't bark to Morris how to negotiate. The Biafrans fled from these stinky negotiations to NATO in Brussels. Kissinger pursued them, rather, the Nobel Peace Prize, through Morris: Morris sent a backchannel message to Eagleburger, its former NSC daddy, now a Foreign Service aide to Ambassador Ellsworth at NATO, to meet secretly with the Biafrans. Unfortunately, this message reached the State Department via the National Security Agency, rather than Brussels. Eliot Richardson, the Under Secretary of State, was supporting the Nigerians. Privately Kissinger and Morris found all this a big joke. 'Henry understood the issues perfectly and had no bureaucratic rationale (unlike the State Department) of protecting an interest. There really is a streak of compassion in it, yet everything is expendable. It had no rational reason for letting those kids starve; it just did cause it was scared to alienate Richardson cause it and Richardson have other fish to fry,' woofed Morris.

In order to save the Biafrans Don Quixote wrote a private letter to President Nixon and gave the letter to a sailor. The sailor gave Nixon the letter. The letter said: WHAT WE CAN DO: WRITE LETTERS TO YOUR LOCAL CONGRESS-DOGS 'I'm writing this letter on my deathbed. (Whenever Don Quixote arrived late to examinations, which she invariably did in school, she explained away this lateness by the fact that her grandmother had died that morning. Actually, one of Don Quixote's grandmothers was a Bowery bum and the other, never wanting to have a kid, had disappeared before her kid in the incubator had known what she looked like.) This is my deathbed. I'm writing in my own name and in the name of all Haitians. I am hereby informing you that you have to give back that task with which, or the hype is that *with which we the AIDS of Haite have entrusted you.* What is that task? Voodoun. You are too emotionless and too similar to our former husbands to fill any role. Maybe others, maybe anyone else, can fill anything since Voodoo is reality. It seems that traitors to humaness such as you're having a good time when humans walk in blood. Unfortunately, the New Yorkers and Haitians don't have any blood cause they're living in shit. Who're the Third World countries now? As for my friends the Biafrans – you forgot to teach them how to eat food. For that, we're going to slice off your stomach cause you don't have a head. Meanwhile, please accept my apology that my left hand isn't forming these letters correctly. I wasn't sent to Oxford or anywhere, so what I do to write is cut crosses into the insides of my wrists. I write in fever. I hope these letters find you in good health.'

The Failure Of My Writing
    Upon receiving this letter, Nixon telephoned Kissinger. 'They're going to let them starve, aren't they, Henry?'
    Kissinger: 'Yes.'
    Then, Kissinger and Nixon began barking about some of the foreign policy passages.
    Biafra had fallen. In the five weeks since the fall, fifty thousand puppies and noncombatants starved to death.
    No one wants my writing now.

What Can We Do?: The Failure Of Revolution
    A bitch walked past Nixon and the sailor. It was munching a piece of bread. It turned around to Nixon, took the chewed-up bread out of its mouth, and gave it to it. 'What was the American Revolution? What's this American freedom? Commerce's thriving in this country: the Heads of Commerce're

getting wealthier. Reagan barks commerce's thriving in this country. Free trade, freedom: what're they? In peace as now: freedom is starvation. What if freedom revolts? What if we, due to our freedom, revolt? When freedom revolts and wants to name itself, it leads people to the torture cells of the secret police's prisons.'

'There's no such thing as revolution,' Nixon barked to the bitch. 'There's only big business. We dogs've seen enough butcheries. We know the canine anatomy inside out.'

'But you,' the sailor woofed, 'can say there's no revolution cause you own. It's easier to talk about how a revolution must necessarily fail, as all intellectuals talk, when your kids have food shelter. When bitches can actually have kids. When we the living dead will awake and want to name our own freedom which is nothing that has ever been known'

'Do you know freedom?' the fat bitch woofed to Nixon. 'Do you know what freedom is? Like everything else, freedom must be paid for in blood. How can you who don't even pay taxes understand freedom? Freedom is nothing until it's used.

'I was there when the people stormed the Bastille. I was there when the last head of the last of the Bourbons finally dropped into the basket. Bam! Blood. We have reaped the heads of aristocrats, and now their tails – the bourgeoisie – 're raping us. Who're we? Is freedom to be without identity? Is this another form of freedom?'

Nixon Gave Them The First Definition Of The Freedom Of America

'I'll tell you about this country. That is I'll tell you why I support nuclear weaponry. I Richard Nixon support nuclear weaponry because. This cunt stinks. No wonder I have to work with the Mafia. Bitches never get enough. We all have to make it as fast as possible, ALL OF US, cause if we don't . . . we'll be drier than the Sahara that's raping us. Cause the Mafia're no longer committing crimes, this cunt, now a dead fish, no longer stinks. Her putrefying bones crack and splinter poisonous shards into living flesh. You know who I am? America is now a piece of diarrhea, no, of wormy shit in the flux and flow of the music of the Third World. Rape America the Cunt! (I do. Yay.) Give her revomited puke to drink so that you, even

108

you, can see with your very own eyes that she doesn't know the difference between one kind of puke and another. America: our land of liberty. What is liberty?' Nixon pulled its wad of bills out of its pocket.

The sailor looked curiously at it. 'I've delivered your letter of doom.' The sailor walked away.

A Conversation Between Nixon And The Angel Of Death
What We Can Do: The Imagination: Now, Throw Food Down On Nixon's Fucking
Nixon, content that it still had a wad, went home to its bitch, Mrs Nixon, and there they started to copulate. This is about Nixon because it all occurred in the past.

The Angel of Death appeared to them, while they were fucking, and barked, 'I am the Angel of Death which is Despair.'

'Dicky. Can't you keep those Secret Service queens out for a moment? We're trying.'

The Angel of Death tried again. 'I am here, Mister So-and-So, cause you summoned me to level the spirits of Americans. I've done so. The only English (or language) is despair. Americans don't even bother to bark anymore. The only way Americans can now communicate is pain. Most of them don't dare. My mistress is Terror. While you fuck, look:'

Mr and Mrs Nixon looked toward the heavy green curtain where they saw a slowly dying body turning into a white worm that had always been in its abdomen. 'This,' the Angel of Death woofed, 'is Despair and Terror fucking. This world is holy, so whenever one and one members of it such as you fuck, Despair and Terror fuck. Hell whispers.

'Do Despair and Terror have children? Hope is their child. The only hope any dog can have is Death. My child lives in the image of myself. Your children shall do the same.

'Nixon. I am the knives the Puerto Rican bitches, the homeless bitches, and all other bitches're now sticking into their cunts. Why? They can't have children anymore and they can't not have children. I am the knives, the only knives, that must bust through the vagina of hegemony. You asked for total Despair. I am the knife, that is, the new Jesus Christ: I am the cause, Despair or the knife, and the effect, the bloody tears that are dripping from our eyes/I's. The only selves there now can be are tears. You have summoned the Despair and Nothingness of your constituents: you have summoned your own destruction.'

'I'll tell you about despair,' Nixon barked in loud tones, while he was fucking, to the Angel, 'Kissinger and I believe that it's good to spread nuclear weapons around the world. But we're constantly being hampered in every way, shape, at every step: we can hardly do anything for the world. Everyone hampers us. Everyone's against us. The Soviets want disarmament talks. Our own people woof about the nuclear plants. The Europeans're barking foreign (that is American) economic control which they think is their starvation. If they're starving, it's their starvation. England's starving cause it won't accept our teachings on how to use nuclear and computer technology and think tanks on democracy.

'I have one message to Europe. This is a nuclear world so if you're not sci-fi, you're not canine.

'Isn't this despair? But I'm an American, I don't go along with suffering and despair as do those Europeans. For instance: I have to do SALT talks. SALT talks are a piece of shit. So I don't not do them like some arrogant son-of-a-bitch and I don't just suffer them like a nampy-pampy fag. I'll give you an example,

'It was early '67, April. Tax time. They, you know, the American so-called dogs wanted me to send Cyrus to Moscow to agree on strategic arms limitations or something-or-other. You know what I did? How I handled this sticky situation? First of all, I instructed Cyrus to make strategic whatever-they-are, but only on outmoded weapons. Please everyone. They weren't going to touch our MIRVS. Furthermore, Cyrus was to make these agreements if and only if the Russkies settled their Vietnam War. They were the ones who had started the war. Reds never take responsibilities for their responsibilities. We take responsibilities for nuclear weapons; we even take responsibilities for primitive cultures such as Vietnam which they started.

'I am a wily son-of-a-bitch. No one touches me. No dog

gives me advice. Whatever I have to pretend, I don't pretend because I'm not English, I do exactly what I want because I'm steel and every other dog is mush.

'But what about the internal affairs of this country? I'll tell you about our internal plumbing: The White House set-up is mishuganah. You wouldn't believe that anyone in its right mind could think that even a corpse's brain works this way: beaurocracies, committees, meetings, discussing issues . . . I'm issuing all of them out. I set up meetings, committees like Kissinger's unofficial nuclear weaponry committee, so they all have something to do and, then, I have nothing to do with them. No wonder we have to have a national deficit: democracy costs. The only real fact is, and this doesn't need discussion, our economic enemies're making more powerful weapons.'

Mr Nixon completely stopped fucking Mrs Nixon. It touched its shrivelled red quivering cock. 'This is America, disgrace of the West, slave manufacturer in the void of two oceans.'

The Angel of Death tried to bark back to this dog who had summoned it. But it was unable to talk for the same reason. Kissinger's small ad hoc group of arms experts had been unable to bark to Kissinger.

The Angel knew that Nixon had summoned it not to bark but to be used to kill us off. Is the American inability to speak, is despair a mask of revolution?

Being unable to talk to anyone, it said to itself,

The Angel Of Death Or Thomas Hobbes Barks Arguments To Itself On Whether Evil Is Necessary In The Canine World

'Is there any reason for me to be alive, though I'm not alive? In short, I'm asking "What is canine?" or "Who am I?"

'Part of me functions just cause it functions. Examples: shitting, sleeping, wanting to not be cold, heart beating. Are there any other parts of me? Yes. I can make decisions. I imagine or fantasize. These activities are dualistic and conditional worlds. Canine worlds, then, are material (just are), dualistic, and conditional.

'What is it to decide? Decision either involves thinking or it doesn't. This is only true in the dualistic world. A decision that doesn't involve thinking resembles shitting. A decision that's composed of thinking's composed of more than one thought,

111

for it's difficult to think only one thought. For a dog. It's more difficult to stop thinking completely. If decision involves thinking, the dualistic world of canines is ideational.

'How do I have such decisive thoughts? Either my mind, where thoughts occur, if they do, resembles a radio receiver. Or, I want. Does such wanting resemble shitting? Is it thoughtless? Have I been taught to learn whatever and however I want?

'What I'm asking is whether there's any possibility that a dog's life can have meaning.

'Look at particulars. If you're American, always look at particulars. These are the particulars of my life: When I was a puppy, I lived among rich dogs because my family was haute bourgeoisie; I was a special mutt in dog society because I was trained to think that way. I lived on the outskirts of, in the lowest part of, society because I worked a sex show; then I believed that I deserved to be shat on, that if I didn't pull myself up by non-existent bootstraps out of the muck I would die, and that I had to be very tough. I was a member of a certain group – the art world – whose members, believing that they're simultaneously society's outcasts and its myths, blow up their individual psychologies into general truths. Do these three canine identities have anything to do with each other? What meaning can such a life or voyage possibly have?

'Are my actions ever free? Can I behave totally intentionally? America's the land of freedom. That is, America's the land of the myth or belief of freedom. Why? Cause in England, the Motherland against which America revolted for the sake of freedom, a dog's life had been (and is) determined by the class and history into which it was born. The American dogs didn't want to live dogs' lives. They wanted to make their own lives and they succeeded. The self-made American dog has only itself and it must make success, that is, survive. It isn't able to love, especially, another living dog.

'What, then, is a dog's life? When I was alive, dogs regarded me as a wise dog because I was so stupid. So I said to the dogs who were disgusted by these prisons of self-determinacy, "You have to understand that we don't know anything. Don't kill

each other for no reason at all freedom revolution. I don't even know if what I'm saying at this moment means anything."'
A Tenant Speaks Back To The Angel Of Death, Thomas Hobbes

'But when we're starving, we don't think. Thinking and thinking about revolting rather than revolting's for the élite who're educated to think.'
The Angel Of Death, Thomas Hobbes

'Are you dogs, dogs? Do you act without thinking? Will you always act stupidly and thoughtlessly? Do you even know what gives you pleasure?'
The Puerto Rican Tenants Reply

'We don't know what pleasure is, Mister.'
The Angel Of Death, Thomas Hobbes

'As I've already said, but I have to say it again, don't I, I act from thoughts or I don't act from thoughts. In order to feel pleasure, I have to know I'm feeling pleasure. Pleasure happens to a dog only in the ideational world.

'"I like my life." "I feel good about my life." Consider these statements. In this context, meaning and pleasure, both forms of consciousness,'re intertwined.

'So how can you, dogs, feel good about your lives? How can the lives of the poor be worth anything?'
The Puerto Rican Tenants In Unison

'Our lives aren't worth anything.'
The Angel Of Death, Thomas Hobbes

'So the hell with your lives. As for my life. Do I feel pleasure? I'm dead. The cut-off head is moving across the floor. The monster has entered the museum of wax. When do I feel good about my life? When I feel my life's full of possibilities – hope – and when I feel I'm useful to my society – good actions. Canine pleasure and meaning, then, reside in hope and good actions.

'What is this hope and good actions? As I've said before so I have to say it again: I think either by receiving thoughts or by wanting. Wanting's either thoughtless or, being taught, resembles receiving. In short, I'm a dog. My hope and actions're mechanical.

'Am I contradicting myself? Contradictions only exist in the dualistic world, whereas machine parts operate non-dualistic-ally. Machine parts can have any relations to each other; machine parts need power, not certain logical relations, in order to work.

'What is this power which is the basis of a dog's life? Think of any example. Any example. Money. A dog has to make money. Especially in this city with rents or landlords the way they are. A dog has to make multo money in this city. Now how can a dog, a dog, make money? It rolls its joint and sells it to a sucker. There're lots of suckers who're dogs. Thus, the joint-roller or dog makes money by owning something another dog who might not be a joint-roller wants. The maintenance of a dog's life or of dog-like life depends on unequal (power) relations between the subjects or dogs. In this case, the relations are those of ownership and desire. The operations of machine parts depend not only on power but also on unequal power relations (a definition of power).

'All of this is true. Doggish life depends on unequal power relations or the struggle of power. This is the society in which we live. The life of a dog, even if the dog's dead like me, is solitary, poor, nasty, brutish, short. The condition of a dog is a condition of war, of everyone against everyone: so every dog has a right to everything, even to another dog's body. This is freedom.

'What, then, holds canine society together? Is it only war?'
The Puerto Rican Tenants In Unison
'The only thing we know in our lives is death.'
The Angel Of Death
'Does war have to depend on death?' It looks at the Puerto Ricans. 'Against what, then, can you revolt? Yourselves? If all is death?'
The Puerto Ricans
'We're not revolting. We're revolting.'
The Angel Of Death
'Death's revolting. This is the Free World. What was the first political revolution that caused this Free World? Baby Doc. Is canine historical cause-and-effect this simple? How do I know what I don't see or know? Every day what I see is death. My only pleasure in my daily life is absence.'

114

The Tenant Who First Spoke Out Speaks Softly

'So it doesn't matter if we think or not.'

The Angel Of Death

'The American Revolution or American freedom is a mask of death. Our nihilism and dying must be the mask of our revolution.' Having barked this, the Angel of Death turned back to Mr and Mrs Nixon, who had stopped fucking and were staring wide-eyed.

Mr Nixon

'Our country doesn't allow negativity,' Mr Nixon barked. 'There's no nihilism in this country.'

The Angel Of Death

'What is my nihilism?' asked an angel rhetorically.

A Portrait Of An American Family

'I was in the middle age of my life,' an angel barked to Mr Nixon. 'Ahead of me there was (I saw) nothing. Behind me were only events that had ended and become memories or regrets. I was in lightlessness doubly: I didn't understand; everything (in my life) had failed and ended.

The Dreaming Of The Doggish Heart Is Death

'I ran away from New York back to my family. I ran into my father's arms.

'"Why have you come back here?" daddy barked to me.

'"New York is hell. You don't know how hellish capitalism really is. Daddy, I was wrong to leave here. I ran away to the city because I didn't feel normal in a normal household and, wanting to be me, I wanted to express me. In the city, in order to stay alive, I sucked cocks while their owners held guns to my head. At the same time, I was scared. All the time I was so frightened of men, I kept running after men who might protect me, especially, cause I was so frightened of men I didn't want anything to do with them, after men who didn't want me. Love was rape and rejection. If I wasn't loved, I couldn't fit into this marketplace or world of total devaluation. I fit in perfectly. I believed I was on Mars. I had no conceptions how to live on Mars. Either my education had been inadequate or faulty or I wasn't who I was born to be.

'"Day after day, I grew older. None of my characteristics changed. I was still unbearable and dream-ridden. Day after

115

day, I cried more and more. My only reaction to continuous devaluation was autism and, now and then, hatred. What could I hate? What did I know? I was totally powerless because I couldn't exist. Crying was the only activity I was capable of doing. A few days ago, I totally left. You're the only sweetness I've ever known."

'"You were perfectly right to come back here." Mommy was cooking corn muffins. "This is where you belong; you've never belonged anywhere else. The family is the only refuge any of us has. Daddy and I've been discussing this."

'I ate part of my corn muffin. My father hugged me and got part of my corn muffin all over me. "Do you really want me?" I couldn't believe it was possible for me to be happy.

'"Your mother and I have always loved you. That's who parents are. Because of our love, baby, you came into this world; you came into this world with our love."

'I couldn't reply.

'"You ran away from this. It's normal for children to break from their parents. You wanted to wallow in the outside world. You wallowed in all the hatred and filth that is outside. Nowadays, only the family stands against hatred and filth. On a political level, hatred is revolution. On a social level, it's chaos. On a personal level, self-destruction. You existed in revolution, chaos, and self-destruction. That is your and your kind's banner.

'"Our love can save you from the graveyard of the poor of the city. Being part of a family is safe."

'I was crying so deeply because I had been so scared and scarred by fear that I was no longer able to accept love, I had to run to the bathroom to cry.

'"You've come back to prison of your own free accord," my mother barked when I returned from the bathroom.

'"You're my property," daddy amended. "From now on, you will do whatever I woof you to do and, more important, be whoever I order you. This is a safe unit."

The Angel Of Death Recounted Its Death

'My father further barked that since the US prisons had become privatized so that, in accordance with NBC, electrocutions could be televised, my family was going to strap me

116

into a leather chair. They strapped me. They left the room. On a TV set in its bedroom, my father watched me be electrocuted.'

The Angel of Death finished its speech to Mr and Mrs Nixon, 'Get out of this country as quickly as you can. The only way it's possible to be canine and survive is to be a traitor. Traitors're stupid and Jewish. That's history for you. May your only freedom be and is suffering until you can die.'

The Impossibility Of Dreaming
Don Quixote got rid of Nixon. Death had won Don Quixote's first assault against America. Death lies everywhere. The green and yellowed plains house nuclear weaponry. The cities stink. Of beggars with real cut-off legs held together by wires, sitting next to four-million-dollar buildings. Of artists who're so uneducated they don't know there's no chance of becoming anything else but a beggar, of becoming a successful artist. There's no sexuality. When dying takes all the time, there's no time. Nature is abomination. Nixon, a minor fact in nature, no longer mattered.

Don Quixote realized that defeating Nixon isn't defeating America and that to defeat America she had to learn who America is. What is the myth of America, for economic and political war or control now is taking place at the level of. language or myth.

'First,' Don Quixote asked, 'how did America begin? What are the myths of the beginning of America?'

Answer: The desire for religious intolerance made America or Freedom.

Explanation: Puritans and Quakers founded the north-eastern portion of the United States. In the Massachusetts Bay Colony, the method of instruction was the sermon and the place of instruction, the New England meeting-house. Theology, or politics, took place, not as in the Mother Country on the level of theory, but in terms of praxis: these New Worlders had left England not because they had been forbidden there to worship as they wanted to but because there they and, more important,

117

their neighbors weren't forced to live as rigidly in religious terms as they wanted.

In 1656, Christopher Holder and his friend were sent to Boston to be punished for preaching Quakerism in New England. The Boston Governor and its Deputy-Governor as good Puritans gave these two dogs thirty stripes each with a three-knotted cord. Then they threw them into a bare cell. For three days and nights Christopher and friend were given no food, liquid, bedding. They spent nine more winter weeks in an unheated jail cell. Winters in northern America are cold. Twice a week the boys got whipped. They were whipped fifteen times the first time. Each time thereafter the lash number increased by three.

In 1658, the Massachusetts Bay House Deputies passed the Death Penalty against Quakers.

Answer: American freedom was the supremacy of technology over ideology (as in nuclear government).

Explanation: The New Englanders were concerned with the organization and effectiveness of their society, rather than with its nature and overall determination. 'There is a straine in a dog's heart that will sometime or other runne out to excesse, unlesse the Lord restraine it, but it is not good to venture it: . . . It is therefore most wholsome for Magistrates and Officers in Church and Common-wealth, never to affect more liberty . . . than will do them good . . .' Behavior – whatever the behavior or the intentionality – must be modulated; all places of eating are modulated to McDonald's. The preamble to *THE BODY OF LIBERTIES,* the first compilation of Massachusetts law: 'The free fruition of such liberties Immunities and priveledges as humantie, Civilitie, and Christianitie call for as due to every dog in its place and proportion without impeachment and Infringement hath ever bene and will ever be the tranquillitie and Stabilitie of Churches and Commonwealths.' Individual liberty or behavior must be modulated for the sake of the institutions of religion and state.

Answer: Freedom was the individual embracement of nonsexual masochism.

118

Explanation: One form of such freedom or modulated behavior occurred in the Quaker, rather than the Puritan, society. Since behavior had to be both modulated and religious, the Quakers embraced and ran after martyrdom; they 'as joyfully entered prisons as palaces, and in the prison-house, (I) sang praises to (my) God and esteemed the bolts and locks upon me jewels.' They elected Reagan.

Answer: Individual freedom was the choice between militarism and the refusal to partake in government.

Explanation: Being martyrs, the Quakers were pacifists. The Indians, steadily losing their lands, started to massacre whites. The Quakers refused to fight. The beginning of American liberalism. '. . . you are unfit for government,' John Fothergill of the London Yearly Meeting told the Quakers, '(because you have accepted a) publick trust, which . . . you cannot discharge. You owe the people protection, and yet withhold them from protecting themselves. Will not all the blood that is spilt lye at your doors?' From hereon in, the Quaker or civilian rested itself on the grace or chance of God.

Answer: Freedom and money must be intertwined.

Explanation: 'A dog who is equal in ability, only to the fourth part of a laborer, (and many such there are,) we will suppose to earn four-pence per diem, five pounds per annum, in London; its bitch and a puppy of above seven years old four-pence per diem more: upon a fair supposition (because it is the common cause) it has another puppy too young to earn anything. These live but wretchedly at an expense of twenty pounds per annum, to defray which they earn ten pounds; so that they are a loss to the rich and industrious part of the nation of ten pounds per annum. In Georgia the same family can raise rice and corn and tend cattle, earning from the prodigious fertility of that soil not less than sixty pounds per annum. Britain will grow rich by sending her Poor Abroad.' In this way England 'carried off the numbers of poor puppies and other poor that were pestering the streets of London.'

Virginia was the fairest territory in the New World and became the most beautiful state in the Union. She had bred most of the revolutionary families out of her finest families. 'In the greatest fortune there is the least liberty. It sinnes doubly, that sinnes exemplarily: whence is meant, that such, whose very dogs should bee examples or patternes of vigilancy, providence and industry, must not sleepe out their time under the fruitlesse shadow of Security. Canines in great place (saith one) are thrice servants; servants of the Soveraigne, or state; servants of Fame; and servants of Businesse. So as they have no freedome . . .' The more politically and socially important the dog, the less freedom it has. After John Robinson, Speaker of the House of Burgesses and Treasurer of the Virginia colony, died in 1766, his estate's administrators discovered that Robinson, while Treasurer, had drawn on the public funds to the tune of £100,761:7:5d. It had lent its friend William Byrd III £14,921, its friend Lewis Burwell £6274, its friend Carter Braxton £3848, its friend Archibald Cary £3975, its estate administrator Edmund Pendleton £1020. Out of its generosity it had helped every prominent Virginian family with pubic funds to public funds. In this way England 'carried off the numbers of poor puppies and other poor that were pestering the streets of London.' The Burgesses who selected Virginia's governors, council-members, judges, military officers, and Federal convention delegates almost exclusively from their own membership were unwilling to separate the offices of Speaker and Treasurer and to audit the colony's accounts. 'The aristocrats like Washington, Henry, Marshall, and Harrison have the country sewn up. This's what's meant by representation.'

Don Quixote Destroys Nuclear Power

'I am standing among dogs who're strange to me. I am miserable in this place. In this cage of steel and bricks. Of half-hollowed-out buildings. Of walls of holes. Nothing means anything to me anymore. Help me. My head hurts. I'm a worker. I don't have any work. I don't have any work in this place. Since I don't have any work, I don't sleep, but there's no reason for me not to sleep because there's nothing for me to be anxious about. I just have all these useless emotions. I

120

will have to phone my boss. Excuse me, please. My boss lives on the sixteenth floor. Excuse me, please. Even though I don't work, I have a boss because everyone has a boss. My boss lives on the fourth floor or the twentieth of this building. This building, as do most of the buildings in this area of New York, has six floors. My boss lives in three of them. It charges the others of us, twenty of us, one million dollars each every year so that we can live here. Excuse me, please. I, myself, live in the basement of this building because the basement doesn't have windows through which junkies can be seen and I can't live with junkies because I'm a widow. It's becoming easier for a bitch to be safe in this city because the air's polluted. For this reason, in my large basement, there are many out-of-date air raid shelters the English government sent me as thank-you's for our cruise missiles. The air raid shelters are my favorite color. Now I don't have a favorite color. There's something I have to do.

'I suppose there's something I have to do. There must be something I have to do. I went to the bathroom. Excuse me, please. Even though I'm poor, there's one thing I'd like to own. I would like to own a mirror. I would like to own a mirror so I could see myself. I can't expect another dog to tell me what I'm like: I can't expect the truth from another dog. Most dogs know what they look like cause they know how to live in this world. I'm the only one who has feelings. When I'm standing on the building stairs and I see a dog, I have so many feelings I run into a corner. The flight of stairs right above me leads to floor 4. I really want to run into the corner. I suppose I have to see my Boss. I'm going to force myself to see the Boss. And yet I know I have no reason to be scared because I'm a very good subject. I have always done everything every dog barked to me to do and thanked them for it afterwards. Except when I acted out. Then I was bad, but I am not bad now because I am wearing a watch. I always arrive on time whenever they want. If I'm a minute early, I drink a cup of coffee only because I'm a coffee junky. If I'm a minute late, I set back all their clocks because I know I'm clever. Whatever they think about me – and I know sometimes they're able to

121

think a lot – I never let myself be anything. I'm not on time: I am time.

'It is now 10:53:08. At 11:07:00 the Boss is going to phone me. I have been waiting by the phone all day. Since I am the only one who has feelings, I have started to cry. But I have to figure out why I'm crying so fiercely. I'm crying because I have too many feelings: feelings must be evidences of dissatisfaction. Since dissatisfaction's an appearance, I have to get rid of this dissatisfaction before I appear to the Boss. I must show up. In a few minutes I'll be no longer existing up in the Boss's office on the fourth or the twentieth floor. I have to stop existing. If the office is on the fourth floor, I'll walk there. If it's not on the fourth floor, I'll race up the remaining steps: I'll be so anxious I won't mind the number of remaining steps. If the office isn't there, I'll throw myself out a window. There're no windows in my basement. Then it'll learn what it's lost. The Boss'll begin to recognize and respect me. Once I'm dead, I'll be someone. I have to get to the office on time. I am time."

The Office

Out of nervousness, the old gangly knight looked down at her watch. On the sands of time. Her watch had stopped ticking. Her memories had gone; she was nothing, almost nothing. How could nobody see The Boss? Since it didn't matter, she strutted and flounced right into The Boss's office right in front of it. It had wanted to see her, but it didn't see her. Time changes everything. The knight, who was ticking because the Boss wasn't able to see her, threw herself, ticking or time, a bomb, out the window.

There was no more time.

The world beyond time. The bloody outline of a head on every desk in the world. The bloody outline of alienated work. The bloody outline of foetuses. There's no more need to imagine. Blood is dripping down our fingertips while we're living dreams. When the living have woken wake will wake up, the veins of the night are metal. Her head is the foetuses of nuclear waste . . .

122

A Conversation At The End

Another Dog: Let's get out of here, master. This country isn't worth living in.

Don Quixote: Yes. I love this country. I was going to save it.

Another Dog: Well you didn't. Everything's the same as it ever was. (They look at the dust of the desert.)

Don Quixote, crying: I did what I could.

Another Dog: You didn't even become a bitch. Whereas I, like every born bitch or bitch by birth, have had to be the idiot the token at the dinner table parties of upperclass closet fags: I was there because I was their token. My ass was their kick-board, for I a bitch became an ass. What a come-down. I was the pinboard into which they stuck drunken cigars, and for what? Why're we asslicking the rich's asses? So they can deign to throw us a few more mange scraps of mangy life?

Don Quixote: That can't be the reason. They don't want your diseases. (Drawing away from the dog.)

Another Dog: Dogs don't notice that sort of thing. So how can you, a member of the élite, destroy the élite? Why do you want to save the world? To throw it to the dogs you're drawing away from? Are you mindless, or an idealist?

Don Quixote: It's impossible to be free, isn't it? The European working classes and bitches at least have learned that they're not human.

The Deserts Of Time

Another Dog: Woof.

Don Quixote: I shall never understand brutality. In all countries millions are miserable and scared of their misery. You ask about the intention of revolution. What is America what is freedom what is Reagan to these people? They only know their own misery. Finally people remember and the only history is that of liberation.

Another Dog: You're not an idealist, you're mad.

Don Quixote: Ask me why I'm mad.

Another Dog: How can you tell me why you're mad if you're mad?

Don Quixote: Because out of the mouths of madwomen comes something-or-other. I'm mad because I'm a failure. I failed to save the United States. The United States is exactly as it was started: religiously intolerant, militaristic, greedy, and dependent on slavery as all democracies have been.

I, Don Quixote, am too old. I'm an old weak failing Night. Let me go back to I don't know where. My mind is the desert at the end of time; in the desert the Arabs're revolting. Since all of me doesn't and can't see anything, I'm just a failure: The revolters can't see what they're doing.

Another Dog: Your maddest characteristic is that you take your madness so seriously. No one gives a shit about what you do, night. Why don't you just have some fun?

Don Quixote: Why did I kill so many monks?

Another Dog: Jesus Christ.

Don Quixote: I slew five thousand monks with my trusty sword.

Another Dog: How did you do that? What do I care? Do I know dead monks? Why shouldn't I get up every day without getting up, piddle time away in slime or sleep? What do I care about human pain which is only a lot of pain?

Don Quixote: Yesterday, when I was walking past a bum lot on Houston Street, a huge snake wiggled in front of me.

Another Dog: New York's become too dirty for dogs.

Don Quixote: I crossed through the Lower East Side which is a jungle. Another snake, a blue one, rose up on Canal Street, a seething head. I knew the first snake was Asia and the second snake, Africa. Then there was a voice which said, AND BEHOLD THERE IS LONELINESS AND DESTRUCTION AND CONTEMPT AMONG ALL HUMANS SO YOU ARE THEY WHO BEAR THE CROSS. DESPAIR, BUT ONLY FOR YOURSELVES, AMERICA. Our companions, Liberty Equality and Fraternity, are our jailors. I've lost my beliefs. I've nothing left. I can't get married. I'll have to make myself into something. (She cuts a cross into her right wrist's flesh.)

Another Dog: I'm hungry.

Don Quixote: Wait a second. (She cuts a cross into the other wrist and one into her chest.) OK. Let's go.

Another Dog: I'll be with you forever.

Don Quixote: I love you. I'm scared of loving you, but that doesn't matter.

124

Another Dog: I'm happy.

And so a nameless dog and Don Quixote went away, one with the other. They saw blood wherever they went, bloody abortions screaming with pain that anaesthetics only drive under the surface of consciousness, blood hidden under the clean white male weaponry. They clutched at their memories which were now skeletons moldering on the desert of blood. These memories of America decayed. They no longer knew what they had left. Loneliness-being-lost and lack of liberalism threw themselves upon the Night and her companion like pleasure, like the bliss of a throbbing red cunt dawn.

HETEROSEXUALITY

Don Quixote, along with some dog, descended somewhere. She had no more home. She had left the only land she had ever known – Spain – and there was no land to which she wanted to go, or to which she knew how to go, except wherever she happened to be. As a result, she wasn't quite sure where she was.

Being landless, like a sailor wafting upon always unknown waves, who goes hither and thither and isn't really able to go anywhere, certainly not anywhere he or she wants to, as if he or she wanted to go anywhere, but only going wherever those unknowable forces the waves took him or her either of their own volition or not of their own volition. Don Quixote had no friends except for strangers and passer-bys, the flotsam and jetsam of the world. The garbage. For she had neither family nor any possibility of family, that is, a lover: During Christmastide, when the family gathers around the hearth, and feels the warmth of a central heater or some tiny electric heaters or the Christmas tree that's happily caught fire and so provides a bit of warmth, and discusses, that is the family, divorces sexual inadequacies job losses insane children, or tries not to discuss anything; the sailor wanders through almost black, now deserted streets. Windows show hints hopes of Christmas trees decorated by silver and light. A TV is on and the family is gathered around it.

Don Quixote, walking down some narrow dark street somewhere, turned around to the dog, She wasn't even sure it was the dog.

The dog woofed.

'Can't you actually bark?' Don Quixote asked the dog. 'It's Christmas. Can't you, just for once, give me something?' She wasn't contented with her lot.

The dog, being doggish, that is guilty or Catholic, decided it couldn't give Don Quixote anything because Don Quixote wanted. Nevertheless, the doggish unknown dog was all Don Quixote had.

'Since I love you, dog,' Don Quixote said over and over to the dog, for she loved the dog, 'my world is only dog, for love, by its nature, is total. Being my life and death, though if you went away from me – which, it being your nature, you must – I wouldn't give a shit, you are my being. My very self.

'What, then,' Don Quixote asked nobody in particular, being of a philosophical bent, 'is this doggish being?'

'Since I love you, and that's all I can do because I love you,' she answered herself, 'doggish being, like all being being itself, must be love. What is this, you or my sexuality?'

The dog answered Don Quixote's question by telling her the story of her doggish life:

'Having been treated badly, and even worse, by men, and even worse, caring that I had been treated badly by men about whom I didn't care, I lost my pride,' the dog began. 'Being proud, I couldn't abide losing my pride, so I resolved to have nothing further to do with men. From then on, I would make love only with women.

'My decision to be with women only didn't heal the initial sickness: why I had let myself be treated so badly. Rather: what was it – raving and raging in me – that allowed me to change or descend into what I wasn't? Sleeping with women,' the dog said in a feminine voice, 'didn't solve anything.

'Since I didn't want to sleep with women, sleeping with women couldn't endanger me, didn't touch the ranting, raving unknown. A woman, rather than being the unknown, is my mirror. For the lips of my mouth are the replicas of the lips between her legs. Our desires, repeating each other to infinity, or to the impossibility of infinity like the mirrors in Renaissance paintings, want to keep evolving, rather than die in one orgasm.

'A mother'll never abandon her child whoever the child is; likewise, female lovers're faithful to each other. Whereas a man always rejects: his orgasm is death.

'For these reasons alone, men and women aren't similar. What did I care about?

'Being with another woman was like being with no one, for there was no rejection or death. Therefore, I didn't care. I didn't think I felt anything for my girlfriends.

'But is thinking one doesn't feel something the same thing as not feeling anything?'

'I don't know.'

Nevertheless, the dog continued. 'If a woman is my image, when I make love with a woman, all I experience is myself. I'm very muscular, though I'm not large.'

'My God!' Don Quixote exclaimed. 'You're not the sexual gender I thought you were! And I love you.'

'Though I'm not large, being flexible and able to do what I want physically,' the dog couldn't be bothered to pay attention to her girlfriend, 'when I make love to a woman or to myself, I'm controlling the body. Loving a woman is controlling. Whereas, when I make love with a man, I'm the opposite: I'm so physically and mentally open or sensitive, I simultaneously can't bear being touched and come continuously. Whereas I can't come with women, which is why, for safety's sake, I was making love with them.

'Since women when they make love to each other're both controlling, there's no question of control or power between them.

'I was staying, squatting, in London. Being shy, I was too scared to to talk to anybody. I spent all my time working. There was a theatrical studio near my room. When I became too tired to work, I'd walk down to this theatre where I didn't know anybody. A man whom I didn't know caught my eye. He didn't look anything like me:

'Although his body, like mine, was muscular, his from early

soccer playing, he looked like a girl. He was so aware of his femininity or what he thought of as his failings, he could scarcely raise his eyes from the ground. So passerbys could observe, even more clearly, the white hair floating around his head. When he was so enamoured or respectful of or interested in the person that he forgot his self-hatred and raised his head upwards, two set-far-apart so-black-as-to-be-Russian eyes appeared. Then his hair was the fur hat, camouflaged by snow, of a Slav princess. There was no way this man could be male.

'Then he was animated, forgetful of who he was, talking so rapidly about his work that the person to whom he was talking and whom he had been so interested in might as well not have existed. Nothing was direct in this man. He despised himself so deeply, he didn't even know he was.'

The dog explained her myth of rejection: 'I'm almost never attracted to men, physically. About once a year, I see a man whom I actually want and then . . . the usual happens: Either he walks away or, after a day or two, he walks away. For me, sexuality is rejection. When men don't reject me, when they make the moves on me, they scare me so much I run away. Either way, since it doesn't work out between me and men, I distrusted my immediate desire for this man. I resolved to have nothing to do with him.

'He indirectly looked at me, for that was his nature, and I kept staring at and following him, though I was having nothing to do with him, and both of us did this for a very long time. Fifty-four days. I don't know whether we got to know each other or not. I didn't even know his name. Each day, though I was in a strange country in England, was a pleasure to me because I could look forward to seeing *him*. I hadn't looked forward to seeing someone for a long time.

'One day, I don't remember when, he spoke to me. The first thing he said was that he admired people who wrote because he was unable to speak. Had he always been tongue-tied? Yes. He said something, made some indication that he needed to be punished in order to reach out to another human being. He was as he had been trained to be by his public school. I immediately hinted that, for that reason, we might be able to get along. He became tongue-tied.

'Since he made no indication he sexually wanted me, I decided he didn't want anything to do with me sexually, though he never indicated anything. We were friends.

'I didn't understand the sexuality of English males. A lot of them, except for my friend whom I sexually wanted, at that time, seemed to want me. They wanted me cause they thought I was a boy; not being a boy, I couldn't want them. In England, girls couldn't be wanted because they were the relatives to the Virgin Mary. Their constant flirtation meant that, if they were touched, they'd reject the toucher. Since I was used to men rejecting me, I had no part in this English world.

'I buried my longing, my anguish – all that is loneliness – for I couldn't want my friend unless he was female. De Franville, the unknown man's name, clearly didn't want me. Since clearly he didn't want me, he couldn't be male. But De Franville had never wanted to be male. His father had repeatedly told him that he wasn't acting like and capable of being a man. Since his father was a good man, De Franville couldn't deny him.

'His mother, by worshipping him, also proved to the young boy that he must be obedient. Being good and beautiful, De Franville early in his life learnt and knew, meant he was shit.

'His mother adored him. Since she adored shit, was she shit? A mother has to be good. De Franville saw no escape from this mess, this mess that had to be him, except by erasing it or him. He had to be more than androgynous: he had to erase loving, sexuality, and identity.

'Both men and women adored this creature who, by his/her sexual void, like a magnet, attracted most those whose sexual desires were the fiercest. He/She seemed to be magnificently sexual. For De Franville, wanting a self he/she could love, needed with a desperation that seemed sexual. Whoever wanted him/her, he/she grabbed at, for they might be mirrors of himself/herself, while he/she, being nothing, was incapable of anything including sexuality.

'Without knowing this and without any desire to be involved in any mess, I stepped into this mess.'

The dog continued talking, now in the third person, because she wanted to tell what De Franville felt about her: 'De Franville was immediately drawn to Villebranche, that's my name, because he thought she was his mirror. She didn't look or act like a woman because, she had been so rejected as a woman, she had flagellated herself into being someone she wasn't. Like De Franville, her sexual existence was precarious. This appeared from her appearance:

'Her body normally appeared in male clothing and her muscles had been trained into a tough muscularity. Her mind had been trained by western philosophy and chess. In a country in which women appear to be related to the Virgin Mary because the men want them to appear that spectrally, Villebranche was an apparition. Even though she had to be a boy because there was nothing else she could be, she wasn't a boy. De Franville felt that this identity was the masculine or feminine counterpart to his own. He kept all of this silent, in himself.

'"How," thought De Franville, "can either of us be capable of sexual love? Therefore we're made for each other. In order to fuck you have to appear, and neither of us can appear in this society which demands appearances based on lies and hypocrisies: We are too honest to exist."

'I have always thought,' the dog explained, 'that the world of society or this city is the world of appearances.

'Being rejected was my worst nightmare. Is that related to being female? If I could control my own life, I could make sure I wouldn't be rejected. In order to control my own life, rather than make up an image or be hypocritical as most social people do, I learned to control my own mind and body. Thus, to whatever extent possible, my fate.'

'God,' the mad knight asked, 'how were you able to do that?'

'First of all, by renouncing all I was taught to live by, such as goodness and proper opinions. Then, by renouncing that renunciation, by actually suffering.'

'I've suffered,' said the knight. 'Why don't I control anyone?'

'The trouble is: you're not a Nazi. You've good intentions or thoughts: you suffer because these intentions or thoughts're ineffectual. Your suffering isn't pure. Since Hitler didn't have good intentions or thoughts, his suffering took effect.'

'Hitler was bad,' the knight instructed.

'Since that's a proper opinion, you must be suffering.'

130

'I am.'

'Let's get rid of the proper opinion, or the suffering, by asking "Who was Hitler?"' Or: "Am I Hitler?"

'In order to answer this question, or, get rid of suffering, I decided to be Hitler. That night, there was a fancy party at Area, a disgusting club in London. So I could dress up as Hitler.

'As I said before, as far as I can remember, which isn't anywhere, but time as such doesn't exist anymore, or is it distance? I wasn't interested in men because I was trying to destroy my own suffering. I wasn't interested in fucking De Franville who clearly wasn't interested in fucking me. This commonality allowed me to let slip, barely peep out, for everything's allowed between people who aren't passionately in love with each other, that I was going to the Area ball dressed as a Nazi captain. Since I could no longer have a man, I would become one. We have such strange ways of fucking these days. Of course, my transformation had nothing to do with De Franville's sexual rejection of me, for I'm too proud, being male, to allow rejection.

'The more I didn't want De Franville, the more, I knew, for our minds were communal, he wanted me. Such a situation is usual for humans. Being indirect or perverted, De Franville wanted me the more, indirectly: The more ferocious his passion became, the more he kept it to himself and the more intensely and secretly he followed me. More in his thoughts than actually. For being the son of a doting mother, he knew he could actually get whoever he wanted.'

Again the hound spoke in De Franville's voice: 'In order to secure my possession of the lesbian, I first studied her character: Fear and inordinate pride were her two main motivations. Especially inordinate sexual pride. So that, while I couldn't directly approach her or rape her, I would have to make her fear, for only when she feared could she love.

'How can I excite interest in her, or fear, without making her clam up? The solution was to make her want me thus be scared, but not be able to have me so she couldn't run away. I had to become the impossible object of her desire: I had to become as beautiful, unmoving, or unreachable as possible.

'I happen to be beautiful and unreachable because everybody wants me and I don't want anybody. Because my father kept trying to control me brutally, I learned to become untouchable. I will not be a male like my father. Moreover, I am what I'm not, for I have to control people, especially lovers, in order to ensure they don't get too close to me and I despise control. For this reason, I can't abide sexuality. At the same time, I despise the women I control who, like my mother who put up with my brutal father, are weak. I can be with a woman only in my thoughts. My sexuality, being fixed or inert, is dead, therefore beautiful. Villebranche, as soon as she notices me, will have to want me.'

Then the dog spoke objectively: 'On the day of the party, De Franville made his appearance mirror his desire: A line of black kohl around each eye, unnoticeable, rendered the eyes so large, they questioned. Rouge emphasizing his lips and high cheekbones and a pair of pants, cut with pleated thighs for a young girl, rather than making him seem female, accentuated his sexual ambiguity. He wasn't a man or a boy imitating a woman, but a young girl, for a young girl has no idea neither of sex nor of her own identity. A young girl is not.

'Thus, De Franville went to the party. There, he did not take part. The lonely, horny, and desirous party-goers gathered around the angel just as passerbys on a street gather around the corpse in a car accident.

'Villebranche was no exception. She was always anonymous and fit into whatever society she was in because she was so scared. So if everyone in the world wanted De Franville, Villebranche in her anonymity wanted him. Frightened, masked, she kept her distance.

'De Franville was not masked because he was a young girl.

'Villebranche who could want only girls because she didn't love them fell in love with De Franville.

'This Nazi captain, always so sure of her power, no longer knew what to do. The girl was too innocent, too sweet. He(she) walked around the object; he(she) fumbled; he(she) was tongue-tied. Finally he(she) got up the courage to say something to his(her) love. 'Uh . . .'

'De Franville, caught in her(his) own bind, looked down and couldn't reply.

'"He won't speak to me again," De Franville said, staring at Villebranche. She(He) wouldn't admit aloud she(he) knew Villebranche was female. Faced with an audacity more snobbish than her(his) passivity, De Franville was unable to move as usual.

'The Nazi captain kept attempting to talk to this perfection in the same way. Caught by perfection, he(she) couldn't speak. There being no replies to his(her) speechlessness, feeling his(her) aggressiveness rejected, he(she) was even more attracted by the non-reply. Totally confused and more in love than in the initial attraction, the Nazi captain walked away from the girl.

'De Franville wasn't a girl, but a cunt. She(He) was so unsure of herself(himself), she(he) fucked everyone she(he) could get her(his) hands on. There were plenty of them. Regardless of sexual gender. At the same time, because she(he) was sexually ambiguous, she(he) looked innocent. She(He) always said that she(he) wasn't a whore, she(he) never got near sex. She(He) didn't even feel. Oh, she(he) might have fucked, here and there, now and then, but that didn't matter. In fact, it didn't really happen. Everyone she(he) had touched, she(he) had loved, cause she(he) had nothing to do with lust. Who could be more androgynous?

'Everyone wanted the virgin. Women whom she(he) lied to and treated as if they were her(his) benefactors naturally wanted her(him) to live with them under any conditions. She(He) was fond of *any* conditions. Men, whom De Franville respected, took care of De Franville, for, next to her(him), they felt their own masculine superiority. When lust overcame their rationality, they raped De Franville. She(He) wasn't sure about being raped: As men say, rape is a form of love, and De Franville was a man. De Franville adored and hated his past rapists.

'The Nazi captain watched this degeneracy from his(her) solitude of pride and fear. De Franville's whorishness or ambiguity made him(her) resolve anew not to go near such a cunt unless he(she) controlled the cunt.

'Everyone's always telling me what to do,' the dog whined. 'This's a bitch's life. I don't know what to do about it. My parents told me what to do when I was a child. When I either did or didn't do what they told me to do, they rejected me. My past misformed, rather than formed, me.'

'Have a cup of coffee,' answered the knight.

'Therefore,' the bitch bitched, 'to open this, my self, which has been misformed by rejection to needing love, or something or other, is to open it (me) to fear. I've always been anxious, as far as I can remember, for I've always, in my memory, been hurt.'

'How far can you remember?'

'As far as being hurt. I'm always scared. In order to over-come my fear,' she returned to her past, 'I dressed up as a Nazi captain.'

'That's one way to accomplish the impossible. I've always been fond of the impossible.'

'Dressing up as a Nazi captain wasn't enough. In order to open myself up, I had to eradicate fear totally. I asked myself: "What do I fear most?"

'"Having someone control me so that it's possible I'll be rejected." How could I eradicate, not my being controlled, but my fear of being controlled? By being controlled as much as possible: by willful marriage. I would ask the person whom I loved the most, feared the most, to marry me.

'Finally knowing what I wanted, I shoved my fears aside in order to get through the crowd of people wanting De Franville, to get to De Franville. De Franville didn't see any of these creeps around her(him) because she(he) thought she(he) didn't exist.

'"I want you." I drew her(him) out of her(his) fantasy. "I don't want just another affair, fantasy. All that romance, cause the mind always changes its thoughts, is peripheral. I want something beyond. I want you."

'She(He) nodded her(his) head, slightly.

'"But you're much younger than me. You probably don't want something like this: To settle down."

'She(He) said as usual that she(he) wasn't worth anything.

'"Cut through fantasy." I was amazed at my nerve. But

she(he) was only a girl. Girls don't frighten me, except in the long term, because in the long term, girls're vicious. "I'm talking about love. I want you to marry me. Either marry me or forget me." Of course, she(he) didn't know me. "We can't talk here."

'"Where can we talk since you never do?" We had never spoken to each other before.

'"I think we're going to marry, but it's a bit too soon for me," she(he) whispered. Then she(he) rejected me. She(he) walked away from me.

'Not thinking, I went after her(him). I caught up to her(him) in an empty, dark, large room, far from anyone.'

Again, the dog spoke in the male voice: 'Before the party, I had hired this room in order to bring Villebranche to it.'

The dog was now male: 'I watched him(her) in a corner of the room quickly take off his(her) uniform jacket and pants. Underneath, he(she) was wearing a white Oxford shirt which should be spotless, but wasn't. The white shirt came down to and nearly covered the spot between his(her) legs. He(She) was obviously shy. He(She) never took off his(her) shirt. Watching him(her), while he(she) was too shy to watch me and kept his(her) back to me, I unbuttoned the tiny buttons of my shirt and undid the front button of the softly flared pants. I undid each button, knowing that behind his(her) façade of not watching, he(she) over his(her) back was watching me. I stripped down to cotton briefs. Villebranche turned full-face to me. There was obviously nothing there between her legs.

'I wasn't surprised, for I had known she was female. She was shocked to realize I had known she was female.

'She didn't show her shock directly, but just looked at me as if she distrusted me at the same time wondering if I was shocked by her deception. Caught in a maelstrom of deceit, I refused to notice it.

'We looked at each other without even noticing that for the first time not only were we alone together but we were, almost, naked.'

The dog regained her own voice: 'The main thing to me was that she(he) accepted my femininity. I no longer had to lie. I no longer had to be someone I wasn't. I was easy, yet I was still in control, for we were totally in the world of women. Though I was in control, since I didn't want to scare this innocent, honest young girl(boy), I decided she(he) should control:

'She(He) did whatever she(he) wanted and didn't do whatever she(he) didn't want to do. All she(he) wanted to do was hug and kiss me. Her(his) need for love must have been tremendous, for the only way she(he) could touch was to grab violently. Since she(he) didn't want or know anything else, her(his) communication was through violence only. She(He) wanted nothing to do with her(his), or anyone else's, sexuality.

'I knew there was a way this girl(boy) and I could make love, but I didn't know how. I wasn't, unfortunately, in control of myself, for I was horny, as I often am. I had to control myself in order to let this young girl(boy) control me. Not only didn't I know how we could make love, I couldn't even name the problem we had.

'De Franville reacted to my inability to act by doing nothing, defiantly giving nothing. I wanted to slap her(him) to hell, but I didn't have her(his) permission.

'"Since I can't make it with you sexually, we'll be friends." This is the most passive, that is defiant, statement of all.

'The young girl(boy), being a young girl(boy), was too unsure of herself(himself) to utter a word. She(He) was unsure of herself(himself) partly because she(he) had never had anywhere to live. Being young and having upper-middle-class parents, she(he) preferred playing house to having one. She(He) preferred playing poor to acknowledging her(his) family's wealth. For this reason, as I said before, she'd(he'd) sleep with anyone for a night's lodging. The person's sexual gender was hardly an issue. Each night, at first she(he) stood passively and didn't talk in some bar while drinking as much as possible. If someone didn't pick her(him) up, she(he) passed out on someone-she(he)-knew's floor or in the bed. She(He) was just playing. When she'd(he'd) play being very desperate, she'd(he'd) run back to her(his) wealthy home. Since in this world those who didn't own had to pretend to own in order to stay alive, those who owned pretended not to. So Ville-branche's home, in the eyes of this young girl(boy), transformed Villebranche from an exciting Nazi officer into a dull house owner, even though De Franville agreed to go to Villebranche's home.

'The house was a three-room flat overlooking the Thames. Villebranche had taken this flat simply because it had been the first one which had been offered her. Though it had neither heat nor hot water, she had done nothing to it. She didn't understand household chores. She despised attempting what she didn't understand. Her minimal attempt to get rid of the middle-class grottiness of the walls, the gray wall-to-wall carpeting, the nice tables was to maintain superficial cleanliness in the joint. Outside her windows, though she never raised the filthy blinds, young women tugged their two-in-one prams to and fro. De Franville cared about her(his) living quarters as much as Villebranche did.

'Not being appalled by the lack of anything, De Franville made no attempt to leave Villebranche's home.

'Villebranche was too polite to show surprise and hesitancy. She politely, or out of fear, asked the girl(boy) to stay the night, even though she was pissed to be bothered with a girl(boy) who didn't want to fuck. Politely, De Franville agreed aloud to stay the night.

'If a progressive "second revolution" still does not take place in England, then a conservative counter-revolution will; and in that case the movements toward Scottish, Welsh, and even Ulster independence will acquire added progressive impetus and lustre, as relatively left-wing causes saving themselves from central reaction.

'Despite her politeness, Villebranche grew more and more angry that she was housing someone who was sexually rejecting her. Villebranche had lost control.

'This must be how sexual desire tears down the fabric of society.'

The dog ignored this tendentious remark. ' "You'll do exactly as I tell you to do from now on," Villebranche said to the young girl(boy) as she slapped her(his) cheeks hard, then proceeded to snap handcuffs around her(his) wrists. Villebranche was out of control.

' "You'll do exactly as I tell you to do", she repeated as she doffed her Nazi jacket.

'Since I knew what I was saying more than I knew why I was saying it,' the dog explained, 'I knew I was simply acting obsessionally, as I've always acted.

'"You cannot stay the night free, slut, because nothing is free. Slut. Nothing. If you want to stay the night here, you do as I want. This's a contract. If you want, you can go. Right now.

'"I believe only in marriage," I added.

'De Franville knew damn well that she(he) needed anyone's correction because she(he) was nothing. Did she(he) have any money? No. Had anyone heard of the slut? No. Such things are unimportant. What signifies and signified is that she(he) thought she(he) was nothing: she(he) was unable to love; everything had to be given to her(him); she(he) was so bad that, given even one milli-second of self-control, she(he) would shit on whoever was loving her(him); more than anything else she(he) felt, she(he) wanted to be loved.

'If bad is worse than nothing, in her(his) heart of hearts De Franville knew she(he) was worse than bad: she(he) wasn't a girl.

'"Even though I don't care about you because you're bad," I naïvely informed the tied-up girl(boy), "I'm going to give you what you want and's good for you."

'"No one ever gives me what I want because everyone's always rejected me."

'"Cut out that masochistic scenario because you know the truth is that you're a shit to whoever loves you. Women've given you everything they could for years. I don't know why I should bother about someone like you." Slightly bored, I didn't know whether I should bother to punish her(him). I had to make a definite decision. "I'm going to hurt you badly," I informed her(him), "because I'm good."

'"You're mean." Even her(his) thoughts were bad. She(He) was trying to get back control, and she(he) no longer had it. She(He) was never going to reject me again. I didn't bother telling her(him) off, for speaking was a form of agreeing or allowing her(him) to be bad, so I slapped her(him) down.

'For the first time, she(he) smiled.

'Whatever her(his) confusions, De Franville knew she(he)

had never felt such sweetness: sweetness and gentleness had never existed in the realm of love. Not with the young actresses who had tried to give her(him) everything, for all women, like her(his) mother, loved too much. Not with the older men, tutors and professors, who had separated sex (punishment) from love. No one had wanted her(him) until now.

'Since this was the first time she(he) was wanted, she(he) was in a strange world. She(he) didn't know how to travel in this world. More scared than she(he) had ever been, she(he) spat at me.

'I was too in control to be upset. I reached for a whip, a short single strap with one knot on its end, a little one that was hanging from a nail near the window. Outside it was snowing.

'It was my responsibility, because I could do anything to this strong body, to give it exactly what it needed and no more: I had to know how to give exactly the right stroke. I had to know how to control each inch of flesh that wasn't mine. I had to be able to feel as this other person feels: I could no longer be selfish. I loved her(him) for giving herself(himself) to me.

'I not only was totally in control, I also had to be totally in control, for love controlled me and this world isn't dualistic.

'"Now, you're going to tell me exactly how you've been bad."

'Being bad, she(he) didn't answer me.

'I emotionlessly or responsibly informed her(him) exactly what was going to happen to her(him). "You're going to be whipped ten times. Every time you refuse to tell me why you deserve the next lash, you'll receive an extra lash. Get those pants off."

'Using her(his) bound-together hands as one hand, the clever bitch(dog) pushed her(his) pants off as fast as she(he) could. I drew a black leather line slowly across the small of her(his) back until the back became accustomed to the feel.'

The dog continued, 'Finally I calmed down enough to perceive what I was doing. Then, in a controlled manner, I increased the brutality of my strokes until her(his) body began to writhe. Due to my increasing ferocity, she(he) twists so much that for the first time just as my whip strokes have become hard enough to make her(him) realize that the pain isn't pretense that pain is only pain and eradicates all pretense and stupid thinking, she(he) reveals a fault that is absolute. She(He) had actually tricked me.

'Then, I hit him without control. I hit him cause I hated him. After a while, my hatred and immolated self-pride, via my right arm's constant action, became a more reflexive under-standing. This man had no intention of taking responsibility, for he hated and feared his masculinity as much as I did. By making all this pain clear, both he and I for the first time accepted that sex.'

The dog talked as the man: 'Because I loved her, I knew she needed what had just happened to me, because she had been as permanently frightened as I had. I told her to lie down on the mattress, on her stomach. She complied like a child. She pulled her hideous olive pants down her legs without my having to say anything. Since I was her slave, I told her she would have to tell me exactly how many whip strokes I was going to give her. "Tell me how many times I should hit you."

'For a moment she thought. "Ten."

'"How hard?"

'"Start lightly and increase the force. Don't damage me." Her fear of not being in control was coming out full force. She was going to let me give her so much pain she was going to lose control. I looked at her ass shaking.

'"Each time I whip you, tell me the number of the lash, so your pain is continuously what you want."

'"One."

'"Two."

'"Three."

'"Four."

'"Five."

'"Six."

'"Seven."

'"Eight."

'"Nine."

'"Ten." Afterwards, she looked up at me in a way that I recognized, for I had looked up to her before in the same way.

'Being for a split second mirrors of each other, we had to be other than we were.'

The dog said in her own voice to Don Quixote, 'I've never done anything like this before.'

'Huh?'

'"I've never gone out of my way for anyone," I told the man or fake man or whoever he was. "Especially for a man.

'"No: I've never gone out of my way for anyone. Before."

'"Men believe only in what they imagine," he replied. "They don't have any idea nor do they care what a certain relationship's really like:

'"Before I actually met you, I was already in love with you. Since I was watching you all the time, we had met long before you knew it, so that I knew, when we met, we already loved each other. Love doesn't need human understanding. I told you the exact truth when I told you I needed to be punished, for I had been bad, you had no conception, how much, I had been deceitful."

'"For that you're going to have to agree to let me punish you forever and ever. God – or someone – forbid, you should ever end up being good."

'De Franville agreed. "Furthermore," De Franville added as a coda, "since you're now giving your life to punishing me, if you ever deviate, falter, or alter in the slightest way, I will turn on you and treat you in a manner so horrendous you will wish you had never, in the beginning, turned to women for happiness."'

Don Quixote was disgusted that human heterosexuality had come to such an extreme end, even though the dog wasn't human, only female. She covered her disgust. 'What happened to you that you ended up this way?'

The dog explained her innocence:

'My childhood is a river:

1. The River

'I have to get out of this house. All the time. I guess I have to wander. Around the ugly river, which should be full of garbage, but isn't. I love this river. Today I ran along the dark riverbank for an hour. The cold wind blew around my sides so that, while running, I felt it. The dirt and leaves beneath my feet were so damp and puddly, it must have just rained, and deeply. I thought it was going to rain. Obviously it was too cold to run.

'I gather my legs up in a "V" as, on my belly, on the stone wall surrounding the river, I look at the river.

'I'm glad I'm in this tired, tedious, hedged-in country. Even though it's colder than hell and the wind is ripping through my untouchable – or so I feel – flesh, I don't want to go inside. I hate going into that empty, cold apartment. It is alien. Someone, there, is going to yell at me. My nurse is always telling me there's something wrong with me. I'm always cold in the apartment cause no one hugs me. They don't hug me cause I'm unlike other people: I'm neither male nor female. My nurse likes my sisters and brother unlike me, because they, unlike me, 're normal. I'm weird. I love the river because it isn't human and I'm not human.

'My sisters and brother're lying around their mother on her bed. She never gets up from her bed. She hugs them and even kisses them. I have to sit at the foot of the bed. Their mother, not my mother, says to me that she's sorry she can't touch me and I'm untouchable, "but until the nurse or any other person who is another person says to me you're normal and you're trying to do the only possible thing you can do to adjust to life – be happy like everybody else in this world – , I cannot allow you to be around happy people, that is, people. Because you are diseased." I love the river because it should be full of garbage, but isn't.

'"What, then, should I do, mommy?" I asked as politely as I knew how.

'"Don't say 'she', Villey." Villey is short for Villain.

'"I didn't say 'she', mommy."

'"I'm not your mother. Don't speak that way to your mother."

'"How can I speak to you?"

'"Children have no right to ask questions. So until you learn to be quiet, keep your fat trap shut."

'I did what she told me, for I did what everyone told me. I passed out of the human world to my worlds of trees and books. Every night I gave my hand in marriage to my favorite book. A child, still being human, has to love. In my bedroom, which wasn't my bedroom because I didn't exist enough to own, there was a bookcase. Each book in that bookcase, when I read it, was a world which didn't contain parents.

'I sit on the windowseat at the bottom of one of the huge livingroom windows where I'm not supposed to sit. Since I draw the thick olive velvet then beige lace curtains past me and I'm hidden between this wall of curtains and the window pane, I'm in my own world. Here, when I read, my own world and the book's world meet. Since there's no room for anything else, I'm safe.

'Since, when humans appear in this world, they're less important than the non-humans: the world outside the window pane also contains no monsters. I would tend to gaze at this world rather than at the small black figures on a page: this world whose meaning is, like a book's, always distant from me. Here, at the edges of meaning, I'm safe. Outside it's raining, as it always does in this city.

'My book says: "There was no possibility of taking a walk that day. We had been wandering, indeed, in the leafless shrubbery an hour in the morning; but since dinner (Mrs Reed, when there was no company, dined early) the cold winter wind had brought with it clouds so sombre, and a rain so penetrating, that further outdoor exercise was now out of the question." My book is about bleakness which I love. Bleakness is Nature storming cold olives and browns something like a sky. Winds blow long drab gray skirts upwards, toward the heavens. Humans're just small figures in the midst of everything or nature, which, immense, proud and arrogant storms fill with cold and frightfulness. Here, a human only revolts and fails because revolution must be failure.

'My step/half brother can't find me. He runs out of the room to tell my fake mother, with whom he's in league, I'm trying to suicide.

'Nevertheless, he's broken through my barricade. Because of him, not only have I lost all my joy in life. They also can now find me. They can put their huge hands on me: I'm in torment.

'This brother, half brother step-brother fake brother, has an angel's face. His torso's a rugby player's. Psychically he's violent. His combination of mental and physical, or he, is powerful and frightening. When he's acting violently expectably, he tears down doors, throws chairs, and beats up people. Since his mother adores him because he acts like this, like a big man, she gives him everything he wants; the more mannish he acts, the more she gives.

'These past few weeks she's been feeding him downers. The family doctor advised this because the family doctor thinks my brother should be caged up. He knows my mother isn't going to do it. The family doctor's responsible. The more violently my fake brother behaves, the more downers she feeds him. One result is he's now spending so much time eating and sleeping – which my fake mother encourages cause when he eats and sleeps he's not violent – that his former physical angelic resemblance is now corpulence and sallowness. Acne covers his puss.

'My fake brother is the human world. Being four years older than me, my fake brother explains to me the reasons why he hates me so that I'll learn them: I don't know how to love sincerely; I care too much what other people think about me.

'If this isn't true, if I don't care what other people think about me, I wouldn't care if he loved me and I'd think he's crazy just as his own mother thinks he is. But, since I do care cause I hate him, what he says about me must be true: I don't know how to love; therefore, he does.

'Since I'm bad and don't even understand my badness, I can't trust myself, so I do everything my fake brother, even though I hate him, tells me to do. I'm always scared.

2. Dreams Of/In The Human World

'This morning,' the dog continued to tell the night about her childhood in order to understand and explain her sexuality, 'this morning I woke up while dreaming I had an abortion in a hospital. I was in the waiting room whose floor was tiled and whose walls paled with yellow. The waiting room was also my hospital room. After the operation, upon feeling tenderness in the area below my bellybutton, I told the nurse, "I think there's something still in there. I think there's something wrong." Whereupon all the nurses took their time doing anything while talking to each other a great deal. The nurse whom I had told, who was very nice, said I should see the doctor, then ran out of the room to fetch one.

'The room I was in was my hospital room. Blood, as if I was pissing, pissing like a man only straight upward without arcing, shot up from my cunt in thin streams. I saw two thin streams. My blood hit the top of the pale hospital walls, even the ceiling. I thought what a mess, just like in a movie. Then, there were more than two streams. The hospital walls had become red, just like in CARRIE. The doctor was taking his time somewhere. The nurse who had gone to fetch him, or some nurse, walking into the room and seeing the bloodiness, rang the emergency bell, just like she had been taught to do. Finally, the nurses put their arms around me and told me they were going to take care of me.

'They put out my consciousness for the necessary operation.

'I calmed myself down enough to fall asleep by fantasizing I had the courage to walk into an S&M club I've wanted to go to and about which I'd been informed. An older but handsome man, who's with his wife, picks me. While I'm hanging suspended from the black leather bands I saw at ——'s house, he's whipping me lightly enough so I can feel he likes me. When he asks me to leave the club with him, I agree. While I'm still chained up, he wraps the rest of my clothes around me to carry me away. I'm wondering if I could be killed or hurt. Of course, as we leave the club, I could scream I'm being kidnapped.

'I'm in no way and don't want to be a victim. I'm pulling back:' the dog explained her fear to the fearless knight, 'fantasy doesn't have the same immediacy as a dream.

'I'll go through (with) (my) fantasy:

'In the cold night, as soon as I see the man outside the club, I say with surprise, "You're not the one I was with inside."

'"You're wrong," he corrects me. "You were so involved in your feelings, you didn't notice when I and the other man changed places."

145

'This man is exactly what I like: short, muscular, hair chopped almost to the flesh.

'This's the fantasy I want. I'm going to say out loud everything I want. I saw him really as a tyrant, a murderer.

'Even though I'm so frightened I can't speak, I control myself and speak: "I'm scared."

'"You'll have to not be scared: (you'll have to trust me). Therefore, I'm going to put this hood over your head."

'Being enclosed in his car and helpless because I'm blind, I have to trust him. He says out loud it's important that people know they need other people.

'When this car stops, he has to lead me, helpless, out of the car, up some steps, across a threshold, to a bed. He straps me so I'm spread-eagled into the four leather bands permanently fixed in the bed's corners. He whips my back until I'm/my consciousness's in another state.

'"Now," the man says to me, "I'll be able to take care of you."

'I resist all the way. A new thing for me. I will not see my fake brother because he, because he doesn't love me, makes me into a victim. Simultaneously all of me wants to be with him because all of me wants his love. My family protests the way I am. The fact is that I *am* this way. I'm conscious that my refusal, my refusal upon refusal, my double mutiny that mutiny, this momentary attempt of mine to be a whole human, renders me liable to their disgusting penalties. Like any other rebel slave, perverse rebel, I resolve, now and forever, with total desperation, always to go to all lengths.'

'If pornography,' mused the night, 'is that which incites its listeners to degeneracy, violence, and rioting questioning, what you're telling me is pornographic. You don't even know how to speak properly.'

'All stories or narratives,' the dog barked, 'being stories of revolt, are revolt.

'These stories or revolts are especially revolts against parents. Why? Because parents have control, not only over children, but also – to the extent that adults're products of their childhood – over everyone. In order to live or be human, the self must seize control:

146

3. Proof That All Story-Telling Is Revolution

'A child's only desire,' the dog told Don Quixote, 'was to kill his parents. Since the parents didn't want to die and since they were unable to kill their child, they did their best to kill their child without actually killing it by treating it as badly as possible. Then they left the kid somewhere so the kid would be an orphan.'

'This explains my childhood,' Don Quixote announced. 'I always knew literature had some purpose.'

'Precisely: these parents have their nurse stick a safety pin into the kid's thigh, then they abandon the kid on some field, as if they can still find a field in the nuclear waste.

'Some people, as if there're still people left in nuclear society, find the kid and bring it up. To the kid, all parents're fake; childhood is fake; fakeness or falsity is good cause fake parents, unlike real parents, love you. This's the definition of childhood.

'As the kid becomes older, he wants to know who he is. Because if the only parents and childhood he can remember or bear to remember're fake, he might not exist. Does he have any control over his own life? How can he become existent and control his own life?

'What is this world of fakeness?' the dog asked meaninglessly. She answered herself, 'Meaningless murders, men, and lack of loving control me.

'In order to find out his identity and to be real, (for knowledge is the same as power), the child must murder his real father. Then the child murders his real father. The child is now terrible and violent. Being evil, the young rebel breaks down chaos or meaninglessness.

'The young boy kills his mother by raping her. Human power comes, at least partly, from sexuality.

'Oedipus: I am the biggest shit in the world. I murdered my father and raped and effectually killed my mother. All righteous people should murder me. Someone, please touch me. Physically touch this mentally diseased flesh. I'd do anything for a hug. There's no end to, because there's no escape from, my being-pain.

'People: Here comes our political leader. He'll be able to help you out. We're, as people, helpless.

'Leader: It's not that you're guilty, son, it's just that you're so foul, you make other people foul, in fact dead, by being around them. Get out of here. Human pain is the most disgusting thing in the world.

'Oedipus: Please, just love me a little. I'm so lonely, travelling from foreign land to foreign land. I don't know what a family is. All other human beings have families. Since I killed mine off, I don't have a family.

'I accept my total loneliness. No, I don't. I talk only for your sake; I'm nothing; only for you, I ask . . .

'Leader: Stop bothering me. I had a tough morning this morning.

'Oedipus: Because I'm so painful don't ever call me or have any human have anything to do with me ever again.

'Leader: At least believe in yourself.

'Oedipus: Who am I? Therefore: what is there to believe in? How hard it is to live with consciousness. (There must be consciousness.) Please touch me, my leader, just once. Just give me one hug and I'll never ask you again.

'Leader: No. I am not going to touch you. I don't want you. Neither are you allowed to rest in the myth of how disgusting or bad you are, for you know the particulars of why you're disgusting. You know consciousness.

'Oedipus: I'd rather be physically hurt than know consciousness or myself. My self is total pain.

'Leader: The point is that you have no choice. You will obey. Chance governs. You have only what you're given or are: yourself. There's no escape: not even exile's escape.

'This is rebellion.

4. The Female Side Of The Oedipal Myth

'Me,' the dog said, 'I'm not male. I want to be touched.

'Since my brother was male, he was mean and cruel. That's how males're. Being mean and cruel, he refused to touch me. That's how males're: they always deny physical affection so that we females'll be tied to them via this double bind: we want them and we hate their guts. Males're insecure,' added the bitch.

'What're my reverse Oedipal relations to women? Nothing.

'Let me explain: I had two kinds of female ties, sister and mother:

'My sisters and I had nothing to do with each other because I wasn't like them. They were English and they spent all their time attracting men, whom they didn't want, by means of no nail polish bad make-up clothing carefully picked out not to emphasize their sexual characteristics and brilliant conversation; whereas I, who couldn't attract a dog, wanted to fuck. Since finding my sexuality repulsive they refused to talk to me, and since I, as I'm always, can't talk, there was no way we could talk, even though we were fake sisters.

'As to my mother – My mother doesn't have sex. My mother doesn't have sex because she doesn't have to because she's found a man and because she's a monster. Because she doesn't need sex and is a monster, she reasonably hates me.

'As for everyone else, that is, the servants. The servants imitate the monsters or their betters by hating me. My only sexuality is fear of everything I know as human. My sexuality is wanting not to exist.

'Please, maybe I can wash your dishes. I want to wash your dishes very badly. I will wash every little dish. I will wash every little dish over and over so many times, until it breaks so it will never be dirty again. Really, I have always wanted to be a maid. Your maid. I don't know how, it just comes naturally, nobody ever taught me. Nobody ever taught me anything. I'm a natural.

'Unlike Jesus Christ, I can't find any joy in wanting to not exist or in suffering.

'The next question about my sexuality is: Why am I lower than Jesus Christ? Why do I suffer more than anyone else suffers? Why is there human unhappiness?

'When I was a child, I thought about this problem a lot. I decided: Since there can't be smoke without fire, such unhappiness is real. There must be something wrong with me. I'm not only not like other females, I'm not like other humans. (I was too young to know everyone's not like other humans. – Does this mean everyone's unchangeably unhappy?) Since I was unlike everyone else, there was no reason my fake family should either love me or care enough about me to hate me.

'Since my only desire is that my fake family love me, my desire or me is reasonless and stupid.

'Are all phenomena meaningless or products of chance? I turned to examining non-human or natural phenomena: the drawing-down away of day; the continuous rain in the beginning month; gray wind, continuous damp which is colder than cold.

'Everything is nothing or chance. I don't know what to do. I'm desperate. I yell aloud the most meaningless thing I can: "Mommy. Please help me. Give me a home. I want to go home, mommy. Mommy, daddy. I'm only a child. Grant me the only pleasure that is love," while I know there's no one to help me.

'I feel someone's helping me. I'm safe: oh, someone's taking care of me. I can cuddle. I grasp this thought like flesh to, into me. Actually, there's only nothingness. I'm pretending there isn't only nothingness. I have to admit to what's real. I cry, only this time crying's no relief.

'Someone runs into the room. The nurse. Someone's, finally, going to take care of me.

'My fake mother comes into the room and tells her to let me alone cause, since I deserve nothing, I'm just acting selfish. I must learn I can't always get my own way.

'When the nurse is about to leave the room, I beg her to relent because I can't bear my thoughts when I'm alone. Loneliness is the worst punishment they inflict on me cause loneliness forces me to perceive all those thoughts I otherwise can escape.

'"Stop pretending, Villain. You're acting viciously and violently. The only person you ever think about is yourself."

'Not bothering to notice my reply, she turns to the nurse, "Don't pay any attention to her because she lies."

'With that, they leave me. I sink into a stupor in which I'm not thinking.

5. I Dream

'I am here alone and it's very quiet. This is my new bed. Go away from me. You over there. Dog. Go back into your corner. With your mouth so bright it could be a sun. Here, is my terrain. Here, ye cavillers, all ye who till your fields and bang your mistresses into babies: I will have none of that. Populate the lands, fecundate the schools that are the burning houses of murderers, but do not do so in front of Your Virgin Queen:

'My flesh, being the whitest of white, even a soap fleck will turn spotty and pimply. My eyes can bear neither the glare of moon nor of days. Thus I need sheets, endless reams of realms of thick sheets unto the infinity of the never-disappearing waves, to pull over and over and over me.

'Being nothing, The Virgin, I can create my own characters: A tall thin blondish too-delicate-to-exist-in-this-world giraffe is an arrogant son-of-a-bitch. An angel, a veritable angel, cheeks pumped full up like that bum-boy of Caravaggio's, hair flowing out more Ariel-ly than any queen's, with a smile as sweet and tender as a babe's, looked at a just-sucked nipple. He is foul. He's the demon Beelzebub not even in disguise. He lies, and, worse, swears he is honest by his own virginal soul. Since, being virgin, he doesn't have any flesh, how can he be telling the truth? How can he be the virgin, for I am the Virgin Mary the Dream the Laughter? May the world be, it is, always joyous, for so am I.

'Oh, my lords, the Christmas season approacheth fast upon us so we must make this land ready. Bring forth the animals: the bear whose curly-clawing palm holds the dove; the truncated-trunked elephant and the arrogant giraffe whose neck had stolen the elephant's truncated trunk; the dog who's the ugliest thing in the world. Shall we tell the stories of all these singular creatures?

'"Tell only one, for night fast approacheth, and soon it is time we shall die."

'"The earth turneth black, and all to ice. Speak now, as quickly as possible. You must. For this Christmas is the last Christmas of all Christmases."

'Yay, and so I will tell you the story of THE RAVEN AND THE LAMBKINS

'Once upon a time, there was a raven who gave birth to a lamb. Since lambs don't usually come out of ravens, the little

151

lamb lambkins felt thats he was a freak therefore unwanted by the world. "No one wants me," the little lamb cried. "How can you be my mother? How can there be any mother, for those such as me?"

'"Come, love," the mother cried back, "for this is neither the season nor any season nor reason nor time: it is the flesh. Let our fleshes touch. Come here, hands who have never touched. Come, and open your flesh. Come, lamb. Come lions. Come, the gray elephants who've wandered lonely, human children, nosing around in every tree pocket they can find. All the flesh, all the animals must relax before you can come.

'"Lamb: Do you not want to come into me?

'"Kiss, lamb. Kiss your mother, the raven." The raven explains herself to her daughter. "The raven's been a very bad person because she made friends with Herpes and gonorrhea but now she's recovered, and flies through nothingness and chaos, soaring, her wings more magnificent than eagles', midnight, as were your eyes when you were born. Lamb."

'The mother talks about her child: "When you were born you were very red, no one wanted you, mange and worm-filled spots lay in the bits of your hair. You were a child I didn't want. I didn't want you because I'm a raven and you're a lamb."

'"I know this."

'"You hated yourself throughout your whole life because you're a lamb, not a raven. Briars tore your wool to bits on the tors. Wild foxes yapped at your paws. But you were safe, for your foulness made you too foul for wolves' food and wolverine delight. How many times when the mental heart shies from suicide, the physical body listening to its mental counterpart becomes sick. In a cold, gray country, no one cares whether a bum lives or dies. Not being able to be a raven, you tried to make yourself into a wolf. But, being a lamb, you were too dumb. You, lamb, were too dumb to live in this world and too dumb to die in this world."

'The lamb didn't say anything.

'"You ask me," the Virgin Mother said, "if there's anything else. For lambs. Anything except the impossibility of being alive and of dying. There is everything else. There're animals who live only at night; there're animals whose beings are mirrors, who are only what they imitate; there're animals whose physical movements're sexuality; there're animals who speak to each other in complex ways.

'"All of these animals," the mother made her child know love, "who're more capable than you rejoice in you, for you need love so desperately."

6. Actuality Repeats The Dream

'The family doctor came to me.

'Doctor: What's making you suffer so much?

'Dog: I'm sick.

'Doctor: How're you sick? Are you physically ill? Are you genetically defective? Are you insane? Are you poor? Have you been beaten down by the system?

'Dog: They've beaten every bit of inside flesh to a pulp; they've bruised into cowering my ability to feel. They've made me into such a fountain of hate, I hate myself. I don't hate them. But these can't be the reasons I'm so miserable cause many children who come from the most horrible mean families turn out OK.

'The doctor thrusted further: What's making you suffer so much?

'Dog: My family's locked me in this room. I live in a mental world or according to beliefs which're false. The physical and the mental aren't separate, for there's only the body. My body's physically sick.

'Doctor: Every human being lives in a mental world that's false. But everybody doesn't suffer as much as you.

'Dog: The deaths of my real parents shaped me. If children come out of parents, I come out of and am nothing. My body's physically sick.

'Doctor: You're canine: you're not just the mechanical results of incidents.

'Dog: My mind is the results. I have neither parents nor friends nor a home so I can't get away from being miserable. I hate it here. I hate myself.

'Doctor: Since you're unhappy, your mind's sick. Can't you learn to think, or unthink, in some other way?

'Dog: Since there is nothing but this, if I stop feeling unhappy, I'm nothing. I'm scared of nothingness.

'I screamed.

'That's the only fact, so I have to face nothingness.

'I'd like to know something.

'The doctor and my fake mother agreed to send me away to school. I was able to leave the hateful home.'

'I agree with you,' Don Quixote, while interrupting the garrulous dog, got everything wrong, 'that our only sexuality's imaginative. I'm imaginatively saving the world.'

A DOG'S LIFE, cont.:

AN EXAMINATION OF WHAT KIND OF SCHOOLING WOMEN NEED

1. What I Really Learn In School: Isolation

'Winds. Howl by yourselves. Do you scream more when there's no one around or when there's someone to hear you?

'I want to get out all my anguish. These past few months. I will talk. I lived with a man. I can't talk directly. Will put down one sentence each space. I'm lonely unto sickness. Those humans who decide to leave their homes or the normal (conditioned) paths of living open their hearts to loneliness and to the violence of the SE winds.

'Blow. Winds. Rage rage more rage all that you can. I would have my heart caught by a demon and kissed.

'I proved beyond doubt,' the dog continued talking to Don Quixote, 'that I was the most wicked and abandoned child ever reared under a roof. For I felt only bad feelings foam in my breast.

'In the corridors of sex, my father whom I've never known is partly pain. Right now it's painful for me to come because no one's fucking me. Sex's a necessary physical ailment because it

154

changes one. So every day I talk to my unknown own lover. I walk by ——'s side down through these unknown beautiful English gardens. While I eat the food of his eyes, I eat with his eyes. I hurt because he doesn't exist. Do you understand why every orgasm's, partly, painful?

'Is sexual pleasure only pleasure?' asked the dog.

'I came to school and to my knowing loneliness on a cold wintry day, a day which was itself grabbing for breath. Rain and wind and cold and, worst of all, dullness darkness fill my eyes, so I no longer recognize even an idea of happiness. The mind is driven to a point next to nothingness. The long slate river: my heart.

'Alone, I don't know what I'm doing because I'm a child, I walk through some door on some house. It is too dark for me to see here. A faint figure which is sort of human is sitting, maybe, I can barely see it.

'"Is this the first time you've left your parents, child?"

'"I don't have parents."

'As of yet, I don't know what that means.

'First day.

'The first night's over. I know what's loneliness. I would rather have this loneliness than be with people who're supposed to love me because they're my only home but hate me. I know, now, I've no home. I'm lonely because the flesh and the rest of me is never touched. Blow, winds, because you're honest. There's nothing here, this cold gray country, but there's nothing anywhere, anymore.

'These're the actual aspects of loneliness: (1) This food stinks because they make us eat chipped beef which is rotten gray liquid with specks of floating solids or shit in it over white toast which is our protein. Everything else which is food is gray gush porridge which stops up sinks and pregnant women. (2) My "learning" is when I either do meaningless, that is so stupid as to be unquestionable, tasks, or else when I'm lost in doing nothing in uselessness. This "learning" is when my actions can never be meaningful. (3) I can't even masturbate because all the spaces here're public. Since my sleep is public, I can hardly go to sleep. (4) Since no one touches me, my own body's hideous. I wear dull brown rags, old women's shoes, and thick stockings all over me, a uniform.

'I hate myself. Do all other people hate themselves? Must every single person be apart from every other single person? Now that I'm alone, I won't commit suicide. Maybe it's possible: maybe most people're lonely, so I in this lonely, hating this loneliness, at least I'm not queer. No matter how I rationalize this, when loneliness and not being sexually touched hurt, they hurt like the human hell they are.

'Now that I'm face to face with loneliness, I'm used to being alone. I'll go on this way. I don't talk to anyone and, I don't expect to talk to anyone. I'm surprised when another living being, who must be a girl, here, addresses me. Since her words have to be dead words, I only mumble back. I live in my own world of playgrounds trees animals books. I will never be intruded upon again. Or touched again. In the distance here, the river of my adoration flows long dull murky, all the way to the right and light. Lambs bleat on either side. Outside the icy air hardly impresses my flesh, for inside I'm all dissatisfactions. A cell-like shell bottles up the dissatisfactions.

'Unable to know any outside, I don't know where I am. Here's a red brick building. Here's a low, dullish brown brick edifice. Beyond's my river. Nothing's real because nothing has meaning for me because no one's touching me. No one tells me what means what. There's no schooling here. Where there's no language, there's no reality.

'This,' explained the dog, 'is why my heart is breaking.

'Cold. Wet. Dead. Low moors sitting over hidden rivers. Earth so heavy it could sink and is, into its lower geographical stratum of mud. Human heaviness heavier than death.

'Russian Politics. I've two recurring fantasies: Alone, I fantasize a human wanting me. But if I have someone to like, even if it's only a fantasy, I fantasize that I don't understand what's happening between that other person and myself. A third person tells me, for his or her own purposes, that my lover's with another person and that I should go see them. Or else, by chance, I catch sight of my lover petting another girl while

156

telling her he loves her. My lover rejects me either in an understood way or openly.

'As I was – as is usual with me – fantasizing I'm a baby, in a small square of dirt called a garden behind the school, a girl reading a book and sitting behind me asked me if I was an orphan.

'"No, I don't have any parents. My parents're dead."

'"Everyone, she explained, here "is one kind of orphan or another.

'"This isn't a school, but an institution for orphans. We are taken up here because we have nowhere to go, and the State, out of its kindness, is a Welfare State."

'"Then where do we go? Is the State our parent?"

'"The State won't give us charity because it believes, and rightly, that governmental charity creates a weak populace. So each of us, since we have nothing – "

'"I have nothing." I interrupted.

'" – must have a friend, or a trust, or a fucker who gives this school five hundred quid a year."

'"Then I can't be an orphan."

'"Oh, yes you are. Five hundred quid isn't even a dole. Orphans're grown-up children who're below dole. You're American, aren't you?"

'"Yes."

'"Since the USA, to make you strong, gives you nothing and takes away from you through taxes, you're below dole or an orphan. Therefore you have to depend on anybody who'll give you anything, even on a worker."

'"Then workers are my parents?"

'"No. They're not," she answered exasperated. "Workers are the people who, though they still have jobs, unlike half the people in this country, think they're the lowest of the low and the most despised. For this reason they're rigidly moralistic, like our school head."

'"Is he a worker?"

'"No, he's a vicar. He has to be kind."

'"You mean he isn't kind?"

'"None of us is anyone else's kind because we're orphans.

157

Therefore: get away from me," she ordered. She was vicious and I was alone. I wanted to be her.

'Endless hole I am an endless hole I can't bear this. I have put myself in exile so I can't be face-to-face with this which is my loneliness.

'On Nature. Today even though my boyfriend's gone from me blow winds because I'm almost happy!

'Today I'm so happy because I must be so happy: it's snowing. A drift forms against the lower window pane. The river is now low, cold and ice-gray. There is a low noise of the sky: the wind's disconsolate moan. Since the wind's disconsolate moan resembles mine, I'm that wind.

'If I was a person who has or had parents who care or cared about her, I'd be crying now because I don't have anyone. This wind would be the sharp separation from the person who loves me. I wouldn't be able to bear such separation, if there was separation. The way in which the strong weather is doing what it's doing without any thought of me would break up my security. But I'm not even anyone.

'So I can be – whoever I want. I can do anything I can be anyone one day and the next day do be anyone else, even the same one. I'm as unpredictable as these winds: these winds or I will make me happy if I run faster, and faster now slower, faster –

'Masochism is now rebellion –

'For a long time I've been a cat whose fur's being rubbed the wrong way but doesn't know how to get touched right. Like the winds, I the cat act without thought carelessly recklessly non-consequentially gaily because without thought, no thought. This's why winds make the air dark. There's no chance I'll know.

'I will love someone, I can. So it is a woman because there're only women. The name of my love, her name is Burn. She's the one the teachers flog.

'Howl, human winds! Howl, all the atoms of this human skin. You do not love me! You who molding me me physically by my pleasure at being hurt would have me love you so much that I can't not love you if you don't love me. You force me to

158

love you solely according to your desires. Now you're molding me by mentally hurting me. Since you want me to be nothing but that which loves you, you treat me as nothing. You're my human destruction. You are my school.

'Loneliness, howl! Real teaching happens via feelings. Howl, the self who fights against suicide.

'This isn't loneliness I'm talking about: this is continuous hurt, the opposite of love. We who are sick because we accept hurt –

'"If anyone tries to touch me, much less beat me up," I scream to Burn, "I'll beat her his (I can't get sexual genders straight) now bloody ass into bloody shreds."

'I calm down. "I've never liked the slightest, even physical, pain, like loneliness. I can't understand why any human should feel pain.

'"If any human being causes any other human being pain," I scream, "I'll rip that human being up!" But whom am I screaming to? I think anyone who lives being lonely and isn't crazy is strong.

'Burn says that by hurting me, the school we go to is teaching me to mold be strong by molding my own violence.

'Since, unlike Burn, I don't have the strength to do anything but scream when I'm in pain, I worship her. "I worship you.

'"I'm a mess," I continue. "Since I objectively know who I am, this's who I am. Since I'm a mess or have no control over any of my emotions, these emotions take me over. These emotions're so fierce, I must be controlled. This's why love's control for me."

'"Then you ought to be punished because you're a bad person and no one's ever punished you for being bad."

'"Even though this can't be true because I never had any parents – " I changed my mind, "then it must be true. Must nothing be nothing? My fake mother punishes me for everything. Then, nothing is only nothing." Having learned this first truth – identity – , I say what I have to say to the girl so that she'll love me: "Yes. I need punishment."

'This good behavior doesn't last long: I start screaming again. "What about love and tenderness?

'"Don't you love me? Don't love and tenderness matter to you?

'"Don't you need someone to love you?" I end my solipsistic speech.

'I don't think she has any idea what I'm talking about.

'My first friend's solipsistic speech: "I see no need for love and tenderness.

'"Why? There's only one good teacher in this school. Miss St Jean Pierre. She teaches us by making us experience what we don't know. Since, when I'm learning from her, I don't have to try to learn, I want to learn because, of course, I want to do whatever I'm doing. Only this's learning. Therefore, learning has nothing to do with either self-discipline or fascism."

'"But it must have to do with kindness and gentleness. Cause when no one loves me, even if I do something, I actually don't do what I do, cause all I can do is want someone to love me."

'"We're all orphans," replied Burn. "Is that any reason to keep punishing ourselves or being ignorant? If we're going to live in this world without love, we're going to have to learn how to live without love. This is our learning . . ."

'I interrupted her solipsism: "When we're struck unreasonably irrationally, either physically or through isolation, we should strike back. Hard. For isolation's a political tool. We should hurt those people those parents whoever made us lonely so goddamn hard that they will suffer irreparably: worms will swim inside their lower legs and their fingers'll crawl. For when a human dies, her guts actually become a giant worm."

'"This statement, this kind of statement, shows me, Villey, that since you've learned nothing therefore have no discipline, you're too dangerous to be touched. By anyone." Even in, especially in friendship, I came face-to-face with my isolation.

'Right now it's the end of an afternoon as if it's already passing on, rather than just passing into, nighttime. I wanted to walk outside today, in through the bare patches of grass and brown muck, for the sensation of these patches that are the hairs on Nature's balding head is the only thing that soothes the pain that is now my skin. But Sunday is the only day

160

they let us out of the inside, the cold claustrophobic inside. Everything is a body. They let us out so we can go to church. After church, we're finally allowed to walk in the outside. The outside is freezing. Freezing doesn't matter because it doesn't matter where you're going because going makes thinking disappear. This cold is my only warmth. My clothes must be rags. My shoes must be thin and light. Rough inflamed bumps from the cold cover my hands and feet. I'm always hungry even when I'm not hungry. Since physical deprivation, like poverty, eats away the mental spirit, I want to return to the regimented pain inside, for it's the only thing I can know.

'Revolt comes from the revolters' self-hatred of their own acceptance of their painful conditions. In order to stave off revolt, they gave us when we returned two slices of wonder bread and real margarine. Just like the miners. The older girls, who're bigger than me, take away my food. Everyone hates me here. I want to die and I don't want to die. Since I'm nothing, I can't hate myself. These political conditions render me apolitical or uninterested in everything.

'Why's being touched so important?' the dog asked nobody in particular. 'Without the touch of another human, I'm nothing. For, being untouched, I can do (be) anything(one) and so, am nothing. Since no one talks to me, I talk to myself. In this world or country, England, we call school, whose head is a head(whip)mistress. Since to me here in this school I'm dead, this country is death. I, all females who're isolated, am the Virgin.

'Virgin Mary, tell me: How can people who can no longer love give birth?

'Even though you don't exist, love: every day in every minute I talk to you because I must. Because if there's someone in me, even only in fantasy, I'm not always up against my own loneliness. I'm not always in the scream which is Death. Death is the one absolute, the object that can be known, the only human knowing. You're my unknowing heart. Virgin. Bitch. If there's chance, there must be love.

'"I can't believe there's no possibility of love," I scream to Burn, now that I've gotten my argument straight, but Burn is dead from typhoid brought on by malnutrition and wet cold of

161

this country. Who, now, is there I can even imagine to hear my screams?

2. Reading: I Dream My Schooling

'I sat in a chair and read. My white stuffed cat sat on my right arm. A white blanket tossed like the ocean over the bottom half of my legs. I read this:

'"""Consumed as you appear to be by the passion to depucelate a girl, or to be depucelated,'" I wasn't sure what *depucelated* meant, but I had a good idea, "'yourself,'" the incomparable Delbène said to me one day, "'I've no doubt that Sainte-Elme has already decided, or may be easily induced, to grant you these pleasures. Should she have to hesitate? She's not running a risk: she's going to pass the rest of her life in holy retirement. But as for you, Juliette, once bereft of your token or identity, you'll be forever refused marriage. Think therefore, and believe me: unsaid misfortunes could well be the consequence of a slight physical flaw in that part that you think nothing at this moment of damaging. Despite the heedlessness of your youth, forgive me my angel, but you know I say this because I care for you, think: play it safe: give up that Sainte-Elme and take me. I'll give you everything you're wanting and more. You yourself choose any girl in this convent whose first fruits you covet, and I'll take away yours in the meantime. There'll be some material injuries to that part . . . don't be scared . . ., I'll take care of you, baby. I can do it; I can't tell you how; it's the secret of this convent. If you want me to tell you, you have to promise me you'll never speak to Sainte-Elme again. Do you promise? Swear! Swear by your cunt. Only your cunt is holy. If you say even one word to Sainte-Elme from now on, I'll be . . . disgusting to you!'"

'Looking at the older woman in her face, "I can't hurt you," though I want to "because I know you care about me. Besides. I want to be physically touched."

'Finally I admitted it. I want to be physically touched.

'I swore I'd never say a word to that nasty Sainte-Elme again. "I'll do whatever you tell me to do."

162

'A month later Delbène: "Have you decided? Have you decided who you want?"

'"What I want most of all is a family. But if I had my sister, she'd be so upset about me, she'd kill herself out of guilt. I'll have Laure. She's not going to be family; I know I'll never have a family. But it's – she's – something: it's closeness. Closeness that will last: she has the stability of the upper-middle classes. She's got that security, which I don't have, which'll keep my enormous will from being the control."

'"Since her only relative's an elderly drooling uncle who lives far away in the mountains, I can see no reason why you can't do what you like with the child. Tonight, when all the students retire to their dormitories, you and I Flavie and Volmar'll slip away. I'll arrange the rest. I'm going to be your teacher. Have the courage of your sex, a sex that has endured unendurable pain: be a young knight, for, tonight, you'll learn something."

'The woman who cleaned the floors entered the room: "Laure's gone! She's run away from school!"

'"How can she want to run away from my love?" I cried. I wanted to add *oh, shit,* but I was in school. I restrained my tongue. "Laure! Laure! How could you die? And by dying, abandon me? For you've brutally forced me to abandon all I've ever had of you which is the hope of you: You've taken away my future. Brat. I hate your guts, I do, because when a love affair dissolves, the conceived desires of the one who doesn't want to break up remain in her to torment her."

'My teacher: "There has to be a future."

'"No. For I won't accept that this world must be pain: A future only of torment is no future for anyone. As for you," I had the guts to address my teacher directly, even though I wasn't ever able to be directly angry at my mother who hated me, "how are you going to keep your promise to me? Laure is gone. Nothing. I want only Laure.

'"Your words mean nothing to me, like the words of all the teachers I've ever had. Words mean nothing."

'I woke up from the dream I had fallen into. Like water running down from its source to a place of safety, a levelling: reading to a dream. What miracle of self-power had I dreamed of? Mists chill as death, as my heart now wants to be so it'll no longer be hurt, wander according to the impulses of the easterly winds – winds whose only laws humans can perceive are those of chance – along the purple, half-seen peaks. Here, in England. Mists, teats, fingers roll, down, and hole until they who're born of the night're mingling with the graveyard's frozen fog. My heart, today is Christmas. Is anything being born? Borne? Can a child be born and borne in the joyless helpless land? Yes!

'I will be born: the two bodies of water around the graveyard I stand in, hidden, still under fog, become turbid and careless: wild they rise up. Over their legal boundaries, they throw through the wet non-existent air a chortle, air thickened by rain which is half-sleet.

'I will be born: In this country where the weather is cold. Poor food, lack of heat, and lack of medical care make flu a way of life. Flu, and worse. The doctors can't even recognize the diseases most people're getting. Flu, and worse. Wang Lung was a magician and hated the Emperor; he loved, of course at a reverential distance, the Empress.

'Living here in disease and being diseased strangely bring us closer to each other: we can now have emotions for each other. We don't care about the people who control us. They almost don't exist, the demi-gods of the world. No longer by enforcing their rules can they tell us what to do, for we even they the demi-gods're in the face of total human death. The few who're well enough to roam roam in almost uninhibited undefined space: the world of almost total death's the world of almost freedom. The closer we're living to total human death, the weaker the socio-political constraints on us.

'Those of us who have anyone who can take us away, a friend or a relative, get out. For the rest of us, we live in our future deaths: our present deaths, for the walls're creaking from the rats of death. We talk about diseases only. Soon, my friend who is dead, Burn, something must spring.

'I was desperate to find some way how to live. These people here teach me nothing but isolation. I turn back to my book. To anything that teaches me about somewhere else, for there's nothing in this country but death.

164

'The book continued:

'"The teacher Delbène: 'Love's nothing unless it involves trust.'

'"Juliette the student said nothing.

'"Delbène: 'I know that I promised you could take Laure's virginity away from her. Laure's gone. Do you still trust me? Is trust part of love?'

'"Juliette the student said nothing.

'"Delbène: 'Do you trust me to make things happen in this world?'

'"Juliette answered she trusted her teacher.

'"The teacher blindfolded the student so the student had to trust her.

'"Delbène, Volmar and Flavie who were also students, and Juliette walked through the fogs over the school's graveyard. They walked into the graveyard chapel. Delbène lifted up a tombstone under which was a hole. The woman and the girls descended through the hole down several narrow slippery steps. Though Juliette couldn't see, she wasn't scared because she trusted Delbène.

'"When Delbène, the last, lowered the tombstone, the stone, falling more quickly than she had expected, made a loud noise as it hit the rock floor.

'"Delbène said, 'Shit'. She and her students continued walking around and past the dead schoolgirls' coffins.

'"Delbène again lifted up a tombstone under which was a hole. The woman and the girls descended through the hole down several narrow slippery steps. Delbène, this time more slowly and gracefully, lowered the tombstone. She followed them down seventeen steps approximately.

'"They walked into a sparse but elegant room. The walls the ceiling and almost everything in the room were white. Hidden pipes kept the chamber well-ventilated. Delbène took the black blindfold off Juliette's head and said, 'What we do in this room is be happy. With our bodies. Our bodies teach us who've been poisoned.'

'I turned my head and saw Laure, the person I wanted.

'In my dream, my teacher said to me: "All the accepted

forms of education in this country, rather than teaching the child to know who she is or to know, dictate to the child who she is. Thus obfuscate any act of knowledge. Since these educators train the mind rather than the body, we can start with the physical body, the place of shitting, eating, etc., to break through our opinions or false education.

'"First, we must act against our opinions; we must act exactly in those ways of which we don't approve. This, at this moment, is correct action. At this moment, we can't have any joy, because we don't know what joy is.

'"When we act thus, other human beings, who cling to their opinions, hate us."

'I, appalled, replied: "I'm not like this: I'm not horrible."

'"You have no idea what you're like."

'"I'm not like this: Horrible."

'"I'm not like this: Horrible."

'"I'm not like this: Horrible."

'Delbène said: "We must do what we consider crimes in order to break down our destructive education."

'"But *crimes* are evil because they're human acts by which humans hurt other humans."

'"But *crimes* are evil because they're human acts by which humans hurt other humans.'

'"But *crimes* are evil because they're human acts by which humans hurt other humans."

'"A good reply," answered my teacher, "according to the world."

'"A good reply," answered my teacher, "according to the world."

'"A good reply," answered my teacher, "according to the world."

'"Wrong," my teacher thundered, "for any answer that seems to be the correct answer denies this world whose nature is chance and relativity. There is no correct answer."

'"Wrong," my teacher thundered, "for any answer that seems to be the correct answer denies this world whose nature is chance and relativity. There is no correct answer."

'"Wrong," my teacher thundered, "for any answer that

seems to be the correct answer denies this world whose nature is chance and relativity. There is no correct answer."

'"Wrong," my teacher thundered, "for any answer that seems to be the correct answer denies this world whose nature is chance and relativity. There is no correct answer."

'"Then how do I know an answer? How can I make decisions?"

'"Then how do I know an answer? How can I make decisions?"

'"Then how do I know an answer? How can I make decisions?"

'"Then how do I know an answer? How can I make decisions?"

'"That," said my teacher, "'s what we're going to find out. It's not simply the case that we can't know anything. We do know."

'"That," said my teacher, "'s what we're going to find out. It's not simply the case that we can't know anything. We do know."

'"That," said my teacher, "'s what we're going to find out. It's not simply the case that we can't know anything. We do know."

'"That," said my teacher, "'s what we're going to find out. It's not simply the case that we can't know anything. We do know."

'"This is something new."

'"This is something new."

'"This is something new."

'"This is something new."

'Yes. This's something new.'

'What do we know?' the dog rhetorically asked the knight.

'How do I know what you know?' the knight replied. 'I'm not a dog.'

'You still don't know anything,' admonished the dog. 'All for you is worse than doubt, night. Hear my end.' said the dog, as she wagged her tail: 'Since the body is the first ground of knowledge, my teacher made me take off my clothes. A mouth touched and licked my ass. A finger stuck into my asshole. A dildo thrust into my asshole and a dildo thrust into my cunt. Both dildoes squirted liquid into me which I saw was white. I was so over-the-top excited, I came. The main thing for me was my body's uncontrolled reactions.

'Since the body is the first ground of knowledge, my teacher made me take off my clothes. A mouth touched and licked my ass. A finger stuck into my asshole. A dildo thrust into my asshole and a dildo thrust into my cunt. Both dildoes squirted liquid into me which I saw was white. I was so over-the-top excited, I came. The main thing for me was my body's uncontrolled reactions.

'Since the body is the first ground of knowledge, my teacher made me take off my clothes. A mouth touched and licked my ass. A finger stuck into my asshole. A dildo thrust into my asshole and a dildo thrust into my cunt. Both dildoes squirted liquid into me which I saw was white. I was so over-the-top excited, I came. The main thing for me was my body's uncontrolled reactions.

'Since my body is the first ground of knowledge, my teacher made me take off my clothes. A mouth touched and licked my ass. A finger stuck into my asshole. A dildo thrust into my asshole and a dildo thrust into my cunt. Both dildoes squirted liquid into me which I saw was white. I was so over-the-top excited, I came. The main thing for me was my body's uncontrolled reactions.

'My teacher told me it wasn't enough for me to know that my body (me) reacted this way. I had to know more precisely all my complex reactions. Did I feel or react more strongly in my asshole or in my cunt?

'My teacher told me it wasn't enough for me to know that my body (me) reacted this way. I had to know more precisely all my complex reactions. Did I feel or react more strongly in my asshole or in my cunt?

'My teacher told me it wasn't enough for me to know that my body (me) reacted this way. I had to know more precisely all my complex reactions. Did I feel or react more strongly in my asshole or in my cunt?

'My teacher told me it wasn't enough for me to know that my body (me) reacted this way. I had to know more precisely

all my complex reactions. Did I feel or react more strongly in
my asshole or in my cunt?

'"I can't tell you because I'm reacting so fiercely," I answered. "I can tell you that a combination of fear that isn't so
intense it loses its pleasure and emotional need and physical
delight in the combination that causes ungovernable exploding
reactions in me."

'"I can't tell you because I'm reacting so fiercely," I answered. "'I can tell you that a combination of fear that isn't so
intense it loses its pleasure and emotional need and physical
delight is the combination that causes ungovernable exploding
reactions in me."

'"I can't tell you because I'm reacting so fiercely." I answered. "I can tell you that a combination of fear that isn't so
intense it loses its pleasure and emotional need and physical
delight is the combination that causes ungovernable exploding
reactions in me."

'"I can't tell you because I'm reacting so fiercely," I answered. "I can tell you that a combination of fear that isn't so
intense it loses its pleasure and emotional need and physical
delight is the combination that causes ungovernable exploding
reactions in me."

'Volmar said, "That thought is barely the beginning of
thought. You must perceive exactly what is. We will do it all
over again so you can try to begin to perceive just what is.":

'Volmar said, "That thought is barely the beginning of
thought. You must perceive exactly what is. We will do it all
over again so you can try to begin to perceive just what is.":

'Volmar said, "That thought is barely the beginning of
thought. You must perceive exactly what is. We will do it all
over again so you can try to begin to perceive just what is.":

'Volmar said, "That thought is barely the beginning of
thought. You must perceive exactly what is. We will do it all
over again so you can try to begin to perceive just what is.":

'Delbène placed her cunt lips lightly on my mouth. I didn't
like the taste of her cunt lips. But I had to keep tasting them. I
learned about like and dislike. At the same time I flicked her
nipple with my second right hand fingertip back and forth,
right and left, black and white, here and disappeared, which

my second right hand fingertip liked to do. When I placed my tongue on the very tip, my clit by wiggling became the nipple. I liked doing this.

'Delbène placed her cunt lips lightly on my mouth. I didn't like the taste of her cunt lips. But I had to keep tasting them. I learned about like and dislike. At the same time I flicked her nipple with my second right hand fingertip back and forth, right and left, black and white, here and disappeared, which my second right hand fingertip liked to do. When I placed my tongue on the very tip, my clit by wiggling became the nipple. I liked doing this. 'Ashè.

'At the same time: Volmar who was a young girl pressed her body against all of mine that she could which was all except for the face. Then she slipped down below the body. She disappeared. Her head came back up between my legs. Similar to how Delbène had placed her cunt lips lightly on my own mouth, I placed my cunt lips lightly on this girl's mouth.

'At the same time: Volmar who was a young girl pressed her body against all of mine that she could which was all except for the face. Then she slipped down below the body. She disappeared. Her head came back up between my legs. Similar to how Delbène had placed her cunt lips lightly on my own mouth, I placed my cunt lips lightly on this girl's mouth.

'Laure was hotter than any of us. Laure's right hand rubbed Flavie's cunt and her left hand rubbed Volmar's cunt. Watching these sexual actions which I couldn't actually feel made me feel my own physical sensations less. My decreasing sexual abandonment let me feel a more general spreading or less focused sexual interest.

'Laure was hotter than any of us. Laure's right hand rubbed Flavie's cunt and her left hand rubbed Volmar's cunt. Watching these sexual actions which I couldn't actually feel made me feel my own physical sensations less. My decreasing sexual abandonment let me feel a more general spreading or less focused sexual interest.

'Delbène asked me, "Are you beginning to understand?"

'Delbène asked me, "Are you beginning to understand?"

'Volmar interrupted again by asking me: Did I feel or react more strongly in my asshole or in my cunt?

'Volmar interrupted again by asking me: Did I feel or react more strongly in my asshole or in my cunt?

'"I come harder when my ass is penetrated than when my cunt's penetrated, though my ass hurts more."

'"I come harder when my ass is penetrated than when my cunt's penetrated, though my ass hurts more."

'"Does this mean physical sensation's stronger for you when physical pain's involved?"

'"Does this mean physical sensation's stronger for you when physical pain's involved?"

'"I'm too young to know."

'"I'm too young to know."

'"Age has nothing to do with perception or knowledge. I'm not asking you what you've been taught or about your false self."

'"Age has nothing to do with perception or knowledge. I'm not asking you what you've been taught or about your false self."

'"I haven't any experience of all this."

'"I haven't any experience of all this."

'"I'm not asking you about your overlays of memories, like the overlays of culture in Europe, culminating in a decayed seaside hotel whose walls peel away from themselves into the literature they think is supporting them. I'm asking you what you know. What do you know, what do you perceive?"

'"I'm not asking you about your overlays of memories, like the overlays of culture in Europe, culminating in a decayed seaside hotel whose walls peel away from themselves into the literature they think is supporting them. I'm asking you what you know. What do you know, what do you perceive?"

'"I'm too scared to talk to you because I'm too scared to talk to anyone, especially older people: I'm scared because I have or know no self. There's no *one* who can talk. My physical sensations scare me because they confront me with a self when I have no self: sexual touching makes these physical sensations so fierce. I'm forced to find a self when I've been trained to be nothing. Therefore, I perceive that physical pain, if it doesn't scare me because it's happening without my expectation and consent, helps out and enlarges sexual excitation."

'Delbène said, "What do *you* perceive? *You* must speak. Here, all of us who're women, who no longer have men around us, in the death of Europe this crypt, must now speak."

'When Flavie a young girl said "One speaks with the body," the teacher reproved her, "You're not speaking yet."

'The teacher herself spoke: "Fuck me! One of you! I'm so desperate to be fucked! My cunt is swollen because it's crying out in its own way to be fucked! I'll abandon my belief that I'm worth something in order to fuck!

'"I'll be your slave. I would have you place leather bonds around my wrists. I would have you place whatever you wanted of yourself on whatever part of my body you want.

'"I would have you, Laure, because I'm in love with you, so I want only you. Put some part of your body in front of my overexcited face. I won't even notice whatever the other girls do to me as long as I can do something to you.

'"Do something, something. Please I have to have one orgasm. I need to orgasm or love so much. I can't orgasm. Will anybody help me?

'"I'll kill Laure. I'll kill one of you. Hit me. Flay me. Oh shit. Oh, oh yes. Oh shit. Yes.

'"I'm so irritated, my flesh's diseased. I don't care. Hit me. There . . . I'm going. Oh. Thank you.

'"As for marriage, I, for one, don't know men. So much for marriage.

'"There're no males here, in this place, for there can be no men around when we're speaking. Therefore marriage has nothing to do with us."

'My teacher's words now mean nothing to me. I who've been without speech speak. "I love a young woman. She's sitting on a stool. I love her because, or else I love her and, she is the most beautiful kindest and in the future intelligent person right now. (Don't be real.) Only her thin tight buttocks're hitting the cold wood. I can't think about her in this way. There's no possibility she could want me. I know she's in love with me. I have her. I can touch her right now as if lust's allowed, as if she's my object. She's sitting in front of me. Her ass which's touching the stool in some way detrimental to her identity/self-determination/separation-from-me is now mine to touch whenever I want to/it.

'"She can't stop whatever I do to her because being in love with me has forced her helpless in my face. Cords fastened to the wood stools fixed to the floor spread her legs open, as far as is comfortable for her. Since she through her love's open to me, inside her I'll be softer than her, less of an identity. As I'll make her come, I'll fade. This isn't possible, though I know she loves me. Her arms are as fixed as her legs. *Fixed* means *abandoned*. Held up and out in the real cross which is the girls' cross, the cross of taking me in her arms.

'"Who am I to have her? I'm about to graduate, while she's the youngest student in our school. She's the most beautiful student in the school. And she's female.

'"My speech is this:"

'I say: "Laure," I said, "come here." She couldn't come cause she was chained to the stool. "Laure, come. Bring your vicious little cunt over here. Even though I know you love me, you're inscrutable so I'm, since I'm a cunt, vicious:

'"Are you thrusting your cunt out at me, twat? Tart-face. Fish-teats. Vomit-bag. They've taught us that, above all, our bodies, especially that part of our body, should be hidden. Secreted. Shoved anywhere, any which way. To them nuclear bomb leakage's less dangerous than ours. Even our tongues shouldn't leak: above all, we must be polite or nondescript or non-existent. These're my words: Cunt, you are an asocial cunt. I'm going to have to whip you badly, cunt."

'"Oh yes," Laure answered, "whip me badly."

'"I'll whip you by breaking you down by breaking through your virginity or identity. As soon as you're no longer a virgin, you're going to leak. You'll keep on leaking so you won't be able to retain any more of their teachings."

'"Oh, whip me badly."

'"I have to warn you. As soon as you start leaking, you're going to need desperately. You won't be secure ever again."

'"What could I need?"

'"You'll need me to stop up your leaks. That's why I'm going to take away your virginity. Let me tell you every detail, Laure, of how I'm going to do it:

' "This's a rod."

' "That's a finger," the evil girl said.

' "This finger is a rod." I corrected her. "Of the proper size. Four inches long and less than an inch in diameter. There's a myth that women experience pleasure only when their cunts're being bruised. Women know better. A small rod is the correct size of a rod. Since such a rod, unlike larger rods, whose material're similar to this one, can bend and swivel, such a rod stops up your leaks while causing leakages of pleasure.

' "Now, Laure. As soon as I've stuck this rod up you, cunt, you're going to bleed all over it. Probably a lot.

' "Let's examine. What is this blood? It's you, cunt, leaking or identity. You might even die. This is love, when death's involved. By sticking this rod up you and making you bleed, love, I'm making you love me.

' "As soon as you've had so much new experience for the first time, O my love, you'll lose the consciousness you've had. You'll leak again: you'll lose consciousness.

' "When you awake to an unknown – our reality – , you'll be leaking forever so much you'll lose your childhood selfishness. In this way my penetration'll teach you."

' "This's the true state of female human knowledge." Laure replied to me. "I'm going to die."

'Unfortunately I didn't know how to fuck Laure. Desperately I strapped a dildo around my waist. I was aghast: wearing a dildo is like wearing plastic. Is wearing plastic. I was no longer natural.

'I learned that our fierce emotions make us do what we'd never otherwise do. Just as a skinny woman lifts up the part of a bus that's run over her young child, I strapped the dildo on to my waist: but the dildo, unlike the bus, went this way and that way. The straps kept slipping off. It was ambiguous.

'The dildo slipped so much, it slipped in, and out of Laure. Even when I managed to slip the slippery thing in for a whole moment, not only couldn't it slip past that fleshy obstruction in her cunt, that obstruction made it slip out. I became scared.

'Since I was scared, nothing mattered, so I had the courage of one who knows no fear. I knew nothing. I placed my right hand around the dildo's bottom and shoved with my thighs then right hand. How could I know the degree of the pain Laure was feeling? I alone was responsible for the pain Laure was feeling. I was responsible or another whom I couldn't know. By my administration and neglect of unknown pain, the dildo slipped into the now blood-filled cunt and didn't slip out. I made Laure wail.

'Between wails she exclaimed. "I'm fainting."

'I was more terrified by what I was doing now than I had been by my strapping on the dildo. How could I be doing this to one whom I loved? I wailed as loudly as the child.

'Delbène: "Shut the fuck up. What are you: women? Do women always wail? Are women weak? Do women never take responsibility: do they do a thing and then, whatever the thing is, immediately regret it; do their emotions keep shifting and all they pay attention to are these drifting emotions; are women stupid? Do women take no responsibility for their own actions and therefore have no speech of their own, no real or meaningful speech?"

'"No," I managed to reply. "I'm coming." Those were my words.'

With these words, the dog ended her story.

'They certainly taught you how to speak in that school,' Don Quixote agreed with the dog, 'for you obviously haven't shut up since then.'

Since the dog shut up by licking the knight's face, the knight decided she preferred the fictional dog school to the ratty girls' school she had had to attend when she was a girl.

THE LAST ADVENTURE: UNTIL THIS BOOK WILL BEGIN AGAIN

'That's very nice – what you just told me – ' Don Quixote said to the bitch, 'but it all took place in the past. It's all past and gone.

The Present
'Sister dog or bitch,' Don Quixote, 'we have to decide about the present. You and I. I mean: what we're going to do now:

'Now, bitch. If I were capable of action, as any man is, if I wasn't so shy that I had to stay cooped up in this Spanish peasant's hut all the time and through time, as I now do; at this very moment I would be delivering Laure from that convent, where, beyond doubt, the evil Sisters are keeping her against her will. Despite whoever's now opposing me, despite whoever thinks I'm a male pornographer, I would deliver her. But I'm only a woman, and frail.

'Then, sister dog, I would place Laure in your paws, and would say, "Oh sister dog. Deal with this woman as you will, for, dog, I trust you and know that every woman knows that no woman, being a bitch, will deal with any woman against her own pleasure. The body cannot lie."'

'But what if I'm not a bitch?' the dog asked.

'To me,' Don Quixote said, 'these conditions, these *shoulds* and *woulds*, are the same as the past. Either they are past and gone or they don't occur. They don't concern me.

'What concerns me,' Don Quixote added, 'is me.'

'Oi yoi yoi,' the dog said. 'Only a bitch can reason the way you do.'

'I'm concerned with what is,' Don Quixote announced, 'not with what isn't or may be. In the beginning of me, I am. Therefore I am.'

'What about me?' the dog barked. 'If I am to me, am I to you?'

'Your question is really the question of the self. Dog, am I you? Are our politics human, doggish, or both?'

At that moment a bugle rang through all the spheres of Don Quixote's and the bitch's ears and outside.

'Belief in sorcerers,' said the dog, 'is common to black people throughout Africa. *Sorcerers* are people who eat peoples' souls. A *sorcerer* is born a sorcerer; once a sorcerer, does sorcery or magic in private. I'm talking about the power of the self in the world. As soon as a sorcerer's known, as soon as evil's realized, it's no longer evil or powerful.

'The only people who can recognize evil are women. Because you have to be in a trance in order to recognize evil and it's usually women who're in trances.

'Women,' said the bitch, 'understand who's evil in this world, who the evil sorcerers are . . .'

'The evil sorcerers!' Don Quixote repeated, all excited. 'The ones who've stopped me from being loved! Who are they?'

Not hearing anything, the bitch continued, 'These women and their trances or dances' name is Wolof as m'Deup.

'This is what a woman does when she dances: She rolls on the ground and eats dirt.'

'You've taken leave of your senses.'

'Then she recognizes the evil in front of her.'

'Who're the evil sorcerers who've stopped me from being loved?' the night asked again. 'Who haven't loved me?'

At that moment, there was a bugle blast. At that moment, the night, hearing the blast of the bugle, knew that the first spirit, Papa Elegguá, was calling her.

She rose up. She saw a number of men wearing psychedelic garb – filthy white cloths over whatever parts of their bodies they managed to cover. These men are now standing up in numbers because they think they have the power of God. Don Quixote couldn't figure out why these filthy punks were acting like this: she just knew that they were. She thought that these poverty-stricken cultists were stranger than the Born-Agains who were murdering women who tried to get abortions in the United States.

'I find white men so strange. I'm not sure I want to be alive,' Don Quixote explained to the gangs of wild dogs who were now flocking around her. Probably because they smelt she was about to get her period.

'My whole life's involved with these white men,' Don Quixote continued in her mad way.

'You're mad,' said a dog.

'I'm not lesbian,' said Don Quixote. 'Whereas those psychedelic humans are male, white, and they hate women.'

'How d'you know they hate women?' asked the bitch. 'Are you a feminist?'

'I know they hate women because they're kidnapping a woman against her will.'

'That's the Virgin Mary,' said another dog. 'Maybe you

should try looking through glasses which aren't so dark you can't see through them.'

'Religious white men hate women because and so they make women into the image of the Virgin Mary,' the night concluded. She felt sad because no man loved her.

The knight knew that theft is evil therefore the theft of any woman is evil. Even the Virgin Mary. Therefore religious white men are evil.

But evil must be evil. If evil is evil, how can any one or thing be evil that goes against itself? A man who controls political power does whatever he likes. It's natural for him to do whatever he likes because that's what having power means and is: the power to do. A man who controls other people steals their souls. Therefore, when the poor or soulless steal, they are acting unnaturally, they're redressing through unnatural means the proper balance of human power. This is why women have to get abortions.

All the dogs started barking.

In humans, human sexuality is closely tied to power. What are the sexualities of those white men who have almost complete political control?

All the dogs were barking.

'Valiant beasts,' Don Quixote named the dogs, 'valiant beasts; because your sexuality does not partake of this human sexuality. I, a knight, partly due to the fact that I no longer fuck – though that hasn't been quite my decision – but what is my decision? – I will now lead you in a fight to death or to life against the religious white men and against all the alienation that their religious image-making or control brings to humans.'

The Battle Against The Religious White Men
Even though the dogs were barking in answer to the knight's battle cry, and in response to their own barking, and even though the dogs, becoming more and more excited as dogs do, were biting bits of the night's flesh off the darkening night, neither they nor anyone could stop the knight from attacking the religious white men.

Being Doggish, The Dogs Try To Stop Don Quixote From Battling

One dog, who was part of the mass, cried out: 'Don Quixote! What're you doing with your life? Where're you going to live? How're you going to grow old? You insane night.

'Must humans always be so stupid?' the dog asked.

'Don Quixote. Why are you assaulting our doggish Catholic faith?'

'Yours?' Don Quixote cried out in astonishment, for she was surprised. 'I didn't know Catholicism was for the dogs.'

'Better *for*, than *going to*.'

'If Catholicism is for dogs,' Don Quixote continued fighting for her right to battle, 'how do you think it became that way?'

'In your world, religion disintegrated,' another dog woofed, 'because you humans stopped thinking things through. You no longer perceive clearly, night. Look at those penitents, night. They aren't bearing away a woman, as you saw; they're bearing the image of a woman: the Virgin Mary.'

'Then why are they religious?' the unseeing night queried. 'Why are they ashamed and miserable?'

'They're repenting that they're white. Any thinking human does this. Don't you read your own history books?

'So if you attack those miserable moderns or modernists, knight, you'll be making a miserable historical mistake. You will be preventing whites from hating their own whiteness.'

Don Quixote finally refuted the dogs' attack on her attack: 'Liberalism has never stopped me from doing anything,' said the night.

The Battle Against Religious White Men

Ignoring the howling doggish dogs, Don Quixote stepped right up to the religious white men or penitents. She wasn't scared of them because she felt that she was such a failure as a person and she was so sick of the world in which she was living that she wasn't scared of anyone anymore. Finally, in a manner of speaking, she was a knight. 'Sirs,' she said.

As a child Don Quixote had been trained to be always polite despite whatever she was thinking. To act despite whatever she was thinking.

'Sirs,' she said.

The white religious men didn't want to bother listening to her because she was neither a landowner nor being victimized.

'Sirs,' she said, 'once upon a time there were many hyenas.'

The dogs, hearing about their brethren, began to gather around the knight.

'Hyenas are the greediest and most ambitious of animals. *He* is short for Hyena.

'Oh religious men: One of the hyenas was so greedy for fame that he turned to God Who is our, or whoever-believes-in-Him's Master. God told Hyena that if he wanted to get famous like God, he would have to pay his dues: he would have to suffer and he would have to sacrifice. Since there are a lot of dues to be paid, even for male (as opposed to female) beasts, it isn't enough to suffer and sacrifice just once in order to get fame. Hyena would have to suffer and sacrifice again and again. Just like everybody else.

'Specifically: Hyena would have to suffer and sacrifice once in order to be powerful because a person who's famous in this country has a lot of power. And once in order to get rid of all those jealous people who were trying to stop him from being famous. Jealous people, naturally, are enemies.

'Being naturally greedy Hyena was already suffering once because he didn't have everything he wanted. Hyenas never have everything they want. This's why suffering's natural. For hyenas. As for sacrificing, as opposed to suffering which is natural, Lord knows, and who else knows but the Lord?, he had sacrificed enough in one lifetime for his parents and his wife. Sacrificing isn't natural, but social. This proves that society isn't natural. For hyenas.

'Hyena rightfully or righteously decided that he'd have to suffer and sacrifice only once more, considering how much he had already suffered and sacrificed, in order to get famous.

'God, being good, kept His word: Due to one act of suffering and sacrifice, Hyena became head (HE) of a multi-national corporation. According to Jesus Christ Our Lord, you too can become head (HE) of a multi-national corporation if you, following the teachings of Jesus Christ, give up enough and stop giving head (HE).

'But Hyena hadn't given enough head, I mean he hadn't

given up enough: he hadn't suffered and sacrificed a second time: so he had many cruel even criminal enemies. From pencil eraser and stamp thefts to major embezzlements, criminal acts like termites were gnawing away at his multi-national corporation. From the inside.

'I already taught you about theft, didn't I?'

'Oh, yes,' a dog replied. 'Stealing is one of the first ways by which we can de-control ourselves.'

'That's either right or wrong.'

'Good dog.' The dog who had just spoken patted Don Quixote's head.

'Being headstrong, the more crimes took place, the more Hyena accused and judged, but, like all political leaders, he made a lot of noise without seeing anything. The more hysterical our leaders will grow, the more the company shit or shitted-upon employees will commit every crime they can think of. And more.'

A political theorist dog enquired who the real criminal was in this situation.

'God.'

'Then God exists?'

'Someone has to be making all this up.

'If imagination still exists in this world – which could be doubtful,' Don Quixote explained, 'there must be an Imaginer. Otherwise imagination, imagining only itself, isn't imagination. It is possible that there is no imagination, that this world is dead. Otherwise, there must be an imaginer.

'Since the Imaginer, whose existence I've just proven, imagines other than Her- or Himself, the Imaginer, having the riches of the world, is a thief. Theft is good or holy.

'Therefore Hyena trotted over to the Imaginer, or God, to complain about his enemies. The enemies of the multi-national corporations.

'God said, "Well, son. You ain't no son of mine. I guess you are."

'God explained His indecision: "It's hard for me to accept what I've done, that I've imagined or spawned evil or you into this world. You ain't no son of mine because you haven't given up enough. Have you given up your wife?"

'And Hyena replied, "I don't have a wife: I don't believe in indulging women in their fantasies."

'And The Lord said, "Have you given up your life?"

'Hyena laughed. "What life? This life which the Lord God Our Father, I mean *You*, gave me or threw me into? This life which started out in poverty? This life which passes from desire to desire, desires which as I grow older I'm less able to satisfy, until I have grown to hate my very self? This life which becomes harder, then goes. I'm a mass of hunger lust loneliness unsure if I have value unsure of any meaning deeply bored helpless. Lord God Almighty, what is there to give up?"

'And The Lord said, "Hear this, sinner man. Sinner Hyena. Your only problem is that you are not rich. This is the problem with all of you poor people. Why don't you just give up your damn desire to have our money?"

'The greedy beast replied to The Lord, "Why, Lord, then I'd be giving up everything!"

'The Lord said, "That is the point. You have to give up everything if you want everything. Or anything. I told you already: *you* haven't given up enough! You have to give up your self."

'Hyena the Laugher went home to his crime-riddened multinational corporation and did exactly as he had been instructed. He did his best to force out of himself all his evil love of money and greed. For if he wasn't rich, he wouldn't have enemies, so his multi-national corporation would be secure.

'Hyena clothed himself in whatever squatters had thrown away, which wasn't enough, and, as if that wasn't enough, after 11:00 at night smeared the beer from drunken spillings on pub floors over his rough skin. Then he took, – not knowing what to sacrifice, he went a bit overboard, – all the red animal meat out of his refrigerator, all the liquid assets out of his VISA-ACCESS accounts, about three hundred thousand cowries (this is an African tale), and whatever cunt juice he could get, Hyena wasn't sexist, and took all this, red meat, cowries, and cunt juice, down to the river under the Hammersmith Bridge. In this place the river Thames was full of garbage. It was prior to the breaking of dawn.

'There Hyena saw the squatters who have no bathrooms in

their squats throwing their leavings or livings into the river. Which is why the river under the Hammersmith Bridge's so dirty.

'God does not like to see His animals slaughtered. God does not like red meat. As the squatters were throwing their livings into the left-over river, holding His Nose God shoved a portion of Hyena's red animal meat into every bit of their piss. The piss turned to blood while the meat changed into the bones of the living animal from whom the meat had come. Hammersmith's squatters would never again eat meat. God moves in mysterious ways.

'The squatters ran back to their flats, and told everyone who was awake – who's awake? – what had taken place. No one believed them because no one believes the poor.

'Then Hyena went to the Hammersmith police station and accused the squatters of stealing his red meat. Of course the police and the courts uphold any accusation against the poor.

'The squatters are the criminals, the ones who've been messing up the multi-national corporations in this country, and this country. Having found them out, having eradicated his enemies, having saved his multi-national corporation from decay and decadence, Hyena was now rich and secure, which is securely or doubly rich, in the Eyes of Our Good Lord.'

Busy with bombings of abortion mills the religious white men didn't pay any attention to the words of the knight. The dogs were barking.

'What, then, is crime?' the knight asked no one.

'What is it to imagine?' asked a dog.

'I have a vision.' Don Quixote started being autistic again:

'I'm hanging by and dangling from a rope over a pit. The pit is bottomless.

'This is the human condition,' Don Quixote said.

'I was in the middle of my life when I found myself in a dark wood, for I no longer knew my way. How hard it is to explain to you how lost I was: the wildness roughness harshness of the wood. Even the memory of it shuts my soul up with fear. My life was so hard for me that death could have been easier. As far as I know,' the night began again:

'I had found myself hanging by and dangling from a rope

over a pit which had no bottom and into which I had fallen. Into bottomlessness.

'Though I was in it, I couldn't perceive its bottom. For everything depending on everything else (meaning and value being only contextually definable) was formless and, so, imperceptible. How is, I mean *was*, vision or meaning possible?' the night asked the wild dogs.

'In my despair which is utter loneliness I cried out for help. I cried to anyone because I didn't know to whom to turn. My mother was dead. I even cried to you,' the night told the beasts. 'But I guess you haven't heard me.'

'I know I could perceive or know something because I knew I was lonely. In this sense, the rope, from which I had been dangling, had dropped.

'I further knew that somewhere I had taken a wrong turning in my life, for I was responsible for my loneliness.

'In the middle of the dark wood, in order to avoid suicide, I gave myself over to temporary death, or sleep. There are times when we who aren't loved must do this. There are times when we who aren't loved must be celibate and frigid.

'The realms of dreams are that of death because the dreamer doesn't expect,' the night mused. 'The dreamer knows what is happening and the world. Dreams which resemble death heal the wounds from living.

'So having no expectations, when I least expected it – as always happens – , I was unexpectedly thrown again into waking reality which I'm unable to know. To my surprise, I found myself in paradise.

'Awake.

'I rubbed my eyes almost out to see if I was really awake. It was morning's beginning: the sun was slowly but steadily rising with the stars that were with it when this world was and is wholeness. My heart, exalted, quivered.

'How could I know whether my heart had any right to be so exalted: to dance, prance, and glance in play? How could I know if what I was seeing was real? How could I know if I was real? How could I know? I know that I saw because seeing is knowing. Necessarily I knew then as I know now. If I was dreaming, I am dreaming,' concluded the night.

'I saw the most beautiful castle that has ever appeared to any seer. Mirrors made up all its surfaces. Since it reflected everything, it must have been invisible.

'This is what I saw:

'Two mirrors, beings doors, opened. I saw an old male creep.

'"Old male creep," I would have said if I hadn't been dreaming.

'This old male creep had no arms. Medals of literary honor hung down from his armless school tweed. In the midst of this jacket, a salt-and-pepper beard made out of snot reached down to its bottom edge. As is the case with Oxford intellectuals who aren't artists, a rosary lay around a red pimply neck. The rosary's beads were large, as befit them. This appearance, this inner confidence, and this great dignity filled me with the utmost respect. 'Old male creep,' I said.

'Upon hearing these words, he walked up to me and hugged me. 'Don Quixote. I have been waiting for you for a long time in this paradise which is England. Finally you have come here. For you are the one, oh valiant knight, who can make me giggle.

'"How can I make you giggle? How can anyone make all of you giggle?" I asked while I looked around paradise or England. I was a tourist. 'You seem perfect.'

'"No," he reprimanded me in his kind schoolmasterly way. "The more our ruling classes, who have knowledge, have, the more they want. This is the nature of paradise, but this is besides the point.'

'"What is the point?" I asked. Being a female, I'm not used to points.

'"The point is just what you've been trying to avoid all your adult life. The point is that you're the one who can show us how to be pointless or dream. For you, night, live in the clouds."

'At this point, I asked him if he was the one who had carved out his friend Duranduran's heart with a tiny dagger, then carved up the material and carried the carved-up bits off to Belerma, who was a beautiful girl. He said yes, loudly. It was in his ancestral blood, for his ancestors had had an empire. I told him it was a great pleasure for me to meet him: just as my former country, the United States of America, had been his country's colony and pupil' may I be his sevant and student.

'Thereupon he took me around his castle of mirrors. Inside one morror: a stone-like man lay horizontally on a rock slab. His right hand lay over his heart.

'"This is Duranduran," the old creep said, proudly. "As he was dying, he told me to cut out his heart. For he loved.'

'I didn't understand how any man could want to be cut up and lose his heart.

'"The point, which you still haven't gotten," my teacher taught me, "is that all of us are enchanted.

We can't dream. But we don't know who our evil enchanters are."

'"I know who the evil enchanters are."

'Not hearing his pupil, "we don't know why they commit the atrocities they commit. Even though my friend's dead, you can still hear him screaming. Don't you hear his screams? Can't you hear the screams of all the people who're dead?"

'"I hear their screams."

'At this point, Duranduran screamed,

   Old male creep. You said

   you were my friend. Then you murdered me.

    Is this why I'm hurting so much?

   If I were dead, my pain wouldn't be such.

   Rather than enchanted I want to be dead,

   for now I can feel this cold stone, my bed.

   This life is bad.

'As soon as the old male creep heard his friend's poem, he kissed his feet. 'Oh my friend, my friend. You can't really be dead! I didn't really kill you! This world must be reasonless.

'"In such a reasonless world, isms such as capitalism, rationalism, imperialism, socialism, communism can't make sense!

'"In such a world, time which is measured therfore rational can't exist. Time is now annihilated, annihilation: for us the future doesn't exist.

'"Since no one believes in cause and effect anymore, – why else would rich people be polluting their own home? – any one does anything. Such freedom is what we name *paradise*.

'"The political mirror of this individual simultaneity of freedom and imprisonment is a state of fascism and democracy: the United States of America.

'"What is your choice?'

'I was stunned. "I have a choice?' I asked, though I had no idea what I meant by what I was saying, for I was stunned.

'"Since you have no choice and you must choose," the old creep answered, 'this is what being *enchanted* means – tell me: who are you?"

'"Who can I be?" I looked at the victimizer and his victim, who were tied to each other by friendship. I have started to cry and I cannot stop crying,

    for those who, having nothing, homeless,

    would flee,

    but there is nowhere to flee;

    so we travel like pirates

    on shifting mixtures of something and nothing.

    For those who in the face of this mixture

        act with total responsibility:

I cried so much I bothered everyone around me.

'"She – "'

Upon hearing this, all the dogs barked.

'"*She* who can tell us who victimizers are, *She* who can see and tell us because *She*'s loony because *She* has become the ancient art of madness, or literature. *She* is in front of us right now." The old fart and his corpse stared at me.

'I stared back.

'"Because by killing the enchanters *She*'ll disenchant us, great deeds are done by great women."

'His words made me so nervy I looked behind me. I saw a beautiful woman about whom they had been speaking.

'"My love," the corpse screamed.

'The most beautiful woman in the world was white. In my vision I asked my guide why the most beautiful woman in the world has white skin.

'"Because black people lived in Africa." He further explained so I had to understand. "The lands comprising Nigeria were the most magnificent of the human realm due to the power of Ogun who wields the tool of war.

187

' "It is the beginning of day.

' "At the beginning of day, Ogun, robed in his bloody garment, gleaming oranges and reds and pinks which are light, leaves his home which is at the top of a hill. With machetes like rays he clears his way through the unmappable tangles. Finally, in glory, he reaches the surrounding waters. In the waters all the hidden monsters, fish that liquid gravity has flattened into steel-like weapons, crocodiles whose teeth burn more than the rays of light, whales materially or actually beyond human perception, our monsters hold Ogun as their king.

' "Nigeria was the most powerful nation in the world.

' "One day, Ogun, the Holder of Power and Decisions, met the most beautiful woman in the world. She was white. Since beauty is the fount and the human creation, she was the mother of all people.

' "Of course she walked right into Ogun's heart and he into hers, and they walked, around and around while morning burst into gleaming and into the light of day, and their creative sources their love and hatred which is love blazed for three years.

' "Because for three years the white woman kept Ogun, black Power, in her bed, and so almost decimated Nigeria, black people out of hatred fear white people. Black people think white people're able to do anything."

'I laughed at the white male creep who had just told me this story.'

The dogs started barking.

' "Blacks don't fear white people."

' "You should have respect for your elders," the old creep reprimanded me.

' "Why? If there's no time, there's neither age nor old age anymore. If you were an elder, you'd at least have old age, but, as far as I can tell, you've so few brains in your head, you have nothing. How, then, can you have visions?"

' "Don Quixote. Here none of us can see truly anymore because we're enchanted." '

At this point the dogs, who had been eagerly listening to Don Quixote's tail, asked the knight what it's like to be enchanted and enslaved. 'Do those who're enchanted eat, shit, and fuck just like we do?' asked the dogs.

'In my vision, those who're enchanted, since they're no longer in touch with their own bodies, have no ideas what their needs are. Therefore they don't need to to eat, shit, or fuck, and they don't care who they elect as their political leaders.

'Since Jesus Christ made his disciples sleep on beds of thorns, religion is enchantment.'

'Don't the enchanted sleep?' asked a young hound who had read *ENDYMION*.

'The enchanted, as all prisoners know well, don't sleep because all through my vision, no one I saw shut an eye and neither did I.'

'It isn't possible for people not to sleep,' a bitch yapped. 'You're just putting us on.'

'How can I not see what I see? How is a lie possible – for a seer?'

'If we can't trust you,' the dogs barked, 'we can't trust anything in this world, even ourselves.'

'I saw Queen Guinevere and Sir Launcelot.' Don Quixote continued her vision.

'Where's this leading, night? Where're you leading us?'

'I'm not leading you anywhere because I'm not leading you.

'I addressed our Queen, but She didn't reply to me. Thus I recognized English royalty.'

'Is Queen Guinevere enchanted?'

'Right when I saw Queen Guinevere,' Don Quixote explained, 'two of my girlfriends who had OD'd about four years ago so were now enchanted asked me for forty quid for a shitted-up black rag they were holding to my nose. Enchanted, they thought this was a skirt. Since I highly value friendship, I never lend money to friends, especially dead ones and more especially junkies.

'But I was upset about my friends. "Do enchanted or dead people live in poverty all the time?" I asked my guide.

'"Of course they do. Do you think that only living humans are poor? Do you think that people who have endless power, which is wealth, and so can do whatever they want, elect to

189

control a limited realm? The powerful of this world can control everyone: living and dead.

'"Know this, Don Quixote," my guide taught: "Those who control political and social power are determined on total annihilation. Poverty and want are everywhere, all the time, in the imagination, in all living and dead being."

'I was so scared of being poor, I refused to give my friends the forty pounds they wanted. Thereupon,' the night explained, 'my vision ended.'

'Is it possible,' all the dogs cried, 'is it possible that all the enchantments – poverty, alienation, fear, inability to act on desire, inability to feel – have made you unable to see and feel visions?'

'Yes. I am a failure.'

Intrusion Of A Badly Written Section
A real vision: There's no longer nature: trees bushes, mainly: unboxed space and time. There're only rooms. Whatever you do, whether you're successful or unsuccessful, you only are in some room.

The vision is: there's no joy.

TV's sit in most of the rooms. While I was watching TV, my TV moved away from the wall. The TV became blacker and the wall became whiter until the blackness was completely divorced from the whiteness.

No thing in this world or room had anything to do with any other thing. Each thing by itself was beautiful. Each thing had no meaning other than itself, or meant nothing. The room was existing surfaces, as TV.

There's no way out of any appearance because an appearance is only what it is. The room was my nightmare or jail. I, a night, want to escape: I want to stop being a knight, the night. I want to escape myself.

How can I escape being? How can I do myself in?

Suicide's no answer, is no way of getting rid of the night, for my mother accomplished nothing by suiciding except a legacy of anger and fear. The self must be more complicated than life and death, more complicated than duality.

If I can't escape from the room by kiling myself, I must be

190

able to escape, if I can, by being happy. By embracing and believing myself, just appearances, the night. By embracing, and believing, my deepest being which is not knowing.

Therefore my vision has ended.

The Madness Of Don Quixote

By definition, being unable to know anything, Don Quixote was mad. 'We must turn to madness, or Voodoun, in order to set Queen Guinevere free,' Don Quixote announced to the dogs.

The dogs didn't understand Don Quixote because they spoke a different language: 'Who's Queen Guinevere?'

'She's the woman whom the white penitents in front of us are holding in chains and raping.'

Since the dogs still didn't understand what her words meant, they thought she was mad. In her madness, she turned to poetry which, as is the nature of poetry, no one, rightfully, hears.

Don Quixote Explained Poetry To The Dogs

'I write words to you whom I don't and can't know, to you who will always be other than and alien to me. These words sit on the edges of meanings and aren't properly grammatical. For when there is no country, no community, the speaker's unsure of which language to use, how to speak, if it's possible to speak. Language is community. Dogs, I'm now inventing a community for you and me.

'I who am at the edge of madness. Mad, all I have vision: what I alone see.'

Don Quixote Actually Attacks White Religious Men

Now totally mad, Don Quixote sang to the white religious men in order to make them release the Virgin Mary or Queen Guinevere:

'Going going gone.

'Going somewhere. (Pirate-piracy.) Going anywhere:

'Going through time, the memories. The first streaks of daylight in the sky, over the ocean.

'Coming into port. Ugly city not mine.

'At first gray, gives way to lavenders and pinks. The first fishing boats.

'This is what the homeless see.

'But what do homeless dogs see?' Don Quixote asked the dogs.

'Joy.'

'This memory of joy makes me aware of my present suffering.

'My consciousness now is a bumpy road which is plunging its head into a hole where a few shacks lay scattered in deep and burning sands; an unending, unstoppable road which is charging ahead as fast as possible; at its bottom brutally it quicksands into a pool of clumsy houses; a road foolishly climbing up, recklessly descending . . .

'Mad language is consciousness in myth.

'The carcass of wood comically perched on cement paws I call "home". The style of its hair is corrugated iron that exists in the sun like skins being dried. In the diningroom, nailheads glisten from the rough floor, lines of pine and shadow run across a ceiling; the chairs are phantom; the light leaks out a gray light; the cockroaches buzzing seem about to hurt . . .

'This's vision because it's what I see.

'At the end of time before the morning, when I'm now homeless. When I, now, have no one. A country and a cunt are a lack of alienation. The most essential country in which dream's possible, this lack of alienation given to me needy, restored to my decision to allow neediness and desperation, therefore not restored in spreading tenderness, but given as a nipple. I don't need my actual mother who's dead, but I have the desperation of a baby who must suck her nipple. Restored in desire.

'Accidentally, the morning's teat is beside a palm-tree. The palm-tree's the cock, a type of teat, which's being rubbed until it is spurting out semen. From the torrents of semen, the Grand-Rivière in Haiti – our desire, our morning, – having been born, is hysterically sucking.

'As a child I never get enough food.

'As a child, Christmas is the magic time. At Christmas, since

I never get enough presents, I'm not loved. For presence is love. In this world into which I was born, love isn't possible:

'I shouldn't love anyone who can't love me:

'Since I no longer want anyone, I'm not human:

'I want to suck your teat.

'In the evening, during the holidays, there was a church which was little but nevertheless frightened me. I decided to ignore my fear because the experience seemed too valuable. The church was a Haitian church. Being Haitian it held all practices including every sort of fucking and Voodoun. All ways were allowed: all cultures: aloud.

'In this church the singers can't sing. Inside, the priests use nailpolish bottles, raw rums, and whatever they can get their hands on for everything. To eat is to appease hunger; to appease hunger is to touch and be touched.

'The town streets had become deserted. Sometimes I saw up to twenty people in the church. They were singing songs of desire. Music was always playing:

'"You are inside. You are warm, inside. You have eaten well, inside. When you drink their juice, you become happier. Red blood sausages unroll like snakes. One two-fingers-long sausage unrolls in coils. It's a zebra. But the other sausage is longer and thicker. My first sausage is wild thyme, while my second's hot pimento.

'"Then I drink rejoicing – steaming coffee, sugary milk punch – your liquid, until my taste buds arrive at the point of ravishment. Then, you tissue me in gentleness.

'"Laugh now, my baby: it is almost morning . . ."'

And Don Quixote concluded her madness. But, having no memory, only for a moment.

'It is necessary to sing, that is to be mad, because otherwise you have to live with the straights, the compromisers, the mealy-mouths, the reality-deniers, the laughter-killers. It is necessary to be mad, that is to sing, because it's not possible for a knight, or for anyone, to foray successfully against the owners of this world.

'This night I am mad,' Don Quixote concluded proudly.

'And at the end of time prior to the morning, this world in which we are now living is crawling on its hands and knees through its muck without any desire to drill through the sky to reality. To drill through your steel as a protest of our claustrophobia. Howl, dogs.

'And at the end of time prior to the morning, when even your own homes' backs shrink in fear from all skies truffled by gun fire, when your feet fear the soil's erosion and the ground crumbling beneath them, until the point that there is no more ground, when even straights sense this decay of their world, we have the clues to the spirit.

'Nevertheless what they name *reality* is still throbbing out its death throes:
linoleumed halls
white lace curtains
a drab carpeted sitting-room
paint drips like the end of the world
a bird cage
your eyes are reduced to petty binoculars
your lips are chastity-belts
your consciousness is only that of guilt
you cannot even hate.

'May the malevolent tear apart what you have carefully constructed, through holes in your urban paradises. Through holes of rats cockroaches nuclear waste garbage lids, the actual world is coming through.

'At the end of time prior to the coming through of morning.

'At the end of time prior to the morning, my catatonia. I'll no longer speak because you are not hearing and will never hear me no matter how I speak. So I am a mass of dreams desires which, since I can no longer express them, are foetuses beyond their times, not even abortions. For I can't get rid of un-born-able unbearable dreams, whereas women can get rid of unwanted children. So I no longer know what I'm doing,' Don Quixote concluded her poem, lamely. No one reads poetry in this society anymore.

One dog yapped.

The night ended or shitted again. 'I wanted to find a meaning or myth or language that was mine, rather than those which try to control me; but language is communal and here is no community.' Having concluded, Don Quixote turned around and started walking home, although she had no home.

Within her own self in some messed-up language which wasn't quite language, while she was walking nowhere, to herself the night said, 'At the end of the night when mourning's about to begin.

'When morning's about to begin, I don't know any country I don't know any community I don't know which of my memories to trust I don't know what memories to believe. Is there any history? Is there anything, here, but boredom?

'All singing must now be howling.'

The dogs who had been following the aged failure in the hopes that she would age and fail enough to give them fresh (dead) meat, howled.

Since the religious white men didn't give a damn whether she came or went, the image of the Virgin Mary didn't show any signs of noticing, and only the hungry hounds cared, Don Quixote being female started to cry. When Don Quixote cried, she wailed: She fell down, curled in a ball, stuck her hands in her mouth cause her mouth wasn't good for anything else, and attempted to hide from those all the white religious men who were tormenting her, whom she could no longer see.

No longer being able to see their food, the dogs howled:

The Dogs' Lament That Their Food, Don Quixote, Has Disappeared
'Oh, beauteous night. Oh, reflecting glory of this world. Especially to the race of white men. Oh.' The dogs, once they started howling, forgot what they meant.

'Woof.

'Now that you are no longer here, we've nothing to eat. You were our sustenance; you, sustenance, were liberal beyond liberal, for the liberal by their hypocrisies have done in us poor; while you, poor knight, have been too weak and hopeless to do in anyone but yourself. And even that took you a whole eight months. Woof, night.'

The dogs remembered: 'You were humble, knight, because you were scared of everyone. At the same time, because you were mad, no one could scare or humble you. Nihilistic autistic knight, neither religious men nor the image of the Virgin Mary could scare you.

'You are so autistic, knight, that you undertook every adventure any sane human would run away from and after that you ran away. You have failed me.'

The dogs described their love, 'You are so autistic, you don't know when humans're laughing at you and you always think humans're laughing at you. Since everyone must despise you; love, being impossible for you, is an obsession. Whatever your love's recipient happens to feel for you, since you're autistic, doesn't influence your belief that you're not worthy. Therefore, night, you always need love with desperate animalism and you can't actually love, that is clearly perceive your love's recipient.

'Night: Where are your eyes?

'When is there going to be daylight?'

The dogs began to howl out of hunger.

This was the first sign of their having language.

Having Language The Dogs Blame The World

Knowing that the frail flailing failing knight was no longer their fodder, in ravenous hunger the dogs turned their attention to the world.

'World,' they yapped.

'We do not have a home in you because the people who own you, our landlords, charge too much rent.'

Dog Reasoning

'The only way a dog can attack its landlord is by biting its leg. By terrorism, which the landlords call useless. Terrorism is mad,' the mutts yapped.

A Discourse On Madness

'Drug-users must waste their lives or time obtaining drugs.

'Humans who live in and by fantasies so rigidified or needed they are obsessions must make their obsessions fortresses.

'The sole madness which uses precise perception, the perception of each moment or of mutability, is the scream.

'Let our madness be,' the mutts screamed in reason, 'the

anger and the pain which are rising, not out of forgetting or fantasizing, but out of remembering.

'For us remembering is too painful to bear.

'Remember everything and do not bear anything,' one bitch bitched.

At The End Of The Night When Morning Was About To Begin, The Dogs Sang,
'It is you, rotten world. It is you all my memories, the world: now ending.

'It is you mother and father who didn't want a child. Father, you left my mother when she was three months pregnant with me. Mother, you were too scared to get an abortion so you just hated me throughout my life because I was the reason your lover had left you. It is you who never should have procreated.

'It is you, grinding secretarial life. It is you, boss, Hello, boss, I mean *sir*, please excuse me, *sir*, please please excuse me, sir. I don't want to lose my job, for I have no other meaning in life. Therefore I will be whatever you want: I won't exist. I will I will, I will won't exist. Whatever you say, Boss, but I know, Sir Boss, I's never do nothing properly I'm just a good-for-nothing, old clown ho', plowing these here fields. You know, I'm madly in love with you. I'd do anything to kiss your cock, Boss. I shouldn't say those words. I'm bad. I'm very very bad. You're suck a good boss, Sir, because you know how to properly mistreat me, which is all I properly deserves; some bosses whose names I won't mention – actually act as if I'm a real person. You know better than that, Sir.

'It is you, city. Market of the world, that is, of all representations. Since you're the only home I've ever known, without your representation or misrepresentation of me I don't exist. Because of you, since every child needs a home, every child is now a white slave.

'City, owner of me. When you want pain out of me, you throw me amidst your bums and pimp-toads who wield smack needles like knightly swords in ancient or romantic times. When you want joy out of me, you make me famous, for I'm the baby, you're my only parent, and fame is your nipple.

'City my parent, for I have no other parents.

'Let us your children wild packs of dogs now roam down your streets looking for anyone who resembles food.

'For us, what is *purity*? What is *idealism*, world? Slashes and gashes of our blood're cutting the skies of love. Therefore this is our history. What you call *history* and *culture* is the denial of our flowing blood.

'Goodbye, *DON QUIXOTE*.' The dogs howled.

'These are your words, city. *Purity. Idealism*. Your vision is the vision of the end of the world. Your world of landlords is the world of death,' the dogs howled.

The Beginning Of The Dogs' Song
'Because it isn't true that animal life is over,
because we are not worthless dogs,
because we are not slaves, oh landlords, oh J. Paul Getty,
even though now and then you pat us on our heads or fuck us,
throw us scraps of food and love, give us doggie walking suits
to make us slaves,
because your human history which is the history of slavery is
not our history,
because your culture is slavery:'

At The End Of The Night When Morning Was About To
Break, The Dogs Sang:
'The world is not ending. The work and the language of the
living're about to begin:
in the wee hours
where the first pale violet gray and pink rays hit objects at
random, when the eyes/I's see only with pleasure,'

The dogs sang their first words, 'The sun, turning round and round our earth, will never stop in our lifetime. Since you, only you, night, for only you are other than the sun, see this light, – since the see-er is part causer of what he or she sees, – you are the immediate cause or will behind our morning. Night, you are not our light, but you are the one who has freed the morning.

'Their created human history is the history of pain: this nighttime of our living; these tortured lives. Let this suffering,

198

this night, be the lance of the knight. Let this night which all of us can perceive be the lance we shall sprinkle with chicken blood, this lance of our blood and fat and muscle, this heart, be the needle by which we shall draw out the bad blood. The owners' blood.

'And at the end of the night,' having disposed of the knight,

'when morning's about to begin, in the winds of our lusts and emotions, I am a ship about to move.

'I/eye. We/Oui.

'Yes, we the dogs are pirates.'

One Pirate Sang:
'In this total devastation of the heart which is the world, the landlords rule. There is no way we can defeat the landlords. But under their reins and their watchful eyes,

'I sail as the winds of lusts and emotions bare me. Everywhere and anywhere. I who will never own, whatever and whenever I want, I take.

'Every part of the slave ship is cracking open. Its stomach vomits and echoes. Its cargo's ghastly tapeworm or capitalism gnaws whatever fluxam it receives while above on deck we teach each other to steal.

'White world, ho ho ho oy yoi yoi, we're doing everything you've told us and you tell us to do because we're good, and we're stealing you. Soon there'll be none left of you:

'Blood will lay on the cabin quilts blood will flood the hold blood slips along the bridges old blood stinking fish in the new bright sun blood lifts into the winds so that droplets of blood are flowing everywhere until the our newborn sun is glistening red blood being everywhere does what it likes.'

Chorus Of Pirates:
'The lousy cunts.'

Another Dog-Pirate Sings,
'No longer a poor woman: a woman dependent on the kindnesses of men
in a land where there are no kindnesses for there is no land in sight,'

Chorus Of Pirates:
'Where she's going to find love now, the lousy cunt?'

Dog-Pirate:
'No longer wandering because no longer trying to find what she will never find driven driven.'

Chorus Of Pirates:
'She's not going to get love from us, the louse-filled cunt.'

Dog-Pirate:
'By the clanking sun of the noon sea. I the female pirate speak. By this beginning light which came up during the depth of our midnight.

'Listen, men. Listen. By this day of total disarmament, in our total naïveté in our total gleaming helplessness I am sailing over the crumbling European waters. Listen, to your graves.

'Listen. For I am crossing the seas. Listen to the waters. I am totally strong now in my helplessness because I am these waters which glisten and receive.

'Listen, men. Today my skin is aching because the sun is touching it. Listen now to the violent sex between sun and water.

'Rise, sun. Rise into a morning.'

At The End Of The Night When Morning Breaks,
'The sky over northern Haiti already holds pink and orange streaks. The fishing boats're out. Rise, you burning of the sky, you thief of all phenomena. Rise in my flesh. Rise in my now red vagina. Rise against all loneliness which exists.'

And the dogs in reply howled, 'Our suffering has been is and will be the anger, the real history, the hammer and wrench by which we, inch by inch, forge the glorious orb of our sun.'

Thus abandoned the night was crawling back home. As she wobbled her way onwards, and wended, and wandered, as is the way with females, the white religious men, being around, asked the knight, out of curiosity, if she was still mad. Having been defeated by white men and deserted by every dog, Don Quixote replied that she was mad.

200

When the people who lived in Don Quixote's home town, which is called Spain, espied this returning knight, – how different she now was from the insecure shy child they had known, – they jeered at all her characteristics with the full variety of drama native to Spaniards. But being vacant Don Quixote looked vacantly at the bourgeoisie. She had no idea where she was. Where in hell she was. She had never been to Spain.

Having passed beyond the pains of defeat and desertion, now vacant, Don Quixote settled into nowhere and drew up her will:

Don Quixote's Will To The Dogs, Her Only Hopes Of Love
'Dear Dogs,

'The sea retreats a virgin. Inland. England. The huge octopuses stranded on the sands never touch the ocean.

'Though, as you read this, I'm dead, I'm looking through all my memories of the tidal waves for something: joy. But too many evil suns are bursting their angers on the branch-tops; too many liars suck down and are sucked down into the lips' whirlpools.

'The ants polish skeletons. The ants at least have yanked technique from the nothingness, the sands' vagina.

'Is there nothing else in reality but a diseased forest's overly sharp points?

'I want to experience joy.

'Dogs of this world. You are holding bleeding flesh between your sharp reddened teeth. I recognize this flesh because it's mine. *Dogs of this world.*

DON QUIXOTE'S DREAM

Being dead, Don Quixote wrote these recollections after she was dead:

'Now I'm going to speak directly.

'It is true that women are never men. Even a woman who has the soul of a pirate, at least pirate morals, even a woman who prefers loneliness to the bickerings and constraints of heterosexual marriage, even such a woman who is a freak in our society needs a home.

'Even freaks need homes, countries, language, communication.

'The only characteristic freaks share is our knowledge that we don't fit in. Anywhere. It is for you, freaks my loves, I am writing and it is about you. Since humans enjoy moralizing, over and over again they attack us.

'Language presupposes community. Therefore without you, nothing I say has any meaning. Without love or language, I do not exist. We who are freaks have only friendship.

'I haven't told you yet anything about my marriage because I don't know anything about marriage. I'm not thinking about it any longer except when I'm thinking. But I know it's not good for anyone to become too used to habits because then that person is selfish.

'Nevertheless I am unhappy – however far unhappiness goes. Unhappiness goes far. The more tired I am at night, the less I can fall asleep; when I wake up by the morning, I hate myself or every moment I call consciousness. To rid myself of the loneliness of freaks, I'm going to get married.

'As soon as I'm married, I'll be a prisoner; I'll be normal. I'll have to stop having the dreams by which I now act.

'No longer being able to perceive dreams, since perceiving is feeling and touching, will narrow my feelings and touchings into a controllable range.

'But when I'm living alone, I don't touch anybody so I'm immersed in my own selfishness.

'I'm talking about the self and others. Where are there possibilities of lives of feelings and touchings? Where and when have people gotten along together and allowed each other to dream publicly? That is, to do art?

'I dream of Spain:

'The Spanish Republic of 1931 was born in a unique set of circumstances: a conjunction of long-term national political crisis, a severe economic depression occurring through the western world (as now), and an increasingly vigorous national intellectual and cultural renaissance. (Is the latter happening now in England?)

'How did the intellectual and cultural renaissance which helped cause the Spanish Civil War begin?

'Two intellectual currents dominated early-twentieth-century Spain: a discourse derived from Karl Kraus' work and a nationalistic Catholicism.

'From his chair as professor of philosophy in Madrid Julian Sanz, Kraus' main Spanish disciple, advanced the doctrine of "harmonious rationalism". Since reality or the whole is fundamentally harmonious, poverty other forms of human degradation all forms of human brutality and undue suffering are humanly rectifiable. If we are badly hurting each other and we don't know how to stop badly hurting each other, we need to learn other intellectual emotive and behavioral models. Since we have to broaden our education, historical and imaginative, we must adopt temporal and geographical internationalism.

'Thomas Jefferson: "I think by far the most important bill in our whole code is that for the diffusion of knowledge among the people. No other sure foundation can be devised for the preservation of freedom, and happiness . . . Preach, my dear sir, a crusade against ignorance, establish and improve the law for educating the common people." Letter to George Wythe, August 13, 1786.

'What is the model for such education?

'In 1876, Francisco Giner de los Ríos, professor of law, a disciple of Sanz del Río, founded what was to be until 1936 the most influential secondary school in Spain, the Institución Libre de Enseñanza. The school taught that the first principle from which all manifestations come is Creation or Will. A secondary principle was internationalism: the magazine *a Boletín* acted as a forum for both Emile Durkheim, Bertrand Russell, John Dewey, etc., and the Spanish intellectuals.

'Whereas the Spanish Catholics advocated nationalism somewhat in the same way that England today, to avoid the recognition that her empire has gone, claims ownership of language and culture via Shakespeare, Milton, etc. The only or proper way to speak and write is English.

'In the early 1900s a mirror of del Río's reaction against political and cultural chauvinism was the state of the Spanish language:

'The Catalans, who before this time had regarded their own language as a patois – as the Haitians now regard, or are supposed to regard their language, – began to create an impressive weight of writing and simultaneously to rediscover the glorious history of their Mediterranean Empire and the differences between them and other Spaniards. Both the Catalan peasants and the bourgeoisie worked together to produce a Catalan philological, literary, and artistic revival.

'The Basque language is unrelated to any language except for Magyar and perhaps Finnish. The Basque movement was political rather than cultural: until 1837 the Basque provinces had governed themselves.

'How did this situation of language affect Spanish politics?

'When the major debate had occurred between Marx and Bakunin within the First International in 1868, representatives from each side had arrived in Spain. By the 1920s the anarcho-syndicalists had become more powerful than the Marxists, and remained so until the Second Republic.

'Language being a form of communication is a political occurrence.

'The anarcho-syndicalists, advocates of decentralized political power, were trying to create a world-collectivist commonwealth. Since dualism's no longer a usable logical model, regionalism and internationalism, anarchy and collectivity can work hand-in-hand.

'How are the mind and the heart being educated to think and to act? To dream?

'The Spain of the Spanish Republic of 1931 is my dream or model:

'Many of the early anarchist leaders resembled the mendicant friars of former centuries: abstemious wanderers, proud to possess little and to be under-dogs, though physically not developed accustomed to the most strenuous physical battles and physically demanding situations: all to accomplish something-or-other. They were motivated by that inner certainty which by its very being denies human leadership and any

204

hierarchy except for that of gentleness and kindness. The anarchists, being nights, were knights.

'This is my dream of my night:

'My master has left me. He doesn't want me anymore. Minute after minute he doesn't come back for me.

'He had risen out of the bed where he had been lying, the liar, with me, where I am now lying, and threw his hands through his hairs into the air, not thinking that I had already fallen to the wayside.

'For the night before, he had come to me and come into me and come right after he had been fucking some other woman. She must have been some fucking bitch, for his skin was dripping and his clothes were half-put-on and torn.

'The woman he had been fucking was so old no person in her or his right mind would go near much less touch such wet tin foil. No one wants to hear the grunts and sounds they make when they do whatever they do. Old women must take on anybody, for no one will have them; they have to be willing to cover the most feelingless man with their deeply felt caresses.

'Having been abandoned for old age, I'm dying. It doesn't matter whether the man was a creep or a saint, good or evil. I am dying. The more he and she, increasingly wet, dived then plumbed their lust and feelings, the more I was separate from them. Whenever they came, I came as close to dying as a living person can come. Everything and, more important, everyone has been taken away from me. I was as good as dead.

'As soon as I was out of the way, a smell like that of death began to emanate from her growingly lustful armpits and nostril hairs. The nostrils in shame tried to retract from the rest of the nose. The remaining parts of neither of these fuckers paid any attention to the stench coming out of them, for they were so entwined.

'As soon as he was wrapped in this existence of smell, he wanted to eat her. But he respected old women, as his parents had taught him to do. So he turned to men.

'He began to eat a man. Being the same sex, the man began to eat him: equally they slapped each other, back and forth; equally open palms slapped heads shoulders backs, back and

205

forth; equally limbs and torso wrestled limbs and torso, back and forth.

'Being in freedom, with neither ties nor commitments, one simply, with no reasons, walked away from the other.

'The one who was left behind decided he would never again let another person touch him. He would never again allow himself to descend to the bottom or the emotional asshole. He would never again, while living, come close to death. In order to protect his living or self, he would enter a monastery.

'Since he must have nothing more to do with men – a type of feminism, or reverse feminism, – he would enter a nunnery.

'Having experienced a more powerful male than he had experienced, God, and so being even sicker of men than he was, the nuns left the man alone. In the nunnery, dead dwell among the dead. The dead nones live by chanting the same words over and over to nobody or by not communicating, by burning up their senses and incenses, and by bowing down to God.

'My master couldn't bear living in death. Since my master couldn't bear the coldness grayness and horribleness of this society, he died.

'My master has left me forever.

'There will be no more men in my life. That sexual ecstasy or orgasm which appears out of a simultaneous overcoming of the hatred, which is fear, of men and out of an actual play with the myth of rejection is no longer mine.

'I remember. But is what I remember this ecstasy which comes from a mixture of pain and joy, or a pure joy? Are my memories, whose sources might be unknown, actual glimpses of possible paradise?

'This, my first and final dream, is not the dream of capitalism.

'Suddenly, I heard my master's voice. "Shut up.

'"Where, where in hell – from Hell? – did you get your idea that I am Male?

'"Shut up, night.

'"Let the sun sink below its horizon so that there are no more stories, no more tracks, no more memories, night. What, in your darkness, fool night, do you think you remember?

'"What do you think, in your blackness, are your dreams?

206

'"Do you know, night, what I heard Satan said about Me? He said that I, the Lord God Almighty, am a whore – in fact that My Very Existence denigrates the name 'whore' – and that he has no respect for Me because I make love to old women, spinster virgins. That he personally would rather boil over in a fourteen-year-old cunt, even if it is rape, than hide beneath his mother's skirts. He's a real man whereas I'm a mealy-mouth hypocrite, dishonest. I, God, don't do anything directly. I promote morality while I lap at My Mother's cunt.

'"That if I, God, am so frightened that I have to moralize, I should moralize about and condemn Myself rather than other people."

'God continued condemning Him- or Herself: "So now that you know I'm imperfect, night, that you can't turn to Me: turn to yourself:

'"Because with every night's onset the sun sinks below its horizon, because there are no more new stories, no more tracks, no more memories: there is you, knight.

'"Since I am no more, forget Me. Forget morality. Forget about saving the world. Make Me up."

'Obeying these teachings – my last memories, – I said "Goodbye" to God the Monstrous Liar and Monster-Wonder and walked over to my horse. I took Rocinante's reins in my hand, for she was too old and worn-out to ride. The old woman. One should never ride an old bitch. I swore, though I had no one to whom to swear, for Rocinante doesn't understand Spanish, that I would never reveal the reality God had just revealed to me about God, – the gossip, – to anyone.

'The night fell.

'As I walked along beside Rocinante, I thought about God for one more minute and forgot it. I closed my eyes, head drooping, like a person drunk for so long she no longer knows she's drunk, and then, drunk, awoke to the world which lay before me.'

Kathy Acker is the author of *The Childlike Life of the Black Tarantula, I Dreamt I Was a Nymphomaniac! Imagine, The Adult Life of Toulouse-Lautrec* (which three books make up a trilogy), *Kathy Goes to Haiti, Blood and Guts in High School, Great Expectations* and *My Death, My Life, by Pier Paolo Pasolini.* She has written several plays and a filmscript, and has also written for art magazines as an art critic. Kathy Acker lives in London.